Kody Keplinger was born and raised in a small Kentucky town. She wrote her first novel, *The DUFF* (*Designated Ugly Fat Friend*), when she was only seventeen. *The DUFF* was a YALSA Top Ten Quick Pick for Reluctant Readers and a Romantic Times Top Pick. Kody is the cofounder of Disability in Kidlit, a website devoted to the representation of disabilities in children's literature. Currently, Kody lives in New York City, where she teaches writing workshops and continues to write books for kids and teens. Kody's website is kodykeplinger.com.

'I always felt like the "ugly girl" in high school – my best friends are insanely Gorgeous – so when I was introduced to the word during my senior year, I knew I was the Duff. The idea of writing a book with 'Duff' in the title started as a joke, but when I realized that my friends felt like Duffs, too, I knew I had to write this story.'

Also by Kody Keplinger

Shut Out
A Midsummer's Nightmare

Kody Keplinger

The **DUFF** fat friend

designated ugly

Hodder
Children's
Books

A division of Hachette Children's Books

First published in the United States in 2010 by Little, Brown and Company

This edition published in Great Britain in 2015
by Hodder Children's Books

A Catalogue record for this book is available from the British Library

ISBN 978 1 444 92798 6

Typeset in Berkeley Book by Avon DataSet Ltd,
Bidford on Avon, Warwickshire

Printed and bound by
CPI Group (UK) Ltd, Croydon, CR0 4YY

The paper and board used in this book are made from wood from
responsible sources.

Hodder Children's Books
a division of Hachette Children's Books
338 Euston Road, London NW1 3BH
An Hachette UK company
www.hachette.co.uk

For Aja,
whose birthday brought us good luck

1

This was getting old.

Once again, Casey and Jessica were making complete fools of themselves, shaking their asses like dancers in a rap video. But I guess guys eat that shit up, don't they? I could honestly *feel* my IQ dropping as I wondered, for the hundredth time that night, why I'd let them drag me here *again*.

Every time we came to the Nest, the same thing happened. Casey and Jessica danced, flirted, attracted the attention of every male in sight, and eventually were hauled out of the party by their protective best friend – me – before any of the horn dogs could take advantage of them. In the meantime, I sat at the bar all night talking to Joe, the thirty-year-old bartender, about 'the problems with kids these days.'

I figured Joe would get offended if I told him that

one of the biggest problems was this damn place. The Nest, which used to be a real bar, had been converted into a teen lounge three years ago. The rickety oak bar still stood, but Joe served only Coke products while the kids danced or listened to live music. I hated the place for the simple reason that it made my friends, who could be somewhat sensible most of the time, act like idiots. But in their defence, they weren't the only ones. Half of Hamilton High showed up on the weekends, and no one left the club with their dignity intact.

I mean seriously, where was the fun in all of this? Want to dance to the same heavy bass techno music week after week? Sure! Then maybe I'll hit on this sweaty, oversexed football player. Maybe we'll have meaningful discussions about politics and philosophy while we bump 'n grind. Ugh. Yeah, right.

Casey plopped down on the stool next to mine. 'You should come dance with us, B,' she said, breathless from her booty shaking. 'It's *so* much fun.'

'Sure it is,' I muttered.

'Oh my gosh!' Jessica sat down on my other side, her honey-blond ponytail bouncing against her shoulders. 'Did you see that? Did you *effing* see that? Harrison Carlyle totally just hit on me! Did you *see* that? Omigosh!'

Casey rolled her eyes. 'He asked you where you got your shoes, Jess. He's totally gay.'

'He's too cute to be gay.'

Casey ignored her, running her fingers behind her ear, as if tucking back invisible locks. It was a habit left over from before she'd chopped her hair into its current edgy blond pixie cut. 'B, you should dance with us. We brought you here so that *we* could hang out with you – not that Joe isn't entertaining.' She winked at the bartender, probably hoping to score some free sodas. 'But we're your friends. You should come dance. Shouldn't she, Jess?'

'Totally,' Jessica agreed, eyeing Harrison Carlyle, who sat in a booth on the other side of the room. She paused and turned back to us. 'Wait. What? I wasn't listening.'

'You just look so bored over here, B. I want you to have some fun, too.'

'I'm fine,' I lied. 'I'm having a great time. You know I can't dance. I'd be in your way. Go . . . live it up or whatever. I'll be OK over here.'

Casey narrowed her hazel eyes at me. 'You sure?' she asked.

'Positive.'

She frowned, but after a second she shrugged and grabbed Jessica by the wrist, pulling her out onto the dance floor.

'Holy crap!' Jessica cried. 'Slow down, Case! You'll rip my arm off!' Then they made their merry way to the middle of the room, already syncing the sway of their hips with the pulsing techno music.

'Why didn't you tell them you're miserable?' Joe asked, pushing a glass of Cherry Coke towards me.

'I'm not miserable.'

'You're not a good liar either,' he replied before a group of freshmen started yelling for drinks at the other end of the bar.

I sipped my Cherry Coke, watching the clock above the bar. The second hand seemed to be frozen, and I prayed the damn thing was broken or something. I wouldn't ask Casey and Jessica to leave until eleven. Any earlier and I'd be the party pooper. But according to the clock it wasn't even nine yet, and I could already feel myself getting a techno-music migraine, only made worse by the pulsing strobe light. *Move, second hand! Move!*

'Hello there.'

I rolled my eyes and turned to glare at the unwelcome intruder. This happened once in a while. Some guy, usually stoned or rank with BO, would take a seat beside me and make a half-assed attempt at small talk. Clearly they hadn't inherited the observant gene, because the expression on my face made it pretty damn obvious that I wasn't in the mood to be swept off my feet.

Surprisingly, the guy who'd taken the seat next to me didn't stink like pot or armpits. In fact, that might have been cologne I smelled on the air. But my disgust only increased when I realized who the cologne belonged to. I would have preferred the fuzzy-headed stoner.

Wesley. Fucking. Rush.

'What do you want?' I demanded, not even bothering to be polite.

'Aren't *you* the friendly type?' Wesley said sarcastically. 'Actually, I came to talk to you.'

'Well, that sucks for you. I'm not talking to people tonight.' I slurped my drink loudly, hoping he'd take the not-so-subtle hint to leave. No such luck. I could feel his dark grey eyes crawling all over me. He couldn't even pretend to be looking me in the eyes, could he? Ugh!

'Come on,' Wesley teased. 'There's no need to be so cold.'

'*Leave me alone*,' I hissed through clenched teeth. 'Go try your charming act on some tramp with low self-esteem, because I'm not falling for it.'

'Oh, I'm not interested in tramps,' he said. 'That's not my thing.'

I snorted. 'Any girl who'd give you the time of day,

Wesley, is most definitely a tramp. No one with taste or class or dignity would actually find you attractive.'

OK. That was a tiny lie.

Wesley Rush was the most disgusting womanizing playboy to ever darken the doorstep of Hamilton High . . . but he was kind of hot. Maybe if you could put him on mute . . . and cut off his hands . . . maybe – just maybe – he'd be tolerable then. Otherwise, he was a real piece of shit. Horn dog shit.

'And you *do* have taste and class and dignity, I assume?' he asked, grinning.

'Yes, I do.'

'That's a shame.'

'Is this your attempt at flirting?' I asked. 'If it is, you fail. Epically.'

He laughed. 'I never fail at flirting.' He ran his fingers through his dark, curly hair and adjusted his crooked, arrogant little grin. 'I'm just being friendly. Trying to have a nice conversation.'

'Sorry. Not interested.' I turned away and took another drink of my Cherry Coke. But he didn't move. Not even an inch. 'You can go now,' I said forcefully.

Wesley sighed. 'Fine. You're being really uncooperative, you know. So I guess I'll be honest with you. I've got to hand it to you: you're smarter and more stubborn than most girls I talk to. But I'm here for a little more than witty conversation.' He moved his attention to the dance floor. 'I actually need your help. You see, your friends are hot. And you, darling, are the Duff.'

'Is that even a word?'

'Designated. Ugly. Fat. Friend,' he clarified. 'No offence, but that would be you.'

'I am not the—'

'Hey, don't get defensive. It's not like you're an ogre or anything, but in comparison . . .' He shrugged his broad shoulders. 'Think about it. Why do they bring you here if you don't dance?' He had the nerve to reach over and pat my knee, like he was trying to comfort me. I jerked away from him, and his fingers moved smoothly to brush some curls out of his face instead. 'Look,' he said, 'you have hot friends . . . *really* hot friends.' He paused, watching the action on the dance floor for a moment, before facing me again. 'The point is, scientists have proven that every group of friends has a weak link, a Duff. And girls respond well to guys who associate with their Duffs.'

'Crackheads can call themselves scientists now? That's news to me.'

'Don't be bitter,' he said. 'What I'm saying is, girls – like your friends – find it sexy when guys show some sensitivity and socialize with the Duff. So by talking to you right now I am doubling my chances of getting laid tonight. Please assist me here, and just pretend to enjoy the conversation.'

I stared at him, flabbergasted, for a long moment. Beauty really was skin-deep. Wesley Rush may have had the body of a Greek god, but his soul was as black and empty as the inside of my closet. What a bastard!

With one swift motion I jumped to my feet and flung the contents of my glass in Wesley's direction. Cherry Coke flew all over him, splattering his expensive-looking white polo shirt. Drops of dark red liquid glistened on his cheeks and colored his brown hair. His face glowed with anger, and his chiseled jaw clinched fiercely.

'What was that for?' he snapped, wiping his face with the back of his hand.

'What do you *think* it was for?' I bellowed, fists balled at my sides.

'Honestly, Duffy, I have no earthly idea.'

Angry flames blazed in my cheeks. 'If you think I'm letting one of my friends leave this place with you, Wesley, you're very, very wrong,' I spat. 'You're a disgusting, shallow, womanizing jackass, and I hope that soda stains your preppy little shirt.' Just before I marched away, I looked over my shoulder and added, 'And my name isn't Duffy. It's Bianca. We've been in the same homeroom since middle school, you self-absorbed son of a bitch.'

I never thought I'd say this, but thank God the damn techno played so loud. No one but Joe overheard the little episode, and he probably found the whole thing hysterical. I had to push my way through the crowded dance floor to find my friends. When I tracked them down, I grabbed Casey and Jessica by their elbows and tugged them toward the exit.

'Hey!' Jessica protested.

'What's wrong?' Casey asked.

'We're getting the fuck out of here,' I said, yanking their unwilling bodies along behind me. 'I'll explain in the car. I just can't stand to be in this hellhole for one more second.'

'Can't I say bye to Harrison first?' Jessica whined, trying to loosen my grip on her arm.

'Jessica!' I cricked my neck painfully when I twisted around to face her. 'He's *gay!* You don't have a chance, so just give it up already. I *need* to get out of here. Please.'

I pulled them out into the parking lot, where the icy January air tore at the bare flesh of our faces. Relenting, Casey and Jessica gathered close on either side of me. They must have found their outfits, which were intended to be sexy, ill equipped to handle the windchill. We moved to my car in a huddle, separating only when we reached the front bumper. I clicked the unlock button on my key chain so that we could climb into the slightly warmer cab of the Saturn without delay.

Casey curled up in the front seat and said, through chattering teeth, 'Why are we leaving so early? B, it's only like, nine-fifteen.'

Jessica sulked in the backseat with an ancient blanket wrapped around her like a cocoon. (My piece-of-shit heater rarely decided to work, so I kept a stash of blankets in the door.)

'I got into an argument with someone,' I explained, jabbing the key into the ignition with unnecessary force. 'I threw my Coke on him, and I didn't want to stick around for his response.'

'Who?' Casey asked.

I'd been dreading that question because I knew the reaction I'd get. 'Wesley Rush.'

Two swoony, girly sighs followed my answer.

'Oh, come on,' I fumed. 'The guy is a man-whore. I can't stand him. He sleeps with everything that moves, and his brain is located in his pants – which means it's microscopic.'

'I doubt that,' Casey said with another sigh. 'God, B, only you could find a flaw in Wesley Rush.'

I glared at her as I turned my head to back out of the parking lot. 'He's a jerk.'

'That's not true,' Jessica interjected. 'Jeanine said he talked to her at a party recently. She was with Vikki and Angela, and she said he just came up and sat down beside her. He was really friendly.'

That made sense. Jeanine was definitely the Duff if she was out with Angela and Vikki. I wondered which of them left with Wesley that night.

'He's charming,' Casey said. 'You're just being Little Miss Cynical, as usual.' She gave me a warm smile from across the cab. 'But what the hell did he do to get you to throw Coke at him?' *Now* she sounded concerned. Took her long enough. 'Did he say something to you, B?'

'No,' I lied. 'It's nothing. He just pisses me off.'

Duff.

The word bounced around in my mind as I sped down 5th Street. I couldn't bring myself to tell my friends about the wonderful new insult that had just been added to my vocab list, but when I glanced at myself in the rearview mirror, Wesley's assertion that I was the unattractive, undesirable tagalong (more like dragalong) seemed to be confirmed. Jessica's perfect hourglass figure and warm, welcoming brown eyes. Casey's flawless complexion and mile-long legs. I couldn't compare to either of them.

'Well, I say we hit another party, since it's so early,' Casey suggested. 'I heard about this one out in Oak Hill. Some college kid is home for Christmas break and decided to have a big blow-out. Angela told me about it this morning. Want to go?'

'Yeah!' Jessica straightened up beneath the blanket. 'We should totally go! College parties have college *boys*. Won't that be fun, Bianca?'

I sighed. 'No. Not really.'

'Oh, come on.' Casey reached over and squeezed my arm. 'No dancing this time, OK? And Jess and I promise to keep all hot guys away from you, since clearly you hate them.' She smirked, trying to nudge me back into a good mood.

'I don't hate hot guys,' I told her. 'Just the one.' After a moment, I sighed and turned onto the highway, heading for the county line. 'Fine, we'll go. But you two are buying me ice cream afterward. Two scoops.'

'Deal.'

2

There is nothing more peaceful than quiet on a Saturday night – or very early Sunday morning. Dad's muffled snores rumbled from down the hall, but the rest of the house was silent when I crept in sometime after one. Or maybe I'd been deafened by the thudding bass at the Oak Hill party. Honestly, the idea of hearing loss didn't bother me too much. If it meant I never had to listen to techno again, I was all for it.

I locked the front door behind me and walked through the dark, empty living room. I saw the postcard lying on the coffee table, sent from whatever city Mom was in now, but I didn't bother reading it. It would still be there in the morning, and I was just too tired, so I dragged myself up the stairs to my bedroom instead.

Stifling a yawn, I hung my coat over the back of my desk chair and moved over to my bed. The migraine began to subside as I kicked my Converses across the room. I was exhausted, but my OCD was totally calling. The pile of clean laundry on the floor, by the foot of my bed, had to be folded before I'd ever be able to sleep.

Carefully, I lifted each piece of clothing and folded it with embarrassing precision. Then I stacked the shirts, jeans, and underwear in separate sections on the floor. Somehow, the act of folding the wrinkled clothes soothed me. As I made the perfect piles, my mind cleared, my body relaxed, and my irritation from the night of loud music and obnoxious, rich, sex-obsessed pigs ebbed. With every even crease, I was reborn.

When all of the clothes were folded, I stood up, leaving the stacks on the floor. I pulled off my sweater and jeans, which stank from the sweltering parties, and tossed them into the hamper in the corner of my room. I could shower in the morning. I was too tired to deal with it tonight.

Before crawling under my sheets, I took a glance at the full-length mirror across the room. I searched my reflection with new eyes, with new knowledge. Uncontrollable wavy auburn hair. A long nose. Big thighs. Small boobs. Yep. Definitely Duff material. How had I not known?

I mean, I'd never considered myself particularly attractive, and it wasn't hard to see that Casey and Jessica, both thin and blond, were gorgeous, but still. The fact that I played the role of the ugly girl to their luscious duo hadn't occurred to me. Thanks to Wesley Rush, I could see it now.

Sometimes it's better to be clueless.

I pulled a blanket up to my chin, hiding my naked body from the scrutiny of the mirror. Wesley was living proof that beauty was only skin-deep, so why did his words bother me? I was intelligent. I was a good person. So who cared if I was the Duff? If I were attractive, I'd have to deal with guys like Wesley *hitting on* me. Ugh! So being the Duff had its benefits, right? Being unattractive didn't have to suck.

Damn Wesley Rush! I couldn't believe he was making me worry about such stupid, pointless, shallow bullshit.

I closed my eyes. I wouldn't think about it in the morning. I wouldn't think about Duffs *ever again*.

Sunday was fantastic — nice, quiet, uninterrupted euphoria. Of course, things were usually pretty quiet when Mom was away. When she was home, the house always seemed loud. There was always music or laughter or something lively and chaotic. But she never seemed to be home for more than a couple of months, and in the time that she was gone, everything grew still. Like me,

Dad wasn't much for socializing. He was usually buried in his work or watching television. Which meant the Piper house was pretty much silent.

And, on a morning after I'd been forced to withstand all the racket of clubs and parties, a quiet house was the equivalent of perfection.

But Monday sucked.

All Mondays suck, of course, but this Monday *really* fucked up everything. It all started first block when Jessica slumped into Spanish with tear-stained cheeks and running mascara.

'Jessica, what's wrong?' I asked. 'Did something happen? Is everything OK?'

I'll admit it; I always got really freaked out on the rare occasions when Jessica came to class looking anything less than perky. I mean, she was constantly bouncing and giggling. So when she came in looking so depressed, it scared the shit out of me.

Jessica shook her head miserably and collapsed into her seat. 'Everything's fine, but . . . I can't go to Homecoming!' Fresh tears spewed from her wide chocolate eyes. 'Mom won't let me go!'

That was it? She'd gotten me all freaked out over *Homecoming*?

'Why not?' I asked, still trying to be sympathetic.

'I'm grounded,' Jessica sniffed. 'She saw my report card in my room this morning, and she found out I'm failing chemistry, and she flipped out! It's not effing fair! Basketball Homecoming is, like, my favourite dance of the year . . . after prom and Sadie Hawkins and Football Homecoming.'

I tilted my chin down and looked at her teasingly. 'Wow, how many favourites do you have?'

She didn't answer. Or laugh.

'I'm sorry, Jessica. I know it must suck . . . but I'm not going either.' I didn't mention that I considered the whole practice of school dances degrading or that they were just giant wastes of time and money. Jessica already knew my opinions on the matter, and I didn't think reminding her would help the situation. But I was pretty happy I wouldn't be the only girl skipping. 'How about this: I'll come over, and we'll watch movies all night. Will your mom be cool with that?'

Jessica nodded and wiped her eyes with the cuff of her sleeve. 'Yeah,' she said. 'Mom likes you. She thinks you're a good influence on me. So that'll be OK. Thanks, Bianca. Can we watch *Atonement* again? Are you sick of it yet?'

Yes, I was getting very sick of the mushy romances Jessica swooned over, but I could get over it. I grinned at her. 'I never get tired of James McAvoy. We can even watch *Becoming Jane* if you want. It'll be a double feature.'

She laughed – finally – just as the teacher made her way to the front of the room and began obsessively straightening the pencils on her desk before calling roll. Jessica tossed a glance at the scrawny instructor. When she looked back at me, her dark brown eyes sparkled with a few fresh tears. 'You know what the worst part is, Bianca?' she whispered. 'I was gonna ask Harrison to go with me. Now I'll have to wait until prom to ask him to a dance.'

Because of her sensitive state, I decided not to remind her that Harrison wouldn't be interested because she had boobs – big ones. Instead I just said, 'I know. I'm sorry, Jessica.'

Once that little crisis was behind us, Spanish went by smoothly. Jessica's tears cleared up, and by the time the bell rang, she was laughing giddily while Angela, a friend of ours, told us about her new boyfriend. I found out that I'd made an A on my last *prueba de vocabulario*. Plus, I totally understood how to conjugate regular present subjunctive verbs. So I was in a pretty damn good mood when Jessica, Angela and I walked out of the classroom.

'And he has a job on campus,' Angela rambled as we pushed our way into the crowded hall.

'Where does he go to school?' I asked.

'Oak Hill Community College.' She sounded a little embarrassed, and she quickly added, 'But he's just getting his associate's degree there before he goes to a university. And OHCC isn't a bad school or anything.'

'That's where I'm going,' Jessica said. 'I don't want to go too far from home.'

Jessica and I were such polar opposites, it was sort of funny sometimes. You could always predict what one of us was going to want to do just by picking the reverse of the other. Personally, I wanted to get the hell out of Hamilton as soon as possible. Graduation couldn't arrive soon enough, and then I'd be off to New York for college.

But the idea of being so far away from Jessica – not seeing her bounce by me every day or hearing her jabber about dances and gay boys – suddenly scared me. I wasn't entirely sure how I'd handle it. She and Casey kind of balanced me out. I wasn't sure anyone else would be willing to put up with my cynicism once I left town.

'We should get to chemistry, Jess,' Angela said as she shook her long black bangs from her eyes. 'You know how Mr Rollins gets when we show up late.'

They scampered off to the science department, and I started down the hallway heading toward AP government.

My mind drifted to other places, to a future without my best friends to keep me sane. I'd never considered that before, and now that I was thinking about it, it made me really nervous. I knew they'd tease me for it, but I would have to find a way to keep in constant touch.

I guess my eyes lost contact with my brain, because the next thing I knew, I ran smack into Wesley Rush.

That was the end of my good mood.

I stumbled backward, and all of my textbooks slipped from my arms and crashed to the floor. Wesley grabbed me by both shoulders, his large hands catching me before I had the chance to trip over my own feet and slam into the tile.

'Whoa,' he said, steadying me.

We were standing *way* too close to each other. I felt like I had bugs crawling under my skin, spreading from the places where his hands touched me. I shivered with disgust, but he misread it.

'Wow, Duffy,' he said, looking down at me with a cocky grin. He was really tall – I'd forgotten that, sitting next to him at the Nest the other night. He was one of the only boys in our school who was taller than Casey – at least six two. An entire foot taller than me. 'Do I make you weak in the knees?'

'As if.' I twisted out of his grasp, fully aware that I

sounded like Alicia Silverstone in *Clueless* but just not caring. I knelt down and began to gather my books, and to my intense displeasure, Wesley joined me. He was playing the Good Samaritan role, of course. I bet he was hoping some hot cheerleader, like Casey, would walk by and think he was being a gentleman. What a pig. Always looking to score.

'Spanish, huh?' he said, glancing down at the scattered papers as he grabbed them. 'Can you say anything interesting?'

'El tono de tu voz hace que quiera estrangularme.' I stood up and waited for him to hand over my papers.

'That sounds sexy,' he said, getting to his feet and handing me the stack of Spanish work he'd swept together. 'What's it mean?'

'The sound of your voice makes me want to strangle myself.'

'Kinky.'

Without another word, I jerked the papers from his hands, tucked them inside one of my books, and stomped off to class. I needed to put as much distance between myself and the womanizing bastard as possible. Duffy? Seriously? He knew my name! The egotistical jackass just couldn't let me be. Not to mention my skin was *still* itching where he'd touched me.

Mr Chaucer's AP government class consisted of only nine students, and seven of them were already in the room by the time I walked through the door. Mr Chaucer gave me a dirty look through his squinting eyes, impressing upon me that the bell would ring any second. To be late was a felony in Mr Chaucer's opinion, and to be *almost* late constituted a misdemeanour. I wasn't the last one to show up, though. That helped a little.

I took my seat in the very back of the room and started to open my notebook, hoping to God that Mr Chaucer wouldn't call me out on my near tardiness. With my current mood, there was no guarantee I wouldn't start cussing at him. He didn't, and we were both saved the drama.

The last student entered just as the bell rang. 'Sorry, Mr Chaucer. I was putting up signs promoting next week's inauguration ceremony. You didn't start already, did you?'

My heart skipped a beat when I looked up at the boy who'd just come in.

OK, so I'm not quiet about the fact that I hate teenagers who date in high school and constantly rant and rave about how much they 'love' their boyfriend or girlfriend. I freely admit that I hate girls who say they love someone before they've dated them. I don't hide the fact that, in my opinion, love takes years – five or ten at least – to develop, and high school relationships seem incredibly pointless to me. Everyone knew this about me . . . but nobody knew that I was *almost* a hypocrite.

Well, OK, Casey and Jessica knew, but that didn't count.

Toby Tucker. Aside from the tragic alliteration, he was perfect in every single way. He wasn't a testosterone-loaded football player. He wasn't an overly sensitive guitar-playing hippie. He didn't write poetry or wear eyeliner. So he probably wouldn't have been classified as the typical hottie, but that worked in my favour, right? Jocks, guys in bands, and Emo boys didn't look twice at – as Wesley would have so delicately worded it – the Duff. I probably had a better chance with intelligent, politically active, somewhat socially awkward guys like Toby. Right?

Wrong, wrong, *wrong*.

Toby Tucker was my perfect match. Unfortunately, he wasn't aware of this fact. That was mostly because I lost my ability to form coherent sentences every time he got close to me. He probably thought I was mute or something. He never looked at me or spoke to me or even seemed to notice me in the back of the room. For a girl with such a fat ass, I felt pretty invisible.

I noticed Toby, though. I noticed his outdated yet adorable blond bowl cut and his pasty ivory skin. I noticed his green eyes beneath the lenses of his oval glasses. I noticed that he wore a blazer with *everything*, and I noticed the adorable way he bit his lower lip when he was thinking really hard about something. I was in . . . OK, not love, but definitely like. I was deeply in *like* with Toby Tucker.

'Fine,' Mr Chaucer muttered. 'Just keep an eye on your watch tomorrow, Mr Tucker.'

'Sure thing, sir.'

Toby took a seat in the front row next to Jeanine McPhee. Like a stalker, I listened in on their conversation while Mr Chaucer started writing the lecture notes on the whiteboard. I'm not normally such a creep, but lo— *like* makes people do crazy things. At least that's the popular excuse.

'How was your weekend, Toby?' Jeanine asked through her constantly stuffy nose. 'Did you do anything exciting?'

'It was pretty good,' Toby said. 'Dad took Nina and me out of state. We toured the University of Southern Illinois together. That was fun.'

'Is Nina your sister?' Jeanine asked.

'No. Nina's my girlfriend. She goes to Oak Hill High

School. Didn't I tell you about her? Anyway, we both got accepted there, so we wanted to check it out. I'm looking at a few other schools, but we've been together for a year and a half, and we kind of want to attend the same school to avoid the long-distance issue.'

'That's sweet!' Jeanine cried. 'I'm actually considering just doing some classes at OHCC before I decide what university I'll go to.'

My skin had stopped crawling, but now my stomach was doing sickening somersaults. I thought I was going to vomit, and I had to fight the urge to run from the room with a hand cupped over my mouth. Eventually, I won the battle to keep my breakfast where it belonged, but I still felt pretty shitty.

Toby had a girlfriend? For a year and a half? Oh my God! How had I missed that? And they were going to college *together*? Did that mean he was one of those stupid, mushy romantics I mocked on a daily basis? I'd expected so much more from Toby Tucker. I'd expected him to be just as skeptical about the nature of teenage love as I was. I'd expected him to see college as a huge decision, not one that should be swayed by where your boyfriend/girlfriend got accepted. I'd expected him to be . . . well, *smart*!

He wouldn't date you, anyway, a voice in my head hissed

at me. It sounded uncannily like Wesley Rush's unnerving whisper. *You're the Duff, remember? His girlfriend is probably thinner with bigger boobs.*

It wasn't even lunch yet, and I already wanted to jump off a cliff. Well, OK that was overdramatic. I definitely wanted to go home and go to bed, though. I wanted to forget Toby had a serious girlfriend. I wanted to wash the feeling of Wesley's hands off me. Mostly, though, I wanted to erase the word *Duff* from my memory.

Oh, yeah, and things got worse that day, too.

Around six o'clock that night, the guy on the news started talking about some big snowstorm that would show up in the 'early morning hours'. I guess the school board took pity on us since we hadn't had a single snow day so far, because they went ahead and cancelled classes before the storm even hit. So Casey called at seven-thirty and insisted that we go to the Nest, since we didn't have to get up early the next morning.

'I don't know, Casey,' I said. 'What if the roads are bad?' I'll admit it. I was looking for *any* reason not to go. My day had been crappy enough on its own. I didn't know if I could endure the torture of that hellhole, too.

'B, the storm isn't supposed to even start until, like, three a.m. or something. As long as we're home by then it'll be cool.'

'I have a lot of homework.'

'It's not due until Wednesday. You can work on it *all day* tomorrow if you want.'

I sighed. 'Can you and Jessica find another ride and go without me? I just don't feel up to it. It's been a bad day, Casey.'

I could always rely on Casey to act at the slightest sign of trouble. 'What happened?' she asked. 'Are you OK? You didn't look happy at lunch. Is it about your mom?'

'Casey.'

'Tell me what's up.'

'Nothing,' I assured her. 'Today just sucked, OK? Nothing major or anything. I'm just not in the mood to go partying with you guys tonight.'

There was a pause on the other end of the line. Finally, Casey said, 'Bianca, you know you can tell me anything, right? You know you can talk to me if you need to. Don't keep things bottled up. It's not good for you.'

'Casey, I'm fi—'

'You're *fine*,' she interrupted. 'Yeah, I know. I'm just saying that if you have a problem, I'm here for you.'

'I know,' I murmured. I felt guilty for getting her nervous like that over something so stupid. I had a bad habit of holding in all my emotions, and Casey knew that all too well. She was always trying to look out for me.

Always coaxing me into sharing so that I didn't wind up exploding later. It could get annoying, but knowing that someone cared . . . well, that felt nice. So I couldn't really get mad about it. 'I know, Casey. I'm fine, though. It's just . . . I found out Toby has a girlfriend today, and I'm a little bummed. That's all.'

'Oh, B,' she sighed. 'That sucks. I'm sorry. Maybe if you come out tonight, Jess and I can cheer you up. Two scoops of ice cream and everything.'

I let out a little laugh. 'Thanks, but no thanks. I think I'll just stay home tonight.'

I hung up the phone and went downstairs, where I found Dad using the cordless in the kitchen. I heard him before I saw him. He was yelling into the receiver. I stood in the doorway, assuming he'd notice me and immediately lower his voice. I figured some telemarketer was getting an earful of Mike Piper, but then my name came up.

'Think of what you're doing to Bianca!' Dad's loud voice, which I'd taken for anger, sounded more like pleading. 'This isn't good for a seventeen-year-old girl and her mother. She needs you here at home, Gina. *We* need you here.'

I slipped back into the living room, surprised to realize he was talking to my mother. Truthfully, I didn't really know how to feel about it. About the things he was saying. I mean, yeah, I missed my mom. Having her home would have been nice, but it wasn't as if we weren't used to getting along without her.

My mother was a motivational speaker. When I was a kid, she'd written some sort of uplifting, inspirational book about improving self-esteem. It hadn't sold well, but she still got offers to speak at colleges, support groups, and graduations all over the country. Since the book had flopped, she came pretty cheap.

For a while, she'd taken only local jobs. Ones she could drive home from after she finished telling people how to love themselves. But after my grandmother passed away, when I was twelve, Mom got a little depressed. Dad suggested she take a vacation. Just get away for a few weeks.

When she came back, she gushed about all the places she'd seen and the people she'd met. I guess maybe that's what sparked her addiction to travelling. Because after that first vacation, Mom started booking events all over the place. In Colorado and New Hampshire. She'd set up entire tours.

Only this tour, the one she was on now, had been the longest. She hadn't been home in almost two months, and this time I wasn't even sure where she was speaking.

Obviously that was why Dad was pissed. Because she'd been gone for so long.

'Damn it, Gina. When are you going to stop being a child and come home? When are you coming home to us for good?' The way my dad's voice cracked when he uttered that sentence nearly had me in tears. 'Gina,' he murmured. 'Gina, we love you. Bianca and I miss you, and we want you to come home.'

I pressed myself against the wall that separated me from Dad, biting my lip. God, it was just getting pathetic. I mean, why wouldn't they just get a fucking divorce already? Was I the only one who could see that things just weren't working out here? What was the point of being married if Mom was always gone?

'Gina,' my father said, and I thought it sounded like he was on the verge of crying. Then I heard him put the phone down on the counter. The talk was over.

I gave him a couple of minutes before I walked into the kitchen. 'Hey, Dad. Is everything OK?'

'Yeah,' he said. God, he was a bad liar. 'Oh, it's fine, Bumblebee. I just had a talk with your mom and . . . she sends her love.'

'From where this time?'

'Um . . . Orange County,' he said. 'She's visiting your aunt Leah while she speaks at a high school there. Cool, huh? You can tell your friends that your mom is in the O.C. now. You like that show, don't you?'

'Yeah,' I said. 'I liked it . . . but it got cancelled a few years ago.'

'Oh, well . . . I guess I'm behind, Bumblebee.' I saw his eyes drift over to the counter, where he'd left his car keys, and I followed them. He noticed this and looked away quickly, before I could say anything. 'Do you have plans tonight?' he asked.

'Well, I could make some, but . . .' I cleared my throat, uncertain of how to say my next sentence. Dad and I really didn't make a habit of talking to each other. 'I could stay home, too. Do you want me to stay here and, like, watch TV with you or something?'

'Oh, no, Bumblebee,' he said with an unconvincing laugh. 'Go have fun with your friends. I'll probably go to bed early tonight, anyway.'

I looked him in the eye, hoping he'd change his mind. Dad always got really depressed after his fights with Mom. I was worried about him, but I wasn't really sure how to approach the subject.

And in the back of my mind, there was this tiny fear. It was stupid, really, but I couldn't shake it. My father was a recovering alcoholic. I mean, he quit before I was born, and he hadn't touched a drop since . . . but

31

sometimes, when he got all pouty about Mom, I got scared. Scared that he might take those car keys and head to the liquor store or something. Like I said, it was ridiculous, but the fear couldn't be vanquished.

Dad broke our eye contact and shifted uncomfortably. He turned and walked towards the sink, washing the plate he'd just eaten spaghetti off of. I wanted to walk over there and take the plate – his pathetic excuse to distract himself – and throw it on the ground. I wanted to tell him how stupid this whole thing was with Mom. I wanted him to realize what a waste of time these dumb depressions and fights were and just admit things weren't working out.

But, of course, I couldn't. All I could say was, 'Dad . . .'

He faced me, shaking his head, a wet dishrag dangling from his hand. 'Go out and have fun,' he said. 'Seriously, I want you to. You're only a kid once.'

There was no arguing. That was his subtle way of telling me he wanted to be alone.

'OK,' I said. 'If you're sure . . . I'll go call Casey.'

I walked upstairs and into my bedroom. I picked my cell phone up off the dresser and dialled Casey's number. Two rings in, she answered.

'Hey, Casey. I changed my mind about the Nest . . .

and, um, do you think it would be OK if I stayed over tonight? I'll tell you about it later, but I . . . I just don't want to stay at home.'

I refolded the clean clothes on the floor at the foot of my bed before I left, but it didn't help as much as it usually did.

3

'Pour me another one, Joe.' I slid the empty glass towards the bartender, who caught it easily.

'I'm cutting you off, Bianca.'

I rolled my eyes. 'It's Cherry Coke.'

'Which can be just as dangerous as whiskey.' He put the glass on a counter behind the bar. 'No more. You'll thank me later. Caffeine headaches are a bitch, and I know how you girls are. When you gain five pounds, you'll blame me.'

'Whatever.' So what if I gained weight? I was already the Duff, and the one guy I wanted to impress had a serious girlfriend. I could gain seventy pounds and be no worse off.

'Sorry, Bianca.' Joe moved to the other end of the bar, where Angela and her best friend, Vikki, waited to order drinks.

I drummed my fingers on the wooden surface of the bar, my mind far away from the music and strobe lights. Why hadn't I insisted on staying home with Dad? Why hadn't I just made him talk to me? I kept imagining him, wallowing in his misery . . . alone.

But that's how we Pipers handled stress.

Alone.

Why was that? Why couldn't either of us open up? Why couldn't Dad admit that he and Mom were having issues? Why couldn't I confront him about it?

'Hello, Duffy.'

Why did that jackass have to sit next to me?

'Go away, Wesley,' I growled, staring down at my restless fingers.

'I can't,' he said. 'You see, Duffy, I'm not one to give up easily. I am determined to hook up with one of your friends – preferably the one with the fantastic rack.'

'Then go talk to *her*,' I suggested.

'I would, but Wesley Rush doesn't chase girls. They chase him.' He grinned at me. 'It's all right. She'll be over here *begging* me to sleep with her soon. Talking to you will just speed up the process. Until then, you get the honour of my company. Lucky for me, it doesn't look like you're armed with a beverage tonight.' He laughed but stopped suddenly. I could feel his eyes on me, but I didn't look up. 'Are you all right? You don't seem as aggressive as usual.'

'Leave me alone, Wesley. I'm serious.'

'What's wrong?'

'Go away.'

The anxiety inside me needed to escape, to be released in some way. I couldn't wait until Casey and I got back to her house to vent. I needed to let it out *right then*. But I didn't want to cry, not in front of half the school, and there was no way I was going to talk about it with Joe or the douche bag next to me, and punching someone would just get me in trouble. I couldn't see any other options, but I felt like I'd explode if I didn't let it out soon.

Mom was in California.

Dad was drowning.

I was too much of a coward to do a damn thing about it.

'There has to be something bothering you,' Wesley persisted. 'You look like you might cry.' He put a hand on my shoulder, forcing me to turn and face him. 'Bianca?'

Then I did a really fucked-up thing. My only excuse is that I was under an unbelievable amount of stress, and I spotted an outlet. I needed something to distract me – anything far away from my parents' drama – just for a second. And when I saw my chance I didn't stop to think about how much I'd regret it later. An opportunity sat on the bar stool beside me, and I lunged at it. Literally.

I kissed Wesley Rush.

One second his hand lay on my shoulder, and his grey eyes rested, for once, on my face, and the next my mouth was on his. My lips were fierce with bottled emotion, and he seemed to tense, his body frozen in shock. That didn't last very long. An instant later, he returned the aggression, his hands flying to my sides and pulling me to him. It felt like a battle between our mouths. My hands clawed into his curly hair, tugging it way harder than necessary, and his fingertips dug into my waist.

It worked better than punching someone would have. Not only did it help me release the agonizing pressure, but it definitely distracted me. I mean, it's hard to think about your dad when you're making out with somebody.

And as disturbing as it sounds, Wesley was a *really* good kisser. He leaned into me, and I tugged at him so hard that he nearly fell off his bar stool. In that moment, we just couldn't get close enough to each other. Our separate seats seemed like they were miles apart.

All of my thoughts vanished, and I became a sort of physical being. Emotions disappeared. Nothing existed but our bodies, and our warring lips were at the centre of everything. It was bliss! It was amazing not to think.

Nothing! Nothing . . . until he screwed it up.

His hand slid up from my waist, trailing along my torso, and came to a stop right on my boob.

Everything flooded back, and I suddenly remembered exactly who I was kissing. I tore my hands out of his hair and shoved him away from me as hard as I could. Anger – fresh, hot anger – surged through me, completely replacing the anxious worry I'd been feeling a minute before. His hands dropped, one landing on my knee, as he pulled away. He looked surprised but distinctly pleased.

'Wow, Duffy, that was—'

And I slapped him. I slapped him so hard, my palm stung with the contact.

The hand on my knee flew to his cheek. 'What the hell?' he demanded. 'Why did you do that?'

'Asshole!' I yelled. I jumped off my stool and stormed onto the dance floor. I didn't want to admit it, but I was madder at myself than at him.

4

Casey's queen-sized bed was incredibly warm. The pillows were soft, and I felt like I could sink into the fluffy mattress and live there forever. But I couldn't sleep. I tossed and turned on my side of the bed, trying not to wake Casey up. I counted sheep. I did that thing where you relax every part of your body from the big toe up. I even imagined one of Mr Chaucer's rambling lectures on public policy.

Still wide-awake.

I was bottling again, but it had nothing to do with Dad this time. I'd gotten that off my chest after Casey and I had dropped Jessica off earlier that night.

'I'm getting worried about Dad,' I'd told her. I'd waited until Jessica was out of the car to talk about it. I knew she wouldn't have understood. Jessica was from a happy, healthy two-parent family. Casey, on the other hand, had already seen her parents' relationship crumble. 'He's so clueless. I mean, isn't it obvious that it isn't working? Shouldn't they just get the fucking divorce and be done with it?'

'Don't say that, B,' she warned. 'Seriously, don't even think that way.'

I shrugged.

'It'll all work out,' she said, reaching over and squeezing my hand as we sped towards her house. The snow hadn't started falling yet, but I could see clouds moving across the stars in the dark sky overhead. 'She'll come home and they'll talk it through and have makeup sex—'

'God! Gross, Casey!'

'—and everything will be back to normal.' She paused as I pulled into her driveway. 'And in the meantime, I'm here for you. If you need to talk, you know I'll listen.'

'Yeah, I know.'

It was the same Casey Saves the Day speech I'd been hearing for twelve years, any time the slightest problem appeared in my life. Not that I needed it that night, really. Honestly, since we'd left the Nest, Dad hadn't been on my mind that much. I'd released all that stress when I'd kissed Wesley.

And that was what kept me from sleeping. I couldn't

stop thinking about what I'd done at the Nest. My skin itched. My lips felt foreign. Plus, no matter how many times I'd brushed my teeth in Casey's bathroom (after half an hour, she'd knocked on the door to make sure I was OK), the taste of disgusting, womanizing bastard was still in my mouth. Ugh! But the worst part was that I knew I'd done it to myself.

I'd kissed *him*. Yeah, he'd groped me, but what had I really expected? Wesley Rush didn't exactly have a reputation for being a gentleman. He might have been a jackass, but I had to take the blame for this situation. That knowledge didn't sit well with me.

'Casey,' I whispered. OK, so waking her up at three a.m. wasn't very nice of me, but she was the one always telling me to share or vent or whatever. So, technically, she brought this on herself. 'Hey, Casey?'

'Hmm?'

'Are you awake?'

'Mmm-mmm.'

'If I tell you something, will you swear not to tell anyone?' I asked. 'And will you promise not to freak out?'

'Sure, B,' she mumbled. 'What is it?'

'I kissed someone tonight,' I said.

'Good for you. Now go back to sleep.'

I took a deep breath. 'It was Wesley . . . Wesley Rush.'

Casey shot straight up in bed. 'Whoa!' She shook her head and rubbed the sleep from her wide hazel eyes. 'OK, now I'm awake.' She turned to face me, her short blond hair sticking up in every possible angle. God, how did she manage to make even *that* look good? 'OMG! What happened? I thought you hated the guy.'

'I do hate him. I will always hate him. It was just a stupid, immature, thoughtless moment of . . . stupidity.' I sat up and hugged my knees to my chest. 'I feel dirty.'

'Dirty can be fun.'

'Casey.'

'Sorry, B, but I don't see what the problem is,' she admitted. 'He's hot. He's rich. He's probably a fantastic kisser. Is he? I mean, he has those lips that just make me think—'

'Casey!' I put my hands over my ears. 'Stop! Look, I'm totally not proud of this. I was upset, he was there, and I just . . . God, I can't believe I did that. Does this make me a slut?'

'Kissing Wesley? Hardly.'

'What do I do, Casey?'

'Kiss him again?'

I shot her a cold look before falling back onto my pillow. I rolled over so that I faced away from her. 'Forget it,' I said. 'I shouldn't have told you at all.'

'Oh, B, don't be like that,' she said. 'I'm sorry, but I think you should look on the bright side for once in your life. I mean, you haven't had a boyfriend since . . .' She trailed off. Both of us knew the name, after all. 'Anyway, it's about time you started getting a little bit of action. You never talk to any guys but Joe, and he's way too old for you. And now that we know Toby's off the market, what's the problem if you date Wesley? Would it kill you?'

'I am *not* dating him,' I hissed. 'Wesley Rush doesn't date, he fucks – everyone, for that matter. I just kissed him, and it was so stupid . . . stupid, stupid, stupid! It was a huge mistake.'

She nestled back into her side of the mattress. 'You know, I knew even you couldn't resist his charm for ever.'

'Excuse me,' I said, rolling back over to glare at her. 'I'm resisting just fine, thanks. And you know what? There's nothing to resist. I find him repulsive. Tonight was just a lapse in judgment and it will never happen again.'

'Never say never, B.'

She was snoring within seconds.

I grumbled to myself for a few minutes, then fell asleep, inwardly cursing both Casey and Wesley. Strangely enough, *that* was comforting.

* * *

Dad had just gotten in from his job at Tech Plus, a local rip-off of Best Buy, when I walked through the door the next afternoon, shaking fresh snow out of my hair. The storm hadn't been as big as the weatherman predicted, but flurries were still falling outside. The sun was bright, though, so the moderate dusting would be melted by that evening. I took off my jacket and glanced over at Dad, who was on the couch, browsing through the *Hamilton Journal* with a mug of hot coffee in his left hand.

He looked up when he heard me come in. 'Hey, Bumblebee,' he said, putting his mug down on the coffee table. 'Did you have fun with Casey and Jessica?'

'Yeah,' I said. 'How was work?'

'Busy,' he sighed. 'Do you know how many people in this town got laptops for Christmas? I'm sure you don't, so I'll just tell you that a lot of them did. Do you know how many of those laptops were faulty?'

'A lot?' I guessed.

'Bingo.' Dad shook his head and started to fold up the newspaper. 'If you don't have the money to spend on a good laptop, why bother? Just save it and buy a better one later. You'll just wind up spending that extra cash on the repairs if you don't. You remember that, Bumblebee. If I teach you one thing in life, let that be it.'

'Sure, Dad.'

Suddenly I felt like an idiot. How could I have gotten so worked up last night? Clearly it was over nothing. I mean, yeah, he and Mom were having issues, but it would probably blow over like Casey said. He wasn't depressed or sad or even remotely close to touching a drop of alcohol.

Still, I knew Mom's latest absence was hitting him kind of hard. So I figured I ought to try and make it easier on him. I knew he was probably feeling a little lonely lately, and I guess that was partially my fault too.

'Wanna watch TV?' I asked. 'I don't have much homework due tomorrow, so I can wait and do it later.'

'Sounds good,' Dad said. He swiped the remote from the side table. 'There's a rerun of an old *Perry Mason* on right now.'

I grimaced. 'Uh . . . OK.'

'I'm kidding, Bumblebee,' he laughed, flipping through the channels. 'I wouldn't do that to you. Let's see . . . Oh, look. There's a *Family Ties* marathon on TV Land. You used to love this show when you were little. You and I used to watch the reruns when you were about four.'

'I remember.' I settled onto the couch beside him. 'I told you I wanted to be a Young Republican because I thought Michael J. Fox was cute.'

Dad snorted and adjusted his thick-rimmed glasses. 'That didn't happen. My Bumblebee's a liberal now.' He put an arm around my shoulders and squeezed. And I knew this was what he needed. Or maybe we both did. Just a little bonding time so that the house didn't feel quite so empty. I mean, I loved the quiet, but too much of it might drive you crazy after a while. 'What do you say we watch a few episodes?'

I smiled. 'Sure, Dad.'

About halfway into the first episode, I had this weird revelation. OK, so when I was a kid, I had a major crush on Alex P. Keaton (Michael J. Fox's super-Republican character on *Family Ties*), but twelve years later, I was in like with Toby Tucker, a Young Democrat. Did I have a thing for politicians or what? Maybe I was, like, destined to be the wife of a senator . . . or I might wind up being the First Lady.

Nah. Politicians didn't marry Duffs. They didn't look good enough on the sidelines of debates. And I wasn't the marrying type, anyway. I had a better shot of being the Monica Lewinsky of the future. I'd just be sure to burn all, um, incriminating dresses.

Hey, Obama was kind of sexy for an old guy. Maybe I had a shot.

I bit my lip as Dad laughed at one of the sitcom-y

jokes. How was it that even *Family Ties* brought me back to that word?

Duff.

God, Wesley and his damn pigeonholing just wouldn't leave me alone. The word was taunting me, even in my own home. I scooted closer to Dad, trying to focus on the show. On our time together. On anything but Wesley and that stupid label. I tried to forget about that damn kiss and how idiotic I'd been.

Tried, tried, tried.

And, of course, failed miserably.

5

When I was in kindergarten, I had a traumatic monkey bars experience. I'd been halfway across, my legs swinging beneath me, when my hands got sweaty and made me slip. I fell for what seemed like a mile before landing on the ground in a heap. All the other five-year-olds laughed at me and my scraped, bloody knee. All of them but one.

Casey Blithe walked out of the gawking group of grade-schoolers and came to stand in front of me. Even back then, I knew she was beautiful. Blond locks, hazel eyes, rosy cheeks . . . the epitome of five-year-old perfection. She could have been in pageants.

'Are you OK?' she asked.

'I'm fine,' I said through thick, hot tears. I wasn't sure whether I was crying because of the pain in my knee or because of the way all my classmates were laughing at me.

'No, you're not. You're bleeding. Let me help.' She reached out a hand and pulled me up. Then she turned and yelled at the kids who were making fun of me.

After that, she basically appointed herself my personal caretaker, never letting me out of her sight, determined to keep me out of trouble. From that moment on, we were best friends.

Of course, that was before popularity and Duffs got involved. She wound up being tall (almost six one – the girl was an Amazon!) and thin and gorgeous. I wound up looking like . . . well, the opposite. To see us separately, no one would ever think we were close. No one would guess the pretty Homecoming Queen was with the chubby mousy-haired girl in the corner.

But we were best friends. She'd been there for me through everything. She'd even stuck by me freshman year, after I'd had my heart broken for the first – and if I had anything to do with it, *only* – time. She never let me isolate myself or drown in my own misery. Despite the fact that she could easily find prettier, cooler, more popular friends, she stayed with me.

So when she asked me to drive her home after cheerleading practice on Wednesday afternoon, I agreed. I mean, after all she'd done for me over the past twelve years, the least I could do was give her a lift every now and then.

I waited in the cafeteria, staring at the psychedelic blue-and-orange walls (the guy who picked our school colours must have been on some serious drugs), attempting to finish my calculus homework. I was in the middle of asking myself the age-old question – *where will I use this in real life?* – when I felt a hand on my shoulder. That skin-crawly thing happened, and I knew exactly who was behind me.

Great. Just fucking great.

I jerked out from under Wesley's hand and spun around to face him, gripping my pencil like a dart and aiming it right at his Adam's apple.

He didn't even flinch. His grey eyes examined the pencil with feigned curiosity and he said, 'Interesting. Is this how you greet all the boys you like?'

'I *don't* like you.'

'Does that mean you love me, then?'

I hated the smooth, confident way he spoke. A lot of girls thought it was sexy, but it was really just stalker-ish. Everything about him screamed *date rape!* to me. Ugh.

'It means that I *hate* you,' I snapped. 'And if you don't stay the fuck away from me, I'll report you for sexual harassment.'

'Might be a hard case,' Wesley mused. He swiped the pencil from me and began twirling it between his fingers. 'Especially considering you're the one who kissed me. Technically, I could report *you* for harassment.'

I gritted my teeth, still hating to even think about it, not even bothering to remind him that he'd been more than willing to participate. 'Give me back my pencil,' I muttered.

'I don't know,' he said. 'With you, this could be classified as a dangerous weapon . . . along with glasses of cherry soda. Interesting choice, by the way. I'd always pegged you for more of a Sprite girl. You know . . . *plain*.'

I just glared at him, hoping he would spontaneously combust before I grabbed my textbooks and notepads off the table. He dodged my attempt to stomp on his foot and stared after me as I marched down the hallway. I was halfway to the gym, where Casey, the cheerleading captain, should have been wrapping up practice, when he caught up with me.

'Oh, come on, Duffy. That was just a joke. Lighten up.'

'It wasn't funny.'

'Your sense of humour needs some work, then,' Wesley suggested. 'Most girls find my jokes charming.'

'Those girls must have IQs low enough to trip over.'

He laughed.

Apparently, *I* was the funny one.

'Hey, you never told me why you were upset the other night,' he said. 'You were too busy shoving your tongue down my throat. So what was the problem?'

'None of your—' I began, but I stopped suddenly. 'Hey! I didn't . . . there was no tongue!' A shiver of rage ran through me as I noticed his mischievous smile. 'You son of a bitch! Get the fuck out of here. God, why are you stalking me? I thought Wesley Rush didn't chase girls. I thought they chased him, right?'

'You're right. Wesley Rush doesn't chase girls, and I'm not chasing you,' he said. 'I'm here waiting for my sister. She's making up a test for Mr Rollins. I just saw you in the cafeteria and thought—'

'What? Thought you'd torture me a little more?' I clenched my fists. 'Leave me the hell alone. You've already made me miserable.'

'How have I done that?' he asked, sounding a little surprised.

I didn't answer. I didn't want to give him the satisfaction of knowing that *Duff* was plaguing me because of him. He'd enjoy it too much.

Instead, I took off running to the gym doors as fast as I could. This time he didn't follow me – thank God.

I hurried into the blue-and-orange gymnasium (Oh God. Bright colours . . . I could feel a headache coming already . . .) and took a seat on the closest bleacher.

'Great practice, girls!' Casey cried from the other side of the gym. 'OK, the next basketball game is Friday. I want you all to practise the dance, and, Vikki, work on those high kicks. All right?'

The Skinny Squad murmured in general agreement.

'Awesome,' said Casey. 'See you later, guys. Go Panthers!'

'Go Panthers!' the other cheerleaders echoed as they separated. Most of the girls hurried to the locker room, but a few headed for the doors, chatting excitedly with their friends.

Casey skipped over to me. 'Hey, B,' she said. 'Sorry we went a little overtime. Do you mind if I change before we get out of here? I feel a little stinky.'

'I don't care,' I murmured.

'What's wrong?' she asked, instantly suspicious.

'Nothing, Casey. Go change.'

'Bianca, I can tell—'

'I don't want to talk about it.' I wasn't about to get into another Wesley discussion with her. She'd probably wind up defending him like last time. 'I'm fine, OK?' I said, softening my voice. 'Long day. Headache.'

Casey still looked skeptical when she walked, with considerably less pep, to the locker room.

Fantastic. I felt like a total bitch. She'd only wanted to make sure I was OK, and I'd shut her out. I shouldn't have taken my anger at Wesley out on her, even if she did think he was a fucking prince.

But when she came out of the locker room in her hoodie and jeans, her usual cheer had returned. She swung her purse over her shoulder and came to where I was sitting, a smile plastered across her spotless, smooth face. 'Sometimes, I can't believe the shit I hear in the locker room,' she said. 'You ready to go, B?'

'Sure.' I picked up my books and started towards the gym doors, hoping that Wesley wasn't still lurking in the hallway.

Casey must have noticed my anxiety. I could see the tense, worried look on her face, but she didn't bring it up again. Instead, she said, 'So, OK, Vikki is *totally* gonna get a reputation as a whore.'

'She already has one.'

'Well, yeah,' Casey admitted, 'but it's about to get worse. She's dating that junior football player – you know, what's-his-name – but she told some guy from Oak Hill High that she'd take him to Basketball Homecoming. I don't know why she does this stuff to herself. You, Jess, and me will have a front-row seat for the drama when it all comes out that night. BTW, what are you wearing to the dance?'

'Nothing.'

'Hot, but I doubt they'll let you in naked, B.' We were walking through the maze of tables in the cafeteria on our way to the parking lot.

'No. I mean, Jessica and I aren't going to Homecoming,' I said.

'Of course you are,' Casey protested.

I shook my head. 'Jessica is grounded. I promised her I'd come over and we'd watch girly movies.'

Casey looked stunned as we pushed through the blue door and entered the freezing student parking lot. 'What? But Jess loves Basketball Homecoming. It's her favourite after prom and Football Homecoming.'

I smiled a little, in spite of myself. 'And Sadie Hawkins.'

'Why didn't I know about this? Homecoming is getting close. Why didn't you all tell me?'

I shrugged. 'Sorry. I didn't even think about it. And I guess Jessica is still moping. She might not want to talk about not being able to go.'

'But . . . but who will I go to the dance with now?'

'Um, a boy,' I suggested. 'Casey, it's not as if it'll be

hard for you to get a date.' I fished the car keys out of my back pocket and unlocked the doors of my Saturn.

'Right, who the hell wants to go with Sasquatch?'

'You are *not* Sasquatch.'

'Besides,' she said, ignoring me, 'it's way better to go with you guys.' She climbed into the passenger's seat and wrapped herself in the blanket Jessica had used a few nights earlier. 'Damn it, B. You really need to get that fucking heater fixed.'

'You really need to get your own car.'

She changed the subject. 'OK, so back to the dance. If you two aren't going . . . do you guys care if I crash your movie fest? It could be a Girls' Night In. We haven't had one of those in a while.'

Despite my crappy mood, I smiled. Casey was right. We hadn't had a movie night together in a long time, and it would be nice to hang out without the drama of boys or loud techno music. For once, I might actually have fun on a Friday night. So I reached for the volume on my stereo and said, 'A week from Friday, it's a date.'

6

When the Friday of our Girls' Night In finally rolled around, I was more than ready for a nice, relaxing evening with my best friends – and the wonderfully Scottish James McAvoy, of course. I'd shoved the copy of *Becoming Jane* that Jessica had given me for Christmas, a pair of barely used pajamas (yeah, I sleep naked at home – so what?) and my toothbrush into my backpack. Casey was bringing the popcorn, and Jessica promised us big bowls of chocolate swirl ice cream.

As if my ass wasn't big enough.

But naturally, the day couldn't be all good. Mrs Perkins, my English teacher, made sure of that during fourth block.

'So, that's *The Scarlet Letter*,' she said, closing her book. 'Did you enjoy it, class?'

There was a low grumble in the negative, but Mrs

Perkins didn't seem to notice.

'Well, because Hawthorne's work is so extraordinary and applicable to contemporary society, I want each of you to write a report pertaining to the novel.' She ignored the loud sighs. 'The report can be about any part of the book – a character, a scene, a theme – but I want it to be very well though out. I will also be allowing you to work in pairs' – the class buzzed with excitement – 'which I will assign.' The excitement vanished.

I knew I was in trouble when Mrs Perkins pulled out her roll sheet. That meant she would be assigning partners based on alphabetical order, and since there were no kids whose last names started with Q in that class, my partner was bound to be—

'Bianca Piper will work with Wesley Rush.'

Shit.

I'd managed to steer clear of Wesley for a week and a half – since the day he'd harassed me after school – but Mrs Perkins had to go and screw that up.

She rattled off the last few names on her list before saying, 'I expect the reports to be no fewer than five pages long – and that's twelve-point font, double-spaced, Vikki. Don't pull that stunt again.' She laughed good-naturedly. 'Now, I want partners to work together. Both must contribute to the report. And be creative, people! Have fun!'

'Not likely,' I muttered to Jessica, who sat at the desk next to mine.

'Oh, I think you're lucky, Bianca,' she said. 'I'd be thrilled if Wesley was my partner. But my heart belongs to Harrison. It is *so* unfair that Casey gets to work with him.' She glanced toward Casey's assigned seat, all the way across the classroom. 'She'll probably get to see his house and bedroom and everything. Do you think she'll say some good things about me if I ask? Maybe she'll be, like, my wing girl.'

I didn't bother answering.

'The reports are due in exactly one week!' Mrs Perkins announced over the chatter. 'So, please work on them this weekend.'

The bell rang and the whole class stood up at the same time. Tiny Mrs Perkins scurried out of the way to avoid being trampled by the stampede toward the door. Jessica and I joined the crowd, and Casey caught up to us just as we stepped into the hall.

'This is bullshit,' she hissed. 'An essay over nothing? I don't want to pick a topic. That's her freaking job! What is the point of this damn assignment if she can't even give us something to write about? It's ridiculous.'

'But you get to work with Harrison, and—'

'Please, Jess, don't start with that crap.' Casey rolled her eyes. 'He. Is. Gay. It isn't gonna happen, OK?'

'You never know! So you won't play wing girl for me?'

'I'll meet you guys in the cafeteria,' I said, turning in the direction of my locker. 'I need to grab a few things first.'

'Cool.' Casey grabbed Jessica by the wrist and pulled her towards the other hallway. 'We'll meet you by the snack machines, 'kay, B? Come on, Jess.' And they left me alone in the packed corridor. OK, not really *packed*. Hamilton High had only around four hundred students or something, but considering the low numbers, the hallways seemed pretty crowded that afternoon. Or maybe I was just stressed out and getting claustrophobic. Anyway, my friends ran away, and I was left among the beasts.

I pushed my way past the loud jocks and smooching couples – PDAs are so disgusting – and headed for the science hallway. It took only a few minutes to get to my locker, which, like the rest of the fugly school, was painted orange and blue. I spun my combination and yanked open the door. Behind me, a group of cheerleaders ran through shouting, 'Go Panthers! Panthers! Panthers!'

I'd just grabbed my coat and backpack and was about

to close the door when *he* showed up. Honestly, I'd expected him sooner.

'Looks like we're partners, Duffy.'

I kicked the locker shut with a little too much force. 'Unfortunately, yes.'

Wesley grinned, running his fingers through his dark curls as he leaned against the locker next to mine. 'So, your place or mine?'

'What?'

'To do the assignment this weekend,' he said, narrowing his eyes. 'Don't be getting any ideas, Duffy. I'm not chasing you. I'm just being a good student. Wesley Rush doesn't chase girls. They—'

'Chase you. Yeah, I know.' I pulled my coat on over my T-shirt. 'If we have to do this, I was thinking we'd—'

'Wesley!' A skinny brunette that I didn't recognize (she looked like a freshman) threw herself at him right in front of me. She stared up at Wesley with big sappy eyes. 'Will you dance with me at Homecoming tonight?'

'Of course, Meghan,' he said, running his hand down her back. He was tall enough to look down her shirt without any problem. Perverted bastard. 'I'll save a dance just for you, OK?'

'Really?'

'Would I lie?'

'Oh, thanks, Wesley!' He bent down, and she gave him a quick kiss on the cheek before scampering off, not looking at me once.

Wesley turned his attention back to me. 'You were saying?'

Through gritted teeth, I growled, *'I was thinking that we'd meet at my place.'*

'What's wrong with my house?' he asked. 'Are you afraid it's haunted, Duffy?'

'Of course not. I'd just prefer to work at my house. God knows what kind of diseases I could get just by stepping foot in your bedroom.' I shook my head. 'So, my house, OK? Tomorrow afternoon at, like, three. Call before you show up.'

I didn't give him a chance to respond. If he had a problem with it, I'd write the paper myself. So, purposely forgetting to say goodbye, I walked off, darting around the groups of gossiping girls and hurrying toward the cafeteria.

I found Casey and Jessica waiting for me by the old vending machines.

'I don't get it, Case,' Jessica was saying. She slipped a dollar into the only working machine and waited for her Sunkist to drop into the slot at the bottom. 'Don't you have to stay and cheer at the game?'

'Nope. I told the girls that I couldn't make it tonight, so one of our alternates, this cute little freshman, is taking my place. She's been wanting to cheer all year, and she's got skills, but there just hasn't been a place for her until now. They'll be fine without me.'

I was standing right next to them before Jessica spotted me. 'There's Bianca! Let's get the heck out of here! Woohoo! Girls' Night In!'

Casey rolled her eyes.

Jessica pushed open the blue door that led to the parking lot, smiling from ear to ear, and said, 'You guys are the best. Like, *really* the best. I don't know what I'd do without you.'

'Cry into your pillow every single night,' Casey said.

'Think your other friends were "really the best",' I offered, returning her smile. There was no fucking way I was going to let Wesley Rush drag me down. No way! This was Girls' Night In, and it wasn't going to be screwed up by an asshole like him. 'You didn't forget that ice cream promise, did you, Jessica?'

'I remember. Chocolate swirl.'

We crossed the parking lot and climbed into my car. Instantly, Jessica wrapped herself in the old blanket, and Casey, shivering visibly, glowered at her with envy as she pulled on her seat belt. With a quick stomp on the gas, we zoomed out of the student lot and hit the highway, speeding away from Hamilton High like prisoners running from their cells . . . which was sort of what we were.

'I can't believe you weren't nominated for Homecoming Queen this time, Casey,' Jessica said from the backseat. 'I was sure you would be.'

'Nah. I got voted queen at Football Homecoming. There's a rule about people winning more than once in the same year. I wasn't eligible to be nominated this time. It's gonna be Vikki or Angela, I'm sure.'

'Do you think they'll fight if one of them wins?' Jessica sounded worried.

'Doubt it,' Casey said. 'Angela couldn't care less about that kind of shit. Vikki is the competitive one . . . I really was looking forward to seeing the drama tonight, though. Did I tell you that Vikki is thinking of meeting up with Wesley Rush, too?'

'No!' Jessica and I cried in unison.

'Yep,' Casey said, nodding. 'I guess she's really trying to make her boyfriend jealous or something. She's dating a junior, taking an OHH kid to our dance, and telling everyone she has the hots for Wesley. She claims they fooled around after a party recently – I guess her boyfriend doesn't know about that yet – and she's thinking of doing it again. She said it was amazing.'

'He slept with her?' Jessica gasped.

'He sleeps with everyone,' I said, turning the car onto 5th Street. 'If it has a vagina, he'll screw it.'

'Ew! Bianca!' Jessica yelped. 'Don't say the . . . the V word.'

'Vagina, vagina, vagina,' Casey said flatly. 'Get over it, Jess. You have one. You can call it what it is.'

Jessica's cheeks were the colour of tomatoes. 'There's no reason to talk about *it*. It's crude and . . . personal.'

Casey ignored her and said to me, 'He might be a player, but he's pretty damn sexy. Even you have to admit that, B. I bet he's awesome in bed. I mean, you made out with him. Was he amazing? Can you really blame Vikki for wanting to hook up with him?'

'You made out with Wesley?' Jessica croaked, choking on her own excitement. 'What? When? Why didn't you tell me?'

I shot a glare at Casey.

'She's embarrassed,' Casey explained, fluffing the back of her short pixie cut. 'Which is dumb because I bet she had a blast kissing him.'

'I did not have a blast,' I said.

'Was he a good kisser?' Jessica asked. 'Tell me, tell me, tell me! I really want to know.'

'Yes, if you must know, he was. But that doesn't make it any less disgusting.'

'But,' Casey interjected, 'with your experience, answer my last question. Can you really blame Vikki for wanting to hook up with him?'

'I don't have to.' I switched on my turn signal. 'She'll blame herself when she gets a venereal disease . . . or when her boyfriend finds out about it. Whichever comes first.'

'And this is exactly why I wanted to go to the dance,' Casey sighed. 'We could have witnessed it all firsthand . . . like Hamilton's own episode of *Gossip Girl*. Vikki's boyfriend would be getting pissed and plotting revenge as his unfaithful girlfriend screws the hottest guy in school, and Bianca, hiding her secret love for Wesley, would mope and pretend to hate him while silently pining for his super-sexy-hot kiss again.'

My jaw dropped open. 'I would *not* be pining for anything of the sort!'

Jessica snorted with laughter from the backseat, pulling her ponytail in front of her mouth to hide a grin when I scowled at her in the rearview.

'Oh, well,' Casey sighed. 'I'm sure we'll hear all about the drama on Monday.'

'Or tomorrow if the story is good enough,' Jessica said.

'Angela and Jeanine never keep gossip to themselves. If it gets crazy, you know they'll call us and tell us what we missed. I'm sure that they will.' She smiled. 'I hope they give lots of details. I can't believe I'm missing my last Homecoming.'

'At least you're not missing it alone, Jess.'

A few seconds after pulling onto Holbrooke Lane, I turned into the Gaithers' driveway. Yanking the keys from the ignition, I said, 'Let the Girls' Night In officially begin.'

'Woohoo!' Jessica jumped out of the backseat and practically danced up to her front porch. She pushed open the door, and Casey and I followed her inside, shaking our heads with amusement.

I slid off my jacket and hung it on the hook just inside the door. Jessica lived in a coatrack house – clean, neat, shoes off at the front door . . . you know the type. Her parents were super-picky about order. Casey did the same and said, 'I wish my mom could keep a house this nice. Or she could at least hire a maid or whatever. Our place looks like shit.'

Mine didn't look that great either. My mom had never been much of a clean freak, and Dad only believed in cleaning once a year, during the spring. Other than laundry, dishes, and the occasional dust-and-vacuum job (usually all my doing), not much housework got done in the Piper home.

'What time will your parents get here, Jessica?' I asked.

'Mom will be home at five-thirty, and Dad should get here a little after six.' She was waiting for us at the foot of the stairs, ready to run up to her bedroom as soon as we joined her. 'Dad started seeing a new patient today, though, so he might be a little late.'

Mr Gaither was a psychotherapist. More than once, Casey had threatened to ask him if he'd take me as a patient for free. See if he'd help work out my 'issues'. Not that I had issues. But Casey said my cynicism was the result of some kind of internal struggle. I said it was just me being intelligent. And Jessica . . . well, Jessica didn't say anything. Even though it was only ever discussed teasingly, she always got a little awkward when the subject came up. With all the psychobabble she heard from her dad, she probably *did* think my constant negativity was part of an internal struggle.

Jessica *hated* negativity. Hated it so much, in fact, that she wouldn't even say she hated it. That would have been too negative.

'Hurry, hurry! Are you guys ready or what?'

'Let's get this party started!' Casey whooped, running past Jessica and speeding up the stairs.

Jessica giggled like a maniac as she made an effort to catch up with Casey, but I lagged behind, following them up the stairs at a regular walking pace. Once I reached the landing, I could hear my friends laughing and talking in the bedroom at the end of the hall, but I didn't follow their voices. Something else caught my attention first.

The door to the first bedroom, the one on the left, was wide open. My brain told me to walk right past, but my feet weren't listening. I stood in the open doorway, willing my eyes to look away. My body just didn't want to cooperate.

Perfectly made bed with the battered, navy blue comforter. Superhero posters covering every inch of wall. Black light over the headboard. The room was almost exactly the way I'd remembered it, only there were no dirty clothes on the floor. The open closet looked empty, and the Spider-Man calendar, which used to hang over the computer desk, had been taken down. But the room still seemed warm, as if he were still there. As if I were still fourteen.

'*Jake, I don't understand. Who was that girl?*'

'*No one. Don't worry about it. She doesn't mean anything to me.*'

'*But . . .*'

'*Shh . . . It's not a big deal.*'

'*I love you, Jake. Don't lie to me, OK?*'

'*I wouldn't.*'

'*Promise?*'

'*Of course. Do you really think I'd hurt you, Bi—*'

'Bianca! Where the hell did you go?'

Casey's voice made me jump. Quickly, I stepped out of the bedroom and shut the door, knowing that I couldn't walk past it every time I needed to pee that night. 'Coming!' I managed to keep my voice normal. 'God! Be patient for once in your life.'

Then, with a forced smile, I went to watch a movie with my friends.

7

After thinking about it for a while, I decided that there were a lot of benefits to being the Duff.

Benefit one: no point in worrying about your hair or make-up.

Benefit two: no pressure to act cool – you're not the one being watched.

Benefit three: no boy drama.

I figured out benefit three while we were watching *Atonement* in Jessica's bedroom. In the movie, poor Keira Knightley has to go through all of this damn tragedy with James McAvoy, but if she'd been unattractive, he never would have looked at her. She wouldn't have gotten her heart broken. After all, everybody knows the 'it's better to have loved and lost . . .' spiel is a load of crap.

The theory applies to a lot of movies, too. Think about it. If Kate Winslet had been the Duff, Leonardo DiCaprio wouldn't have been after her in *Titanic*, and that could have saved all of us a lot of tears. If Nicole Kidman had been ugly in *Cold Mountain*, she wouldn't have had to worry about Jude Law when he went off to war. The list goes on forever.

I watched my friends go through boy drama all the time. Usually, the relationships ended with them crying (Jessica) or screaming (Casey). I'd only had my heart broken once, but that was more than enough. So really, watching *Atonement* with my friends made me realize how thankful I should have been to be the Duff. Pretty screwed up, right?

Unfortunately, being the Duff didn't save me from experiencing family drama.

I got home at around one-thirty the next afternoon. I was still recovering from the sleepover – where no one slept – and I could barely keep my eyes open. The sight of my house in a state of complete devastation woke me right up, though. Broken glass sparkled on the living room floor, the coffee table was upside down, like it'd been kicked over, and – it took me a minute to register this – beer bottles were scattered around the room. For a second I stood frozen in the door, worried that there'd been a burglary. Then I heard Dad's heavy snoring in his bedroom down the hall, and I knew the truth was worse.

We didn't live in a coatrack home, so it was perfectly acceptable to keep your shoes on when you walked on the carpet. Today it was pretty much required. Glass, which I figured out had come from several broken picture frames, crunched under my feet as I made my way to the kitchen to get a trash bag – one would be necessary to clean up this chaos.

I felt oddly numb as I moved through the house. I knew I should be freaking out. I mean, Dad had been sober for almost eighteen years, and the beer bottles made it pretty fucking clear that that sobriety was in danger. But I didn't feel anything. Maybe because I didn't know how to feel. What could have been bad enough to knock him off that wagon after so long?

I found the answer on the kitchen table, neatly masked by a manila envelope.

'Divorce papers,' I muttered as I examined the contents of the opened package. 'What the fuck?' I stared down at my mother's loopy signature in a twisted state of shock. I mean, yeah, I'd kind of seen the end coming – when your mom vanishes for more than two months, you just get that feeling – but now? Really? She hadn't even called to warn me! Or Dad. 'Damn it,' I whispered, my fingers shaking. Dad hadn't seen this coming. God, no wonder he was suddenly boozing it up. How could Mom do this to him? To either of us.

Fuck this. Seriously. Fuck her.

I tossed the envelope aside and went to the cabinet where we kept the cleaning supplies, fighting the tears that stung my eyes. I grabbed a garbage bag and headed into the demolished living room.

It hit me all at once, causing a lump to rise in my throat as I reached for one of the empty beer bottles.

Mom wasn't coming home. Dad was drinking again. And I was *literally* picking up the pieces. I gathered the largest shards of glass and the empty bottles and tossed them into the bag, trying not to think about my mom. Trying not to think about how she most likely had a perfect tan. Trying not to think of the cute twenty-two-year-old Latino she was probably screwing. Trying not to think about the perfect signature she'd used on those divorce papers.

I was angry at her. So, *so* angry. How could she do this? How could she just send divorce papers? Without coming home or warning us. Didn't she know what it would do to Dad? And she hadn't even thought of me. Let alone called to prepare me for this.

Right then, while I made my way around the living room, I decided that I hated my mother. Hated her for always being gone. Hated her for shocking us with those papers. Hated her for hurting Dad.

As I carried the trash bag full of destroyed picture frames into the kitchen, I wondered if Dad had managed to break those memories – the ones of him and Mom that the photos had captured. Probably not. That's why he'd needed the alcohol. When even that hadn't erased my mother's face from his mind, he must have thrashed around the room like a drunken madman.

I'd never seen my father drunk, but I knew why he'd quit. I'd overheard him and Mom talking about it a few times when I was little. Apparently Dad had a bad temper when he was smashed. So bad that Mom had gotten scared and begged him to quit. Which I guess explained the overturned coffee table.

But the idea of my father drunk . . . it just didn't compute. I mean, I couldn't even imagine him using a swear word more offensive than *damn*. But a bad temper? I couldn't picture it.

I just hoped he hadn't cut himself on any of the glass. I mean, I didn't blame him for this. I blamed Mom. She'd done this to him. Leaving, disappearing, not calling, no warning. He never would have relapsed if he hadn't seen those stupid papers. He would have been fine. Watching TV Land and reading the *Hamilton*

Journal. Not sleeping off a hangover.

I kept telling myself not to cry as I sat the coffee table back up and vacuumed the smaller pieces of glass out of the carpet. I couldn't cry. If I'd cried, it wouldn't have had anything to do with the fact that my parents were getting divorced. That wasn't a shocker. It wouldn't have had anything to do with missing my mother. She'd been gone too long for that. I wouldn't even have been mourning for the family I'd once had. I was happy with the way life was, just me and Dad. No. If I had cried, it would have been out of anger, out of fear, or something else entirely selfish. I would have been crying because of what it meant for *me*. *I* had to be the adult now. *I* had to take care of Dad. But at that moment, my mother, living like a star in Orange County, was acting selfishly enough for the both of us, so I had to put the tears aside.

I'd just rolled the vacuum back into the laundry room when the cordless phone started ringing.

'Hello?' I said into the receiver.

'Good afternoon, Duffy.'

Oh, shit. I'd forgotten about working with Wesley on that stupid project. Of all the people to see that day, why did it have to be him? Why did this day have to get worse?

'It's almost three,' he said. 'I'm getting ready to drive

over to your place. You told me to call before I left . . . I'm just being considerate.'

'You don't even know what that means.' I glanced down the hall in the direction of my father's snores. The living room, while no longer a death trap, still looked rough, and there was no telling what kind of mood Dad would be in when he rolled out of bed. I just knew it probably wouldn't be a good one. I didn't even know what I would say to him. 'Look, on second thought, I'll come to your house. I'll see you in twenty minutes.'

Every town has that one house. You know, the one that is so freaking nice that it just doesn't fit in. The house that's so lavish that you almost feel like the owners are rubbing their wealth in your face. Every town in the world has one particular house like that, and in Hamilton that house belonged to the Rush family.

I don't know if it could technically be called a mansion, but the house was three storeys tall and had two balconies. *Balconies!* I'd gawked at the place a million times as I drove past, but I never thought I'd be going inside. On any other day, I would have been a little excited to see the interior (of course, I never would have told anyone that), but my thoughts were so wrapped around the divorce papers on my kitchen table that I couldn't feel anything but anxious and miserable.

Wesley met me at the front door, an annoyingly confident grin on his face. He leaned against the door frame, arms folded across his broad chest. He was wearing a dark blue button-down shirt with the sleeves rolled up to his elbows. And of course he'd left the top few buttons undone. 'Hello, Duffy.'

Did he know how much that name bothered me? I glanced at the driveway, which was empty except for my Saturn and his Porsche. 'Where are your parents?' I asked.

'Gone,' he replied with a wink. 'Looks like it's just you and me.'

I pushed past him and walked into the large foyer, rolling my eyes with disgust. Once my shoes were positioned neatly in the corner, I turned to Wesley, who was watching me with vague interest. 'Let's get this over with.'

'Don't you want the grand tour?'

'Not really.'

Wesley shrugged. 'It's your loss. Follow me.' He led the way into the enormous living room, which was probably as big as Hamilton High's cafeteria. Two large pillars held up the ceiling, and three beige couches, along with two matching love seats, were arranged around the room. On one wall I saw a huge flat-screen TV, and on another I found a giant fireplace. January sun spilled in through the floor-to-ceiling windows, lighting the space with a natural, happy feeling. But Wesley turned and started walking up the stairs, away from the comforting room.

'Where are you going?' I demanded.

He looked over his shoulder at me with an exasperated sigh. 'To my room, of course.'

'Can't we write the paper down here?' I asked.

The corners of Wesley's mouth turned slightly upward as he hooked a finger over his belt. 'We could, Duffy, but the writing will go much faster if I'm typing, and my computer's upstairs. You're the one who said you wanted to get this over with.'

I groaned and stomped up the stairs. 'Fine.'

Wesley's bedroom was on the top floor – one of the rooms with a balcony – and it was bigger than my living room. His king-size bed hadn't been made yet, and video game cases were scattered on the floor beside his PlayStation 3, which was hooked into a bigscreen TV. Surprisingly, the room smelled nice. It was a mixture of Wesley's Burberry cologne and recently washed clothes, like he'd just put laundry away or something. The bookshelf that he walked towards overflowed with books by different authors, from James Patterson to Henry Fielding.

Wesley bent over at the waist to look at the bookshelf, and I looked away from his Diesels as he pulled his own copy of *The Scarlet Letter* off the shelf and moved to sit on his bed. He gestured for me to join him, and I did, reluctantly. 'OK,' he said, thumbing absently through his hardcover book. 'What should we write the paper on? Any ideas?'

'I don't—'

'I was thinking we could do an analysis of Hester,' he suggested. 'It sounds cliché, but I mean an in-depth characterization. Mainly, why did she have the affair? Why did she sleep with Dimmesdale? Did she love him, or was she just promiscuous?'

I rolled my eyes. 'Oh my God, do you always go for the simplest answer? Hester is way more complicated than that. Neither of those choices shows any imagination.'

Wesley looked at me with one raised eyebrow. 'All right,' he said slowly. 'If you're so smart, then why did she do it? Enlighten me.'

'For distraction.'

OK, so maybe it was a little far-fetched, but I just kept seeing that damn manila envelope. Thinking of my selfish bitch of a mother. I kept wondering what my father was like drunk for the first time in eighteen years. My mind searched for anything – *anything* – that would distract me from the painful thoughts, so would it be too ridiculous to think that Hester felt the same way? She was lonely, surrounded by hypocritical Puritans, and married to a completely creepy, absentee English guy.

'She just wanted something to get her mind off the bad shit in her life,' I mumbled. 'Some way to escape . . .'

'If that's the case, that didn't go well for her. It all backfired in the end.'

I didn't really hear him. My mind was rushing back to a night not long ago, a night when I'd found a way to push my worries out of my head. I remembered the way my thoughts had gone silent, letting my body take over. I remembered the bliss of nothingness. I remembered how, even after it ended, I'd been so focused on what I'd done that my other worries barely existed.

'. . . so I guess that idea could make sense. It's definitely a different angle, and Perkins likes creativity. We might get an A.' Wesley turned to look at me, and his expression grew suddenly concerned. 'Duffy, are you OK? You're staring off into space.'

'Don't call me Duffy.'

'Fine. Are you OK, *Bian*—?'

Before he could say my name, I closed the space between us. Quickly, my lips moved against his. The mental and emotional emptiness took over instantly, but physically, I was more alert than ever. Wesley's surprise didn't last as long as it had before, and his hands were on me in seconds. My fingers tangled in his soft hair, and Wesley's tongue darted into my mouth and became a new weapon in our war.

Once again, my body took complete control of everything. Nothing existed at the corners of my mind; no irritating thoughts harassed me. Even the sounds of Wesley's stereo, which had been playing some piano rock I didn't recognize, faded away as my sense of touch heightened.

I was fully conscious of Wesley's hand as it slid up my torso and moved to cup my breast. With an effort, I pushed him away from me. His eyes were wide as he leaned back. 'Please don't slap me again,' he said.

'Shut up.'

I could have stopped there. I could have stood up and left the room. I could have let that kiss be the end of it. But I didn't. The mind-numbing sensation I got from kissing him was so euphoric – such a high – that I couldn't stand to give it up that fast. I might have hated Wesley Rush, but he held the key to my escape, and at that moment I wanted him . . . I *needed* him.

Without speaking, without hesitating, I pulled my T-shirt over my head and threw it onto Wesley's bedroom floor. He didn't have a chance to say anything before I put my hands on his shoulders and shoved him onto his back. A second later, I was straddling him and we were kissing again. His fingers undid the clasp on my bra, and it joined my shirt on the floor.

I didn't care. I didn't feel self-conscious or shy. I mean, he already knew I was the Duff, and it wasn't like I had to impress him.

I unbuttoned his shirt as he pulled the alligator clip from my hair and let the auburn waves fall around us. Casey had been right. Wesley had a great body. The skin pulled tight over his sculpted chest, and my hands drifted down his muscular arms with amazement.

His lips moved to my neck, giving me a moment to breathe. I could only smell his cologne this close to him. As his mouth travelled down my shoulder, a thought pushed through the exhilaration. I wondered why he hadn't shoved me – Duffy – away in disgust.

Then again, I realized, Wesley wasn't known for *rejecting* girls. And *I* was the one who should have been disgusted.

But his mouth pressed into mine again, and that tiny,

fleeting thought died. Acting on instinct, I pulled on Wesley's lower lip with my teeth, and he moaned quietly. His hands moved over my ribs, sending chills up my spine. Bliss. Pure, unadulterated bliss.

Only once, as Wesley flipped me onto my back, did I seriously consider stopping. He looked down at me, and his skilled hand grasped the zipper on my jeans. My dormant brain stirred, and I asked myself if things had gone too far. I thought about pushing him away, ending it right where we were. But why would I stop now? What did I stand to lose? Yet what could I possibly gain? How would I feel about this in an hour . . . or sooner?

Before I could come up with any answers, Wesley had my jeans and underwear off. He pulled a condom from his pocket (OK, now that I'm thinking about it, who keeps condoms in their pockets? Wallet, yes, but *pocket*? Pretty presumptuous, don't you think?), and then his pants were on the floor, too. All of a sudden, we were having sex, and my thoughts were muted again.

8

I was only fourteen when I lost my virginity to Jake Gaither. He'd recently turned eighteen, and I knew perfectly well that he was too old for me. Still, as a freshman in high school, I just wanted a boyfriend. I wanted to be liked and to fit in, and Jake was a senior with a car. At the time, I thought of that as perfection.

In the three months we were together, Jake never took me out on a real date. Once or twice, we made out in the back of a dark movie theatre, but we never went out to dinner or bowling or anything like that. We spent most of our time sneaking around so that our parents and his sister, who later became one of my best friends, wouldn't find out about us. I actually found that part, the secrecy, fun and sexy. It was like a forbidden romance – like *Romeo and Juliet*, which I'd read in English class that semester.

We slept together several times, and while I really didn't enjoy the actual sex, the sensation of closeness, of connection, felt comforting to me. When Jake touched me like that, I knew he loved me. I knew sex was a beautiful, passionate thing, and it was right to be with him.

Sleeping with Wesley Rush was entirely different. While I definitely got more physical pleasure out of it, the closeness and the love were missing. When it was over, I felt dirty. I felt like I'd done something wrong and shameful, but at the same time, I felt good. Alive. Free. Wild. My mind was totally cleared, like someone had hit the refresh button. I knew the euphoria wouldn't last forever, but the filthy regret was worth the momentary escape.

'Wow,' Wesley said. We were lying in his bed only a few minutes after we'd finished, with a foot or more space between our bodies. 'I definitely wasn't expecting that.'

God, he ruined everything when he talked. Annoyed, and still wading through the emotional repercussions, I sneered. 'What? Ashamed that you screwed the Duff?'

'No.' I was surprised by how serious he sounded. 'I'm never ashamed of anyone I sleep with. Sex is a natural chemical reaction. It always happens for a reason. Who am I to dictate who experiences the joy of sharing my bed?' He didn't see me roll my eyes as he continued. 'No, I just meant that I'm shocked. I was honestly starting to believe that you hated me.'

'I do hate you,' I assured him, kicking off the covers and moving to pick up my clothes.

'You must not hate me too much,' Wesley said, rolling onto his elbow and watching me dress. 'You did pretty much throw yourself at me. Generally, hatred doesn't inspire that kind of passion.'

I pulled on my T-shirt. 'Believe me, Wesley, I definitely hate you. I was just using you. You use people all the time, so I'm sure you understand.' I buttoned my jeans and grabbed my alligator clip from the nightstand. 'This was fun, but if you ever tell anyone, I swear I'll castrate you. Clear?'

'Why?' he asked. 'Your reputation could only improve if people found out you slept with me.'

'That might be true,' I admitted. 'But I have no desire to improve my reputation, especially not that way. So are you going to keep your mouth shut or do I need to find a sharp object now?'

'A gentleman doesn't kiss and tell,' he said.

'You're not a gentleman.' I put my hair back up in the clip. 'That's why I'm worried.' I glanced at my reflection in the full-length mirror on the wall. Once I was sure that

I looked normal – not guilty – I turned to face Wesley again. 'Hurry up and put your pants on. We need to finish this stupid essay.'

It was a little after seven that night when Wesley and I finally finished the essay for English. Or at least, we finished the rough copy. I made him promise that he'd e-mail me the draft later so that I could edit it.

'You don't trust me to get it done?' he asked, raising an eyebrow at me as I put my shoes on in the foyer.

'I don't trust you with anything,' I said.

'Except getting you off.' He was wearing that grin I hated. 'So, was this a one-time thing, or will I be seeing you again?'

I started to snort, to tell him he was dreaming if he honestly thought I'd be back, but then I remembered that I was about to go back home. The manila envelope would probably still be lying on my kitchen table.

'Bianca?' Wesley asked. A shiver ran across my skin when he touched my shoulder. 'Are you all right?'

I jerked out of his reach and moved towards the door. I'd gotten halfway out before I turned to him and said, with a moment of hesitation, 'We'll see.' Then I ran down the front steps.

'Bianca, wait.'

I clutched my jacket closer to me, trying to fight the cold wind, and yanked open the door of my Saturn. He was behind me in seconds, but, thankfully, he didn't touch me this time. 'What?' I demanded as I slid into the front seat. 'I need to get home.'

Home, the last place I wanted to go.

The winter sky had already turned black, but I could still see Wesley's grey eyes in the darkness. They were exactly the colour of the sky before a thunderstorm. He crouched down by my door to get to my eye level, and the way he was looking at me made me really uncomfortable. 'You didn't answer the other question.'

'What other question?'

'Are you all right?'

I scowled at him for a long moment, assuming he was just trying to be a pain in my ass. But something about his lighted eyes made me hesitate. 'It doesn't matter if I am or not,' I whispered. I started my car, and he darted out of the way when I moved to slam the door shut. 'Bye, Wesley.'

And I drove away.

When I got home, Dad was still in his bedroom. I finished cleaning up the living room, avoiding the kitchen altogether, and ran upstairs to take a shower. The hot water didn't wash away the dirty feeling Wesley had left on my skin, but it did relax some muscles that were forming tense knots in my back and shoulders. I just hoped the dirt would wash away in time.

I'd barely wrapped a towel around me when my cell phone started ringing in my bedroom, and I sprinted across the hall to answer it in time.

'Hey, B,' Casey said into my ear. 'So are you and Wesley done?'

'What?'

'You two were working on the English project today, weren't you?' she asked. 'I thought he was meeting you at your place.'

'Oh . . . right. Well, I wound up going over to his house instead.' I was trying hard not to sound guilty.

'OMG, you mean the mansion?' Casey asked. 'Lucky! Did you walk out onto one of the balconies? Vikki said that's half the reason she wants to hook up with him again. Last time, it was just in the backseat of his Porsche, but she really wants to see the inside of that house.'

'Is there a point to this conversation, Casey?'

'Oh, yeah,' she laughed. 'Sorry. It's no big deal. I just wanted to make sure you were all right.'

What was with everyone asking me that tonight?

'I know you hate him,' she continued. 'I wanted to

make sure you were fine . . . and that he was OK, too. You didn't, like, stab the boy, did you? I mean, I totally disapprove of murdering hotties, but if you need help burying the body, you know I'll bring the shovel.'

'Thanks, Casey,' I said. 'But he's alive. Today wasn't as bad as I expected. Actually . . .' I almost told her everything. How Mom and Dad were getting a divorce and how, in a moment of desperation, I'd kissed Wesley Rush, *again*. How that kiss had turned into something much, much more. How my body felt dirty all over, yet at the same time amazingly free. The words lingered on the tip of my tongue, but I couldn't make them come out.

Not yet, at least.

'*Actually* what, B?' she asked, bringing me out of my thoughts.

'Um . . . nothing. He actually had some good ideas for the paper. That's it. I guess he's, like, a Hawthorne freak or something.'

'Well, that's good. I know you find smart boys sexy. Are you gonna admit you want him now?'

I froze, not knowing how to respond to this, but Casey was laughing already.

'I'm teasing, but I'm glad things turned out OK. I was a little worried about you today. I just had this feeling that something bad was going to happen. I guess I was just being paranoid.'

'Probably.'

'I've got to go. Jessica wants me to call her with all the details of my meeting with Harrison. She just doesn't get it, does she? Anyway, I'll see you at school on Monday.'

'OK. Bye, Casey.'

'See you later, B.'

I flipped the cell phone shut and placed it on my nightstand, feeling like a total liar. Technically, I hadn't lied; I'd only withheld, but still . . . withholding from Casey was, like, a mortal sin. Especially when she made such a point of opening herself to my problems.

But I'd tell her eventually. Well, about my parents, at least. I just needed to deal with it myself before I sprang it on her and Jessica. The Wesley thing, though . . . God, I hoped they'd never find out.

I knelt at the foot of my bed and started folding the clean clothes, like I did every night. Weirdly, I wasn't as stressed as I'd expected myself to be. I hated to admit it, but I definitely had Wesley to thank for that.

9

Dad didn't leave his bedroom for the rest of the weekend. I knocked a couple of times Sunday afternoon and offered to make him something to eat, but he just murmured a refusal, never opening the door between us. His isolation terrified me. He must have been depressed about Mom, and ashamed he'd fallen off the wagon to top it off, but I knew this wasn't healthy. I decided that if he hadn't emerged by Monday afternoon, I would bust into the room and . . . well, I didn't know what I'd do next. In the meantime, I just tried not to think of my father or the divorce papers on the kitchen table.

Surprisingly, that was pretty easy.

Most of my thoughts swarmed around Wesley. *Ew*, right? But I really didn't know how to handle school on Monday. What did one do after having a one-night stand (or, in my case, one-afternoon stand) with the school's biggest man-whore? Was I supposed to act nonchalant? Treat him with my normal undisguised hatred? Or, because I'd honestly enjoyed myself, should I act, like, grateful? Tone down the contempt and be *friendly*? Did I owe him something? Surely not. He'd gotten just as much out of the experience as I had, minus the self-loathing.

By the time I arrived at school Monday morning, I'd pretty much settled on avoiding him entirely.

'Are you OK, Bianca?' Jessica asked as we walked out of Spanish at the end of first block. 'You're acting . . . um, *weird*.'

I'll admit, my spy skills weren't exactly smooth, but I knew that Wesley walked past the classroom on his way to second block, and I didn't want to risk an awkward post-sex meeting in the hallway. I peered anxiously around the edge of the door, scanning the crowd for those unmistakable brown curls. But if Jessica could tell something was up, I was being way too obvious.

'It's nothing,' I lied, stepping out into the hall. I looked both ways, like a small child crossing a busy highway, and I was relieved that I didn't see him anywhere. 'I'm fine.'

'Oh, OK,' she said without suspicion. 'I must be imagining it, then.'

'You must be.'

Jessica tugged at a loose strand of her blond hair that had escaped from the confines of her ponytail. 'Oh, Bianca, I forgot to tell you! I'm so excited!'

'Let me guess,' I teased. 'This has something to do with Harrison Carlyle, right? Did he ask you where you got your cute skinny jeans this time? Or how you condition your luscious hair?'

'No!' Jessica giggled. 'No . . . Actually, it's my brother. He's coming to visit us for the week, and he should be getting into Hamilton by noon today. He's going to pick me up from school this afternoon. I'm really excited to see him. It's been, like, two and a half years since he left for college and— Hey, Bianca, are you sure you're OK?'

I stood frozen in the middle of the hallway. I could feel the blood draining from my face, and my hands turned cold and started to shake. There was definite nausea coming on, but I told the same old lie. 'I'm fine.' I forced my feet to move again. 'I just, um, thought I forgot something. It's fine. Now, what were you saying?'

Jessica nodded. 'Oh, well, I'm so excited about Jake! I can't believe I'm saying this, but I've really, really missed him. It'll be nice to hang out with him for a few days. Oh, and I think Tiffany is coming with him. Did I tell you they just got engaged?'

'No. That's great . . . I've gotta get to class, Jessica.'

'Oh . . . OK. Well, I'll see you in English, Bianca.' I was halfway down the hallway before Jessica got the sentence out of her mouth.

I pushed past the stampeding students, barely hearing them as they bitched at me for stepping on their toes or ramming them with my backpack. The sounds around me slowly faded as unwanted memories flooded into my head. It was like Jessica's words had broken the dam that held them back for so long.

'So, you're Bianca? The freshman bitch that's been screwing my boyfriend?'

'Your boyfriend? I haven't been—'

'Stay the hell away from Jake.'

My face burned as the memories rushed back. My feet moved so fast I was almost sprinting toward my AP government class. As if I could outrun the thoughts. As if they wouldn't chase me with a vengeance. But Jake Gaither would be back in Hamilton for a week. Jake Gaither was engaged to Tiffany. Jake Gaither . . . the boy who broke my heart.

I ran into the classroom just as the tardy bell rang. I knew Mr Chaucer's eyes were glaring in my direction, but I didn't bother to look. I took my seat near the back of the room, trying desperately to focus on something else.

But not even Toby Tucker's witty commentary on the legislative branch or the back of his adorable out-of-fashion head could tempt my thoughts away from Jake and his bride to be.

I barely heard a word Mr Chaucer said all block, and when the bell rang, my page of notes, which should have been full of details from the lecture, consisted of only two short, barely legible sentences. God, I was going to fail this class if shit like this kept coming up.

So much drama! If I were a rich Manhattan snob, I could have been a character on *Gossip Girl*. (Not that I watch that trashy show . . . often . . . that my friends know about . . .) Why couldn't my life be a sitcom? Then again, even the *Friends* crowd had issues.

I slouched toward the cafeteria, and I found Casey and Jessica waiting for me at our table. As always, Angela, Jeanine, and Jeanine's cousin Vikki joined us. Angela was busy showing everyone her new Vans, so my sulkiness went unnoticed as I slumped into my chair.

'Cute,' Casey commented, grinning at the shoes. 'Who got them for you?'

'Daddy,' Angela answered, stroking the toe of her purple shoe. 'He and Mom are competing for my love now. At first it was kind of annoying, but I've decided to take the high road and have fun with it.' She crossed her legs and tossed back her dark hair. 'I'm hoping for Prada next.'

Everyone laughed.

'I didn't get anything cool out of my parents' divorce,' Casey said. 'My dad didn't really care if I loved him more, I guess.'

'That's sad, Case,' Jessica murmured.

'Oh, not really.' Casey shrugged and started picking at her orange fingernail polish. 'Dad's an ass. I was thrilled when Mom kicked him out of the house. She cries a lot less now, and when Mom's happier, the world is happier. Sure, we don't have as much money any more, but it wasn't like Dad spent his checks on us, anyway. He offered to buy Mom a car she didn't want, but that's about the extent of his good nature.'

'Divorces are depressing,' Jessica sighed. 'I'd be heartbroken if my parents split up. Wouldn't you, Bianca?'

I felt heat rush to my face, but Casey was switching the subject, so I pretended I hadn't heard Jessica's question. 'Hey, Vikki, what happened on Homecoming night? You never told us how that went down.'

Jeanine giggled knowingly. 'You haven't told them yet, Vikki?'

Vikki rolled her eyes and twirled a strand of her curly strawberry-blond hair around her perfectly manicured finger. 'Oh my God. OK, so Clint is totally not speaking to me anymore, and Ross . . .'

Her voice drifted into the background and my mind wandered. As much as I wanted to stop thinking of Jake, I couldn't bring myself to be interested in Vikki's boy troubles. On any other day, I would have found mild amusement in her story, like she was my own personal soap opera, but at that moment her drama seemed so vague and unimportant. So vapid. So indulgent. So empty.

I couldn't help feeling a little guilty for thinking this. That made me just as self-absorbed as she was. So I halfheartedly tried to listen to the woes of Vikki McPhee.

Then something she said caught my full attention.

'. . . but I did fool around with Wesley for a little while afterward.'

'Wesley?' I said.

Vikki beamed at me, proud of what she viewed as an achievement. Didn't she know more than two-thirds of the girls in school had accomplished the same thing? Including me . . . but, of course, she didn't know that part. 'Yeah,' she said. 'After the fight with Clint, I wound up out in the parking lot with Wesley. We messed around in his car for a while, but my mom called, so I had to get home before we could do anything. Sucks, right?'

'Sure.'

My eyes moved across the cafeteria, searching for a few seconds before they located the back of a curly brown head inches above those around him. He sat with a group of friends – mostly girls, naturally – at a long rectangular table on the other side of the room. He was wearing a tight black T-shirt that, while not really appropriate for the frigid temperatures of early February, showed off his perfect muscular arms. Arms that had twined around me . . . arms that had helped erase my stress . . .

'Did I tell you guys that my brother is coming to town?' Jessica asked. 'He and his fiancée are visiting for the week.'

Casey's worried eyes immediately turned on me and widened when she realized I was on my feet. 'Where are you going, B?'

Everyone at the table looked at me then, and I tried to sound convincing. 'I just remembered,' I said. 'I need to go talk to Wesley about our English project.' Screw avoiding him. I had a better, more helpful idea.

'Didn't you finish that on Saturday?' Jessica asked.

'We got started on it, but we didn't finish the paper.'

''Cause you were too busy making out,' Casey teased, winking at me.

Don't look guilty. Don't look guilty.

'Making out?' Vikki raised an eyebrow at me.

'Didn't you hear?' Jessica laughed, smiling good-naturedly at me. 'Bianca is madly in love with Wesley.'

I faked a gagging noise and everyone laughed. 'Yeah, right,' I said, making sure that my voice was full of irritation and disgust. 'I can't stand him. God, I've lost so much respect for Mrs Perkins since she made me work with him.'

'I'd be ecstatic if I were you,' Vikki said, sounding a little bitter.

Jeanine and Angela nodded in agreement.

'Anyway.' I was feeling a little jumpy. 'I need to talk to him about getting this done. I'll see you all later, OK?'

''Kay,' Jessica said, waving cheerfully.

I hurried through the crowded cafeteria, not slowing down until I was within five feet of Wesley's table, where the only other male occupant was Harrison Carlyle. Then I paused for a second, suddenly a little hesitant.

One of the girls, a skinny blonde with Angelina Jolie lips, was rattling on about her crappy vacation in Miami, and Wesley was listening with rapt attention – obviously trying to convince her of his sympathy. Disgust erased my insecurity, and I cleared my throat loudly, getting the whole group's attention.

The blonde was agitated and angry, but I focussed on Wesley, who looked at me casually, like he would any other girl. I turned up my nose and said, 'I need to talk to you about our English paper.'

'Is it necessary?' Wesley asked with a sigh.

'Yeah,' I said. 'Right now. I'm not going to fail this stupid assignment because of your lazy ass.'

He rolled his eyes and got to his feet. 'Sorry, ladies,' he said to the tragedy-stricken girls. 'I'll see you tomorrow. You'll save a seat for me?'

'Of course we will,' a tiny redhead squeaked.

As Wesley and I walked away, I heard Big Lips hiss, 'God, that girl is a *bitch*!'

When we were out in the hallway Wesley asked, 'What's the problem, Duffy? I emailed you the essay last night, just like you demanded. And where exactly are we going? The library?'

'Just shut up and come with me.' I led him down the hall past the English classrooms.

Don't ask where I got this idea, because I couldn't tell you, but I knew precisely where we were going, and I was sure that this might officially make me a slut. But when we reached the door of the unused janitor's closet, I had no feeling of shame . . . not yet, at least.

I grasped the doorknob and noticed Wesley's eyes

narrow with suspicion. I yanked open the door, checked that no one was watching, and gestured for him to go inside. Wesley walked into the tiny closet, and I followed, shutting the door stealthily behind us.

'Something tells me this isn't about *The Scarlet Letter*,' he said, and even in the dark I knew he was grinning.

'Be quiet.'

This time he met me halfway. His hands tangled in my hair and mine clawed at his forearms. We kissed violently, and my back slammed against the wall. I heard a mop – or maybe a broom – topple over, but my brain barely registered the sound as one of Wesley's hands moved to my hip, holding me closer to him. He was so much taller than me that I had to tilt my head back almost all the way to meet his kiss. His lips pressed hard against mine, and I let my hands explore his biceps.

The smell of his cologne, rather than the lonely, stale air of the closet, filled my senses.

We wrestled in the darkness for a while before I felt his hand insistently lifting the hem of my T-shirt. With a gasp, I pulled away from the kiss and grabbed his wrist. 'No . . . not now.'

'Then when?' Wesley asked in my ear, still pinning me to the wall. He didn't even sound winded.

I, on the other hand, struggled to catch my breath. 'Later.'

'Be more specific.'

I squirmed out of his arms and moved towards the door, nearly tripping over what felt like a bucket. I raised a hand to flatten my wavy hair and reached for the doorknob. 'Tonight. I'll be at your house around seven. OK?' But before he could answer, I slipped out of the closet and hurried down the hall, hoping it didn't look like a walk of shame.

10

I didn't think the final bell would ever ring. Calculus was excruciatingly long and boring, and English was nerve-racking. I caught myself glancing across the room at Wesley several times, anxious to feel the mind-numbing effects of his arms, hands, and lips again.

I just prayed my friends didn't notice. Jessica, of course, would believe me if I told her she was imagining things; Casey, on the other hand . . . well, hopefully Casey was too absorbed in Mrs Perkins's grammar lesson – ha, yeah, right! – to look over at me. She would probably interrogate me for hours and guess everything that had happened, seeing right through my denials. I really needed to get the hell out of there before I was exposed.

But when the bell finally rang, I was in no hurry to walk outside.

Jessica skipped towards the cafeteria with her blond

ponytail bouncing behind her. 'I can't wait to see him!'

'We get it, Jess,' Casey said. 'You love your big brother. It's cute, really, but you've said that . . . twenty times today? Thirty, maybe?'

Jessica blushed. 'Well, I can't wait.'

'Of course you can't.' Casey smiled at her. 'I'm sure he'll be happy to see you, too, but you might want to calm down just a tiny bit.' She stopped in the middle of the cafeteria and looked over her shoulder at me. 'You coming, B?'

'No,' I said, crouching down and messing with my shoestrings. 'I need to . . . tie this. You guys go ahead. Don't stall the reunion for me.'

Casey gave me a knowing look before nodding and pushing Jessica ahead. She started a new conversation to distract Jessica from my lame excuse. 'So tell me about this fiancée. What's she like? Pretty? Dumb as a sack of potatoes? I want the details.'

I waited in the cafeteria for a good twenty minutes, not wanting to chance seeing *him* in the parking lot. How funny that less than seven hours earlier, I'd been avoiding a completely different guy . . . one I was now desperate to see. As sick and twisted as it was, I couldn't wait to be back in Wesley's bedroom. Back on my own private island getaway. Back in my world of escape. But

106

first I had to wait until Jake Gaither drove out of the parking lot.

When I felt confident that he'd gone, I walked out of the school, pulling my coat tight around me. The February wind bit at my face as I moved across the empty parking lot, and the sight of my heat-challenged car didn't hold any comfort. I slid into the driver's seat, shivering like crazy, and started the engine. The ride home seemed to take hours even though Hamilton High was only about four miles from my house.

I'd just started to wonder if I could go to Wesley's house a few hours early when I pulled into my driveway and remembered my dad. Oh, great. His car was in the driveway, but he shouldn't have been home from work yet.

'Damn it!' I wailed, punching the steering wheel and jumping like an idiot when the horn sounded. 'Damn it! Damn it!'

Guilt surged through me. How could I forget about Dad? Poor, lonely, barricaded-in-his-bedroom Dad? I worried as I climbed out of the car and trudged up the sidewalk that he might still be in his room. If he was, would I have to break down the door? Then what? Yell at him? Cry with him? Tell him that Mom didn't deserve him? What was the right answer?

But Dad was sitting on the couch when I walked inside, a bowl of popcorn in his lap. I hesitated in the doorway, not sure what the hell was going on. He looked . . . *normal*. He didn't look like he'd been crying or drinking or anything. He just looked like my dad with his thick-rimmed glasses and untidy auburn hair. The same way I saw him every other day of the week.

'Hey, Bumblebee,' he said, looking up at me. 'Want some popcorn? There's a Clint Eastwood movie on AMC.'

'Um . . . no thanks.' I looked around the room. No broken glass. No beer bottles. Like he hadn't been drinking that day at all. I wondered if that was it. If the relapse was over. Did relapses work that way? I had no clue. But I couldn't help feeling wary. 'Dad, are you OK?'

'Oh, I'm fine,' he said. 'I woke up late this morning, so I just called work and told them I was sick. I haven't taken any of my vacation days, so it's not a big deal.'

I glanced into the kitchen. The manila envelope still sat on the kitchen table. Untouched.

He must have followed my gaze, or guessed, because he said with a shrug, 'Oh, those stupid papers! You know, they had me in such a fit. I finally thought about it and realized that they're just a mistake. Your mom's lawyer heard she'd been gone a little longer than usual this time and jumped the gun.'

'Have you talked to her?'

'No,' Dad admitted. 'But I'm sure that's the problem. It must be. Nothing to worry about, Bumblebee. How was your day?'

'It was good.'

We were both lying, but I knew that my words weren't true. He, on the other hand, seemed genuinely convinced. How could I remind him that Mom's signature was on the papers? How could I bring him back to reality? That would only drive him into his bedroom again – or send him in search of a bottle – and ruin this moment of manufactured peace.

And I didn't want to be the one to fuck up my dad's sobriety.

Shock, I decided as I walked up the stairs to my bedroom. He was simply in shock. But the denial wouldn't last long. Eventually he'd wake up. I just hoped he'd do it with grace.

I stretched out on my bed with my calculus book in front of me, trying to do homework I really didn't understand. My eyes kept jumping to the alarm clock on my nightstand. *3:28 . . . 3:31 . . . 3:37 . . .* Minutes ticked by, and math problems blurred into patterns of unidentifiable symbols, like ancient runes. Finally I slammed the book shut and conceded defeat.

This was sick. I should *not* have been thinking of Wesley. I shouldn't have been kissing Wesley. I shouldn't have been sleeping with Wesley. Hell, barely a week earlier I would have thought *speaking* to him was horrific. But the more my world spun, the more appealing he became. Don't get me wrong, I still hated him with a passion. His arrogance made me want to scream, but his ability to free me – if only temporarily – from my problems left me high. He was my drug. Seriously sick.

Even more sick was the way I lied to Casey about it when she called at five-thirty.

'Hey, are you OK? Oh my God, I can't believe Jake's back. Are you, like, flipping out? Do you need me to come over?'

'No.' I was feeling jumpy, still glancing at the clock every few minutes. 'I'm fine.'

'Don't bottle it up, B,' she urged.

'I'm not. I'm fine.'

'I'm coming over,' she said.

'No,' I said quickly. 'Don't. There's no reason to.'

There was silence for a second, and when Casey spoke again, she sounded kind of hurt. 'OK . . . but, I mean, even if we didn't talk about Jake, we could just hang out or whatever.'

'I can't,' I said. 'I, um . . .' It was five-thirty-three. Still an hour before I could leave for Wesley's. But I couldn't tell Casey that. Never. 'I'm thinking I might go to bed early tonight.'

'What?'

'I stayed up way too late last night watching, um . . . a movie. I'm exhausted.'

She knew I was lying. It was pretty obvious. But she didn't question me. Instead, she just said, 'Well . . . fine, I guess. But maybe tomorrow? Or this weekend? You really do need to talk about it, B. Even if you don't think you need to. Just because he's Jessica's brother . . .'

At least she thought I was lying to cover up my issues with Jake. I'd rather she think that than know the truth.

God, I was such a shitty friend. But Wesley was just something I had to lie about. To everyone.

When six-forty-five finally rolled around, I grabbed my coat and raced downstairs, already pulling my car keys out of my pocket. I found Dad in the kitchen, microwaving some Pizza Rolls. He smiled at me as I put on my gloves. 'Hey, Dad,' I said. 'I'll be back later.'

'Where are you going, Bumblebee?'

Oh, uh, good question. This was a problem I hadn't

anticipated, but when all else fails, tell the truth . . . or part of it at least.

'I'm going to Wesley Rush's house. We're working on a paper for English class. I won't be home late or anything.'

Oh, please, I thought. *Please don't let my cheeks turn red.*

'OK,' Dad said. 'Have fun with Wesley.'

I ran out of the kitchen before my face could burst into flames.

'Bye, Dad!'

I practically sprinted out to my car, and I tried very, very hard not to speed when I pulled onto the highway. I was *not* getting my first ticket because of Wesley Rush. The line had to be drawn somewhere.

Then again, I'd crossed several lines already.

But what exactly was I doing? I'd always mocked girls who screwed Wesley, and yet, here I was, becoming one of them. I told myself there was a difference. Those girls thought they had a shot with Wesley; they found him sexy and appealing – which, in a twisted way, I guess he was. They believed he was a good guy they could tame, but I knew he was a jackass. I only wanted his body. No strings. No feelings. I only wanted the high.

Did that make me a junkie *and* a slut?

My car came to a stop in front of the gigantic house, and I decided that my actions were excusable. People with cancer smoke pot for medicinal purposes; my situation was very similar. If I didn't use Wesley to distract me, I would go crazy, so I was really saving myself from self-destruction and a load of therapy bills.

I walked up the sidewalk and rang the doorbell. A second later, the lock clicked and the knob turned. The instant Wesley's grinning face appeared in the doorway, I knew that, regardless of my reasoning, this entire thing was wrong. Disgusting. Sick. Unhealthy.

And completely exhilarating.

11

I had major sex hair. I stared into the big mirror and tried to flatten the mess of auburn waves while Wesley put his clothes on behind me. Definitely not a situation I'd ever imagined myself in.

'I'm perfectly fine with being used,' he said as he pulled on the tight black T-shirt. His hair was pretty incriminating, too. 'But I would like to know *for what* I'm being used.'

'Distraction.'

'That much I gathered.' The mattress creaked when he flopped down onto his back and tucked his arms behind his head. 'What am I supposed to be distracting you from? There's a chance that if I knew, I could do my job more efficiently.'

'You're doing just fine already.' I scraped my fingernails through my hair, but it was as good as it would get.

Sighing, I turned away from the mirror and faced Wesley. To my surprise, he was watching me with actual interest. 'Do you really care?'

'Sure.' He sat up and patted a spot beside him. 'There's more to this amazing body than awe-inspiring abs. I have a pair of ears, too, and they happen to work superbly.'

I rolled my eyes and sat next to him, pulling my feet up onto the bed. 'OK,' I said, wrapping my arms around my knees. 'Not that it matters, but I found out that my ex-boyfriend is coming back to town for a week this morning. It's so stupid, but I panicked. I mean, the last time we saw each other . . . it didn't go very well. That's why I dragged you into the closet at school.'

'What happened?'

'You were there. Don't make me relive it.'

'I meant with your ex-boyfriend,' Wesley said. 'I'm curious. What kind of misery could cause a hateful person like you to run into my muscular arms? Or is he the one who put that layer of ice around your heart?' His words sounded facetious, but his smile seemed sincere, not the lopsided one he wore when he thought he was being clever.

'We started dating during my freshman year,' I began reluctantly. 'He was a senior, and I knew that my parents would never let me see him if they knew how old he was.

115

So we kept the whole thing a secret from everyone. He never introduced me to his friends or took me places or talked to me at school, and I just assumed it was to protect us. Well, of course, I was totally wrong.'

My skin itched as Wesley's eyes steadied on me. God, that annoyed me. He was probably looking at me with pity. *Poor Duffy.* My shoulders tensed, and I stared at my socks, refusing to see his reaction to my story. A story I'd never told anyone but Casey.

'So I saw him hanging out with this girl a few times at school,' I continued. 'Every time I asked, he just said they were friends and not to worry. So I didn't. I mean, he told me he loved me. I had every reason to believe him. Right?'

Wesley didn't answer.

'Then *she* found out. This girl I'd been seeing him with tracked me down at school one day, and she told me to stop screwing her boyfriend. I thought it was a mistake, so I asked him about it . . .'

'Not a mistake?' Wesley guessed.

'Nope. Her name was Tiffany, and they'd been together since seventh grade. I was the other woman – or *girl*, technically.'

Slowly, I looked up and saw Wesley making a face. 'What a dick,' he said.

'You can't talk. You're the biggest playboy there is.'

'True,' he admitted. 'But I don't make promises. He told you he loved you. He made a commitment. I'd never do that. A girl can believe what she wants to believe, but I don't say anything I don't mean. What he did is the mark of a true *dick*.'

'Anyway, he's back in town this week with Tiffany . . . his *fiancée*.'

Wesley let out a low hiss. 'Ah, that's awkward.'

'You think?'

There was a long pause. Finally, Wesley asked, 'So, who is he? Would I remember him?'

'I don't know. You might. His name is Jake Gaither.'

'Jake Gaither.' Wesley's face twisted in horror. 'Jake Gaither? You mean that *strange* guy? The freak with the acne and hooked nose?' His eyes widened in shock. 'How the hell did he get *two* girls? Why would anyone go out with him? Why would *you* go out with him? He was a beast.'

I felt my eyebrows contract. 'Thanks,' I muttered. 'Did you ever think that maybe that's the best that the Duff could do?'

Wesley's face fell. He looked away from me, examining our reflections in the mirror across the room. After a few moments of uneasy silence, he said, 'You know, Bianca, you aren't *that* unattractive. You do have some potential. Maybe if you hung out with different friends—'

'Just stop,' I said. 'Look, I've already fucked you twice. You don't have to flatter me. Besides, I love my friends way too much to trade them in for the sake of looking hotter.'

'Seriously?'

'Yeah. I mean, Casey has been my best friend since, like, forever, and she's the most loyal person I've ever met. And Jessica . . . well, she has no idea about me and her brother. We weren't friends back then. In fact, I didn't *want* to know her after Jake and I split, but Casey said it would be good for me, and she was right . . . as usual. Jessica can be a little ditsy, but she's the sweetest, most innocent person I know. I could never give either of them up just to look good. That'd make me a real dumbass.'

'Then they're lucky to have you.'

'I just said not to flatter—'

'I'm being honest.' Wesley frowned at the mirror. 'I have only one friend – one *real* friend. Harrison is the only guy who will be seen with me, and that's because we aren't trying to attract the same audience, if you know what I mean.' A small smile spread across his lips when he turned to face me. 'Most people will do anything to avoid being the Duff.'

'Well, I guess I'm not *most* people.'

He looked at me seriously. 'Does the word even bother you?' he asked.

'No.' I knew it was a lie the second the answer passed my lips. It did bother me, but I wouldn't admit that. Especially not to him.

My entire body seemed to be conscious of his eyes on me again. Before he could say anything, I stood up and walked to the bedroom door.

'Listen,' I said, twisting the knob. 'I have to go, but I was thinking we should do this again. Like a fling, maybe. Purely physical. No strings attached?'

'Can't get enough of me, can you?' Wesley asked, stretching out on his back again with a smirk. 'That sounds good to me, but if I'm so fantastic, you should spread the word to your friends. You say you love them, so you ought to let them experience the same mind-blowing pleasure . . . maybe at the same time. It's only right.'

I scowled at him. 'Just when I think you might have a soul, you say shit like that.' The door thudded against the wall when I flung it open. I marched down the stairs and yelled, 'I'll let myself out!'

'I'll see you soon, Duffy.'

What an asshole.

My father was oblivious. I guess his suspicious dad mode was faulty or something because he hardly questioned me as I slipped out of the house to go see Wesley more and more that week. Any sane dad would have been tipped off when his daughter used the 'working on a paper' excuse twice in a row, but four times in one week? Did he really think it took me that long to write a stupid essay? Wasn't he worried I might be out doing exactly what I *was* doing?

Apparently not. Every time I walked out of the house, he just said, 'Have a nice time, Bumblebee.'

But I think cluelessness must have been in the air. Even Casey, who'd been watching me like a hawk since Jake drove into town, hadn't picked up on anything between me and Wesley. Nothing more than her usual jokes about my secret pining for him, that is. Of course, I was doing everything I could to hide the evidence, but more than once, I was sure she'd caught me.

Like Friday afternoon when we were hanging out in my bedroom and getting ready to go to the Nest. Really, Casey was the one getting ready. I mostly just sat on my bed and watched while she posed in front of my mirror. We'd done this a million times, but with Jessica still clinging to her brother every waking moment, the room felt strangely empty. Almost eerie.

Jessica was so different from both of us. I mean, Casey and I were opposites, but Jessica was from an entirely different planet. She was a constant ray of light. The glass half full. She kept us balanced with that big smile and naive innocence that always shocked us. While sometimes it felt like Casey and I had both seen too much of the world, Jessica was, in a lot of ways, still a child. Virginal. Always full of wonder. She was our sunshine, and Casey and I were kind of in the dark without her.

I was wondering how many more days Jake would be in town, when Casey turned to look at me, apparently deciding that she liked her purple skinny jeans after all. (I'm glad *she* did, because I thought they were hideous.) 'You know, B, you're dealing with this whole Jake thing a lot better than I expected,' she said.

'Thanks . . . I think.'

'Well, I kind of figured that when Jake rolled back into Hamilton with his fiancée, you'd be freaked. I was banking on tears, midnight phone calls, and some good old nervous breakdowns. Instead, you're being, like, totally normal . . . or, you know, as normal as Bianca Piper ever gets.'

'I retract my thanks.'

'Seriously.' She crossed the room and sat down next to me. 'Are you dealing with this OK? You've barely complained, which is disturbing because you complain about everything.'

'Do not,' I protested.

'Whatever you say.'

I rolled my eyes. 'For your information, I've found a way to take my mind off it, but that's kind of ruined when you keep talking about it, Casey.' I nudged her playfully with my elbow. 'I'm starting to think that you *want* me to cry.'

'At least that would prove to me that you're not bottling it up.'

'Casey,' I groaned.

'I'm not kidding, B,' she said. 'This guy really fucked you up freshman year. You were a crying, blubbering, panicking mess after what he did, and I know it's hard because we have to keep it from Jess, but you need to deal with it somehow. I don't want to see you go through that shit again.'

'Casey, I'm fine,' I assured her. 'I really have found a way to relieve the stress, OK?'

'What's that?'

Oh, shit.

'What's what?'

Casey frowned at me. '*Duh*. Your way of relieving the stress. What are you doing?'

'Um . . . just stuff.'

'Are you working out?' she asked. 'Don't be embarrassed if you are. My mom does cardio when she's pissed off. She says it helps her channel the negative energy – whatever that means. So is that what you're doing? Are you working out?'

'Um . . . you could say that.'

Damn it. My cheeks were definitely burning. I turned away from her, examining the hairs on the back of my arm.

'Cardio?'

'Mmm-hmm.'

But miraculously, she didn't seem to notice that my face was on fire.

'Cool. You know, these pants are a size bigger than what I usually buy. Maybe we should work out together. It could be fun.'

'I don't think so.' Before she could argue or see the scarlet colour of my cheeks, I stood up and said, 'I've gotta go brush my teeth again. Then I'll be ready to get out of here. OK?' And I ran out of the room.

When I returned a few minutes later, I was forced to lie yet again.

'Wanna stay over at my place tonight?' Casey asked as she fluffed her short hair in the mirror. 'Mom's going to a bachelorette party for a woman she works with, so it'll just be us . . . and a few James McAvoy movies if you want. Jess will be sad she missed it, but—'

'I can't tonight, Casey.'

'Why not?' She sounded hurt.

The truth was that I had plans to see Wesley around eleven that night, but obviously I couldn't just be honest. But I couldn't really lie either. I mean, my lies were always so fucking transparent. So I did what I was getting better and better at these days. I withheld.

'I have plans.'

'After we leave the Nest?'

'Yeah. Sorry.'

Casey turned from the mirror and stared at me for a long moment. Finally, she said, 'You've been busy a lot lately, you know. You never want to do stuff with me much any more.'

'I'm going out with you tonight, aren't I?' I asked.

'Yeah, I guess, but . . . I don't know.' She turned away and examined her reflection one last time. 'Never mind. Let's just go.'

God, I hated being dishonest with Casey. Especially because she clearly knew *something* was going on, even if she hadn't figured out what just yet. But I was going to do everything in my power to keep my thing with Wesley under wraps.

And, of course, Wesley acted totally casual about everything. In public, we treated each other with the same sarcastic indifference as always. I insulted him, gave him dirty looks, and cursed under my breath as he acted like a pig (not that there was any *acting* involved). No one would have guessed we were different behind closed doors. No one could tell that I was counting down the minutes until we'd be meeting on his front porch step.

No one but Joe.

'You like him,' the bartender teased as Wesley, after enduring a verbal tirade from yours truly, went off to dance with a giggling bimbo. 'And I'm thinking he likes you, too. You two have something going on.'

'You're insane,' I said, sipping my Cherry Coke.

'I've told you a million times, Bianca, and I'll tell you again. You're a bad liar.'

'I wouldn't touch that douche bag with a ten-foot pole!' Did my voice convey enough disgust? 'Do you really think I'm that much of an idiot, Joe? He's arrogant, and he sleeps with everything he can get his filthy hands on. Most of the time, I just want to claw his creepy eyes out. How could I like him? He's a jackass.'

'And girls love jackasses. That's why I can't get a date. I'm too damn nice.'

'Or too hairy,' I offered. I took the last drink of my Cherry Coke and pushed my glass across the bar to him. 'Shave that Moses beard and you might have better luck. Women don't want to kiss carpet, you know.'

'You're trying to get out of talking about it,' Joe pointed out. 'That just proves there's something going on with you and Mr Jackass.'

'Shut up. Just shut up, Joe.'

'So I'm right?'

'No,' I said. 'You're just really, really annoying me.'

OK, I definitely had to find some way of avoiding the Nest for a few weeks . . . or, better yet, *forever*.

12

'Your shot, Duffy.' Wesley leaned on his pool stick, a triumphant smirk on his face.

'You haven't won yet,' I said, rolling my eyes.

'But I'm about to.'

I ignored him, focussing my attention on one of the two striped balls still remaining on the table. At that point, I really wished Wesley and I had just stuck to our pattern – walk straight up to his bedroom, bypassing everything else entirely. But that night on the way up the stairs, Wesley had mentioned having a pool table – and proceeded to brag that he was a wizard with a pool stick. For some reason, it sparked a competitive nerve in me. I just couldn't wait to wipe the floor with him and knock that cocky little grin right off his face.

Only, I was starting to regret my decision to challenge him to this game because, as it turned out, his boasts hadn't been too far from the truth. I wasn't bad at pool either, but I was about to get my ass kicked. And there was nothing I could do to wiggle my way out of it.

'Steady there,' he whispered, his lips brushing past my ear as he eased up behind me. His hands settled on my hips, fingers toying with the hem of my shirt. 'Focus, Duffy. Are you focussing?'

He was trying to distract me. And *shit*, it was working.

I jerked away from him, trying to thrust the back of my pool stick into his gut. But of course he dodged, and I succeeded only in knocking the cue ball in the opposite direction of what I'd intended, sending it right into one of the corner pockets.

'Scratch,' Wesley announced.

'Damn it!' I whirled around to face him. 'That shouldn't count!'

'But it does.' He took the white ball out of the hole and placed it carefully at the end of the table. 'All's fair in love and pool.'

'War,' I corrected.

'Same thing.' He eased the stick back, staring straight ahead, before shooting it forward again. Half a second later, the eight ball sailed into a pocket. The winning shot.

'Asshole,' I hissed.

'Don't be a sore loser,' he said, leaning his stick against the wall. 'What did you really expect? I'm obviously amazing at everything.' He grinned. 'But, hey, you can't hold it against me, right? We can't help the way God makes us.'

'You're an arrogant cheater.' I tossed my pool stick aside, letting it clatter to the floor a few feet away. 'Sore winners are way worse than sore losers, you know. And you only won because you kept messing me up! You couldn't keep your fucking hands to yourself long enough for me to make a decent shot! That's just low. And for another thing—'

Without warning, Wesley lifted me up onto the pool table. His hands moved to my shoulders, and a second later, I was flat on my back, staring up at him as he smirked. He shifted so that he was on the table too, leaning over me with his face only inches from mine.

'On the pool table?' I said, narrowing my eyes at him. 'Seriously?'

'I can't resist,' he said. 'You know, you're pretty sexy when you're pissed at me, Duffy.'

First, I was struck by the irony of that statement. I mean, he used *sexy* and *Duffy* – implying I was fat and ugly – in the same sentence. The contrast was almost laughable. Almost.

The thing that really got me, though, was that no one, not even Jake Gaither, had ever called me sexy. Wesley was the first. And the truth was, being with him made me *feel* attractive. The way he touched me. The way he kissed me. I could tell his body wanted me. OK, OK. So it was *Wesley*. His body wanted everyone. But still. It was a feeling I hadn't experienced in . . . well, I'd never experienced it. It was exciting and empowering.

But none of that could erase the stab of pain the last word in his statement gave me. Wesley might have been the first to call me sexy, but he was also the first to call me the Duff. That word had been tugging at me, taunting me, for weeks now. And it was his fault.

So how could he see me as both sexy and Duffy at the same time?

Better question: why did I care?

Before I could manufacture any decent answers, he started kissing me, his fingers already locating the buttons and zippers of my clothes. We became a tangle of lips and hands and knees, and the issue was completely pushed out of my head.

For the moment, at least.

'Go Panthers!' Casey yelled as she and a few other

members of the Skinny Squad did cartwheels along the sidelines.

Beside me, Jessica was waving a two-dollar blue-and-orange pom-pom, her face glowing with excitement. Jake and Tiffany were having dinner with Tiffany's parents that night, which meant I got to spend a couple of hours with her . . . even if that couple of hours was at a stupid sporting event.

The truth was, I hated pretty much anything requiring school spirit, because, obviously, I had none. I hated Hamilton High. I hated the horribly bright school colours, the incredibly generic mascot, and at least ninety percent of the student body. That's why I couldn't wait to leave for college.

'You hate everything,' Casey had said to me early that day when I'd explained to her why I had no desire to attend the basketball game.

'That isn't true.'

'Yes, it is. You hate everything. But I love you. And Jess. Which is why I am going to ask you, as your best friend, to bring her to the game.'

When Jessica had told me she wanted to hang out that night, my first instinct was to just go to my place and watch movies. But Casey's obligations to cheer at the game had interfered. That might not have been a big deal

– Jessica and I could have watched movies on our own – but Casey had to make it so complicated. She wanted to see Jessica, too. And she wanted us to see her cheer. Even if it went against everything I stood for.

'Come on, B,' she said, sounding irritated. 'It's just one game.'

She was irritated a lot these days. Especially at me. And I really wasn't in the mood to argue with her.

So that's how I'd been wangled into this. That's how I'd wound up sitting on an uncomfortable bleacher, bored out of my mind, as the cheers and shouts of the people around me brought on a fucking migraine. Absolutely wonderful.

I'd just decided to drive to Wesley's after the game, when Jessica elbowed me in the side. For a second I assumed it was an accident, like she'd gotten a little too excited waving her pom-pom around, but then I felt her tug on my wrist. 'Bianca.'

'Huh?' I turned my head to face her, but she wasn't looking at me. Her gaze was focused on a group of people a few bleachers down.

Three tall, pretty girls – juniors, I thought – sat in a row, leaning back on their palms, their legs crossed. Three perfect ponytails. Three pairs of hip-hugger jeans. And then, up the aisle, walked the fourth. She was smaller and paler with short black hair. Clearly a freshman. She was carrying several bottles of water and a few hot dogs in her arms, like she'd just come back from the concession stand.

I watched as the smiling freshman passed out the bottles and food. Watched as each of the juniors took theirs from her. Watched as they gave her less than appreciative looks. She took her seat at the end of their little row, and none of the older girls seemed to talk to her, only to one another. I watched as she tried to hop into their conversations, her small mouth opening and closing again as each of the juniors interrupted her, ignoring her entirely. Until, after a moment, one faced her, spoke quickly, and looked back to her friends. The freshman stood up again and walked, still smiling, down the steps and back toward the concession stand. Back to do their bidding.

When I faced Jessica again, her eyes were dark and . . . sad. Or maybe angry. It was hard to tell with her because she didn't show either of those emotions very often.

Either way I understood.

Jessica had been like that freshman once. That's how Casey and I had found her. Two senior girls Casey cheered with – complete cheerleading stereotypes: bitchy, blond, and bimbo-like – had been bragging about some dopey sophomore they kept as a 'pet.' And, more than once, Casey had watched them talk down to her.

'We've got to do something about it, B,' she'd said insistently. 'We can't just let them treat her that way.'

Casey thought she had to save everyone. Just like she'd saved me on the playground all those years ago. I was used to this. Only this time, she wanted my help. Normally I would have agreed just because it was Casey asking. But Jessica Gaither was a girl I had no desire to even meet, let alone save.

It wasn't that I was heartless. I just didn't want to know Jake Gaither's sister. Not after what he'd done to me. Not after the drama I'd been through the year before.

And I'd managed to stand my ground quite firmly . . . until that day in the cafeteria.

'God, Jessica, are you fucking brain-dead or something?'

Casey and I both turned around in our seats to see one of the skinny cheerleaders glaring down at Jessica, who was at least a head shorter than she was. Or maybe that was just the way Jessica slumped, cowering.

'I asked you to do one simple thing,' the cheerleader spat, jabbing a finger down at the plate Jessica was holding. 'One stupidly simple thing. No fucking dressing on my salad. How hard is that?'

'That's how the salad came, Mia,' Jessica mumbled, her cheeks bright pink. 'I didn't—'

'You're a moron.' The cheerleader turned around and stormed away, ponytail swinging behind her.

Jessica just stood there, looking down at the plate of salad with big, sad eyes. She seemed so small then. So weak and mousy. At that moment, I didn't think of her as beautiful. Or even all that cute. Just fragile and skittish. Like a mouse.

'Hurry up, Jessica,' one of the other cheerleaders called from their table, sounding annoyed. 'We're not saving your seat forever. Jesus.'

I could feel Casey looking at me, and I knew what she wanted. And, staring at Jessica, I couldn't exactly pretend I didn't understand why. If anyone needed a little bit of Casey Saves the Day, it was this girl. Plus, she didn't look anything like her brother. That made my decision a little easier.

I sighed and said, loudly, 'Hey, Jessica.'

She jumped and turned to look at me, and the fearful expression on her face almost broke my heart.

'Come sit with us.' It wasn't a question. Not even an offer. It was pretty much an order. I didn't want to give

135

her a choice. Even though, if she was sane, she totally would have chosen us.

Then Jessica was hurrying toward us, and the senior cheerleaders were pissed, and Casey was beaming at me. And that was that. History.

Though it didn't seem so much like the past just then, as I watched the little freshman girl hurry off toward the concession stand. I could see the way her jeans hung on her wrong – she didn't quite have the curves for low-rise pants – and that awkward slouch in her shoulders that made her look strangely unbalanced. Those little things that separated her from her so-called friends. A walking echo of the girl Jessica had been. So long ago. Only now I had a new word for it. For that girl.

Duff.

There was no way around it. That freshman was definitely the Duff in comparison to the pretty bitches bossing her around. It wasn't that she was so unattractive – and she definitely wasn't fat – but out of the four of them, she was the last one anyone would notice. And I couldn't help wondering if that was the point. If they used her as more than just the errand runner. Was she there also to make them look better?

I looked at Jessica again, remembering how small and weak she'd seemed that day. Not cute. Not pretty. Just kind of pathetic. The Duff. Now she was beautiful. Voluptuous and adorable and . . . well, *sexy*. Any guy – except Harrison, unfortunately – would want her. But the strange thing was, she didn't look all that different. Not on the surface, at least. She'd been curvy and blond even then. So what had changed?

How could one of the most gorgeous girls I'd ever met have been the Duff? How did that logic even work? It was like Wesley calling me sexy and Duffy at the same time. It just didn't make sense.

Was it possible that you didn't have to be fat or ugly to be the Duff? I mean, Wesley had said, that night at the Nest, that *Duff* was a comparison. Did that mean even somewhat attractive girls could be Duffs?

'Should we go help her?'

I was startled for a second, and a little confused. I realized Jessica was watching the freshman make her way down the sideline.

I had a horrible thought then. One that officially made me the biggest bitch ever. I seriously considered going and claiming that freshman as our own, so that maybe, just maybe, I wouldn't be the Duff anymore.

I could hear Wesley's voice in my head. *Most people will do anything to avoid being the Duff.* I'd said I wasn't most people, but was I? Was I just like those cheerleaders – now long since graduated – who'd mistreated Jessica or like these three perfect ponytailed juniors on the bleachers?

Before I could make a decision, though, to help the freshman – be it for the right reasons or the wrong – the buzzer sounded over our heads. Around us, the crowd stood, all cheering and whooping, blocking my view of the small, dark-haired figure. She was gone, and so was my opportunity to save her or use her or whatever I might have done.

The game was over.

The Panthers had won.

And I was still the Duff.

13

Valentine's Day might as well have been called Anti-Duff Day. I mean, what other day can hurt a girl's self-esteem more? Not that it mattered. I hated Valentine's Day even before I was aware of my Duff status. Honestly, I didn't even understand why it was a holiday. Really, it was just an excuse for girls to whine about being lonely and for guys to worm their way into getting laid. I found it materialistic, indulgent, and, with all of the chocolate, completely unhealthy.

'It's my favourite day of the year!' Jessica cried as she danced her way down the hall toward Spanish one morning. It was the first time I'd seen her truly bouncy since Jake's departure two days earlier. 'All of the pink and red! And flowers and candy! Isn't it fun, Bianca?'

'Sure.'

It had been almost a week since the basketball game,

and neither of us had mentioned the freshman girl since we left the gym that night. I wondered if Jessica had forgotten about it already. Lucky her. I hadn't. I couldn't. That girl and the thing we had in common – our shared identity as Duffs – had been lurking at the back of my mind ever since.

But I certainly wasn't going to talk about it. Not with Jessica. Not with anyone.

'Oh, I just wish Harrison had asked me to be his valentine,' she said. 'That would have been perfect, but we can't always get what we want, can we?'

'Nope.'

'You know, I think this is the first year that all three of us have been single,' Jessica continued. 'Last year, I was dating Terrence, and the year before that Casey was with Zack. I guess we can all just be each other's valentines. That would be pretty fun. It is our last Valentine's Day together before college, and we haven't really hung out together lately. What do you think? We can hang out at my house to celebrate.'

'Sounds good.'

Jessica threw an arm around my shoulders. 'Happy Valentine's Day, Bianca!'

'You too, Jessica.' I smiled in spite of myself. I couldn't help it. Jessica had one of those contagious smiles that made it really hard to be negative when she was so freaking bubbly.

We reached the classroom door and found our teacher waiting for us inside. 'Bianca,' she said as I walked in. 'I just got an e-mail from one of the secretaries at the front desk. She needs some students to come help distribute flowers people have sent. You're caught up on all your work, so would you mind doing that for me?'

'Um . . . OK.'

'Oh, how fun!' Jessica released me from her one-armed hug. 'You get to deliver flowers. It's almost like you're playing Cupid.'

Right. How fun.

'See you later,' I said to Jessica as I turned and walked right back out of the room. I pushed through the hordes of students, fighting against the current to make my way to the front desk. Couples seemed to be everywhere, displaying their affection – holding hands, batting eyes, exchanging gifts, making out – for the entire school to witness. 'Disgusting,' I muttered.

I was about halfway to the front desk when a strong hand gripped my elbow. 'Hello, Duffy.'

'What do you want?'

Wesley was grinning at me when I spun around to face him. 'I just wanted to let you know that if you plan on dropping by tonight, I might be a little busy. With it being the day of love, I have a pretty full schedule.'

Now he sounded like a *professional* man-whore.

'But if you're desperate to see me, I should be free around eleven o'clock.'

'I think I can survive one night without you, Wesley,' I said. 'In fact, I can survive an eternity.'

'Sure you can.' He released my arm and winked. 'I'll see you tonight, Duffy.' Then he was gone, swept away by the tidal wave of students on the verge of being late for class.

'Prick,' I grumbled. 'God, I hate him.'

A few minutes later, I stood at the front desk, where the secretary, who looked like a nervous wreck, smiled at me with relief. 'Did Mrs Romali send you? This way, this way. The table is over here.' She led me around the corner and gestured to a foldable, square table with a vomit-green surface. 'There it is. Have fun!'

'Not likely.'

The table was covered – I mean *covered* – with bouquets, vases, heart-shaped boxes, and Hallmark cards. At least fifty bundles of red and pink waited to be handed out, and I got the privilege of being the bringer of such joy.

I was debating where to start when I heard footsteps

behind me. Assuming the secretary had returned, I asked, without turning around, 'Do you have a list of the classes these kids are in so I know where to take the gifts?'

'Yes, I do.'

That didn't sound like the secretary.

I whirled around, shocked by the voice that had replied. It was one I knew very well, despite the fact that it had never – not once – spoken directly to me.

Toby Tucker smiled. 'Hi.'

'Oh. I thought you were someone else.'

'I didn't mean to scare you,' he said. 'So you were wangled into this, too, huh?'

'Um, yeah.' I was relieved to find my vocal cords weren't in a state of paralysis.

As always, Toby was wearing a slightly-too-formal-for-school blazer, and his blond hair fell around his face in that old-fashioned bowl cut. Adorable. Unique. Intelligent. He was the embodiment of all the things I wanted in a guy. If I believed in stupid things like fate, I might have thought it was destiny that we were working together on Valentine's Day.

'Here are the class rosters,' he said, handing me a green binder. 'We should probably get started; this could take a while.' His eyes scanned the field of gifts from behind his oval glasses. 'I don't think I've ever seen so much pink in one place.'

'I have. My best friend's bedroom.'

Toby chuckled and picked up a bouquet of pink and white roses. He eyed the tag and said, 'The quickest way to get this done might be to separate these into piles based on which class each student is in. It will make delivery much more efficient.'

'Right,' I said. 'Organize by class. OK.'

I was quite aware of how moronic I sounded with my less-than-eloquent replies, but there wasn't much I could do about it. I mean, just because my voice actually worked didn't necessarily mean I could use it well in his presence. I'd been crushing on Toby for three years, so to say he made me nervous would be a massive understatement.

Lucky for me, Toby didn't seem to notice. As we sorted the various gifts into groups, he even offered up some polite small talk. Slowly, I found myself easing into a semi-comfortable chat with Toby Tucker. A Valentine's Day miracle! Well, *miracle* was too strong a word – a miracle would have been him sweeping me into his arms and laying one on me right there. So maybe this was more like a Valentine's Day benefit. Either way, my awkward, idiotic dialogue began to ebb away. Thank God.

'Wow, there's a lot here for Vikki McPhee,' he said, placing a box of candy on top of a steadily growing pile. 'Does she have six boyfriends?'

'I only know about three,' I said. 'But she doesn't tell me everything.'

Toby shook his head. 'Jeez.' He picked up a card and began to check the label. 'So what about you? Any Valentine's Day plans?'

'Nope.'

He put the card in one of the piles. 'Not even a date with the boyfriend?'

'That would require me *having* a boyfriend,' I said. 'Which I don't.' Not wanting him to start feeling sorry for me, I added, 'But even if I did, I wouldn't be doing anything special. Valentine's Day is a stupid, pathetic excuse for a holiday.'

'You really think so?' he asked.

'Of course. I mean, there is a reason its initials are *VD*. I bet you more people contract syphilis on Valentine's Day than on any other day of the year. What a cause for celebration.'

We laughed together, and for a minute it felt kind of natural.

'And you?' I asked. 'Do you have plans with your girlfriend?'

'Well, we did,' he said, and sighed. 'But we broke up on Saturday, so those plans are now dead.'

'Oh. I'm sorry.'

But I wasn't. Inside, I felt kind of ecstatic and overjoyed. God, I was such a freaking bitch.

'Me, too.' There was a momentary pause on the verge of being awkward, and then he said, 'I think we have all of these sorted. Are you ready to start delivering?'

'I'm ready, but not very willing.' I pointed to a large vase of assorted flowers. 'Look at this. I would wager money that some girl sent this to herself so that she'd look good in front of her friends. How sad is that?'

'You're telling me you wouldn't do it?' Toby asked, a tiny smirk spreading across his boyish face.

'Never,' I said flatly. 'Who cares what others think of me? So what if I don't get a present on Valentine's Day? It's just vanity. Who do I need to impress?'

'I don't know. I think Valentine's Day is more about feeling special,' he said, plucking a flower from the large vase. 'I think every girl deserves to feel special once in a while. Even you, Bianca.' He reached over and tucked the flower's stem behind my ear.

I tried to convince myself that this was completely cheesy and ridiculous. That if any other guy – Wesley, for

146

example – had tried a line like that, I might have slapped him or just laughed in his face. But I felt my face turn pink as his fingers brushed past my cheek. This wasn't any other guy, after all. It was Toby Tucker. Perfect, amazing, dreamy Toby Tucker.

Maybe Valentine's Day could be Duff-friendly after all.

'Come on,' he said. 'Grab that pile and we'll start passing these out.'

'Uh . . . OK.'

We might have been done delivering by the end of first block, but the secretary kept bringing more and more packages to the little vomit-coloured table. It became very clear to Toby and me that we'd be working until at least lunch.

Not that I minded spending the morning with Toby Tucker.

'I don't want to jinx it,' he said as we returned to the table, only five minutes before the lunch bell. 'But I think we might actually be done.'

We reached the empty table and exchanged smiles, though mine was halfhearted. 'That's it,' I said. 'That was the last of them.'

'Yep.' Toby leaned against the table. 'You know, I'm glad they forced you to help. I would have been bored out of my mind if I'd done this by myself. It was fun talking to you.'

'I had fun, too,' I said, trying not to sound too enthusiastic.

'Listen,' he said. 'You shouldn't sit in the back of the room in AP government. Why don't you take one of the desks behind Jeanine and me? There's no reason for you to be alone back there. I think you should join us – the nerds in the front of the room.'

'I might.' And, obviously, I knew I would. How could I refuse such a request from Toby Tucker?

'Bianca Piper?' The secretary rounded the corner and approached us. There were no flowers or candy boxes in her hands this time. 'Bianca, there's someone here to sign you out.'

'Oh,' I said. 'Um, OK.' Weird. I had a car. There was no reason for me to be checked out.

'See you later, Bianca,' Toby called as I followed the secretary toward the front desk. 'Happy Valentine's Day.'

I waved just before turning the corner, trying to remember whether or not I had a doctor's appointment that day or something. Why was I being checked out of school? But before my mind could invent any family tragedies, the answer hit me like a ton of bricks, and I stopped dead in my tracks.

Oh. My. God.

She stood at the front desk, looking like she'd just stepped off a soundstage somewhere in Hollywood. Her blond hair, lightened by the sun, fell around her shoulders in gentle, perfect waves. She wore a knee-length teal dress (without pantyhose, of course) and high high heels. Dark sunglasses covered her eyes – eyes that I knew were green. She lifted the sunglasses as she turned to face me.

'Hi, Bianca,' the beautiful woman said.

'Hi, Mom.'

14

I could tell she was nervous by the way she stepped towards me. She looked shaky, and her eyes were wide with, from what I could guess, fear. For good reason, too. Unlike my father, I knew she'd meant to send those divorce papers, and I hated her for it. For not warning either of us. So I shot her a warning glare and moved away when she approached me. This must have confirmed her worries, because her glance sank to the floor and she focused on the toe of her stiletto.

'I've missed you, Bianca,' my mother said.

'Sure you have.'

'Did you finish signing her out, Mrs Piper?' the secretary asked, returning to her chair behind the tall desk.

'Yes, I did,' Mom said. Her voice found its smooth, natural tone again. 'So are we free to go, warden?'

'You're released,' the secretary laughed. She fluffed her hair and added, 'And I wanted you to know, I bought a copy of your book. It has been *such* a lifesaver for me. I read it once a month.'

Mom smiled. 'Oh, thank you! Glad to meet one of the ten people who've actually read it.'

The secretary beamed at her. 'It changed my life.'

I rolled my eyes.

Everyone loved my mother. She was funny, intelligent, and gorgeous. She looked a lot like Uma Thurman – as far from being the Duff as you could possibly get. All of her flaws were hidden behind that pretty face, and her smile could deceive people into believing she was perfect. The secretary, who giggled and waved as Mom led me out of the school, was just another fool.

'Where exactly are we going?' I didn't bother to shield her from my bitterness. She deserved it.

'Um . . . I don't know,' Mom admitted. Her heels clacked on the smooth pavement as she walked. The sound stopped when we reached her car, a red Mustang that looked like it had been lived in for a few days. It wasn't hard to tell she'd driven here all the way from Orange County. 'Somewhere with heat?' She was trying to sound perky. 'I'm freezing my booty off.'

'If you put some decent clothes on, you might not

have that problem.' I yanked open the passenger's side door and pushed some junk out of the seat before sliding in. 'Sorry this isn't California. It gets cold here.'

'Oh, California isn't all it's cracked up to be,' Mom said. She looked tense as she got into the car, and her bubbly laugh was clearly nervous, not humorous. 'It's not as fun as the movies make it look, you know?'

'Really? That's weird. You seem to like it better than Hamilton. But then again, you like to be anywhere but here, don't you?'

The laughter died, and the car became silent. Mom started the engine and pulled out of the parking lot. Finally, with all of her veils shredded, she whispered, 'Bianca, we have to talk about this. I don't think you understand what I'm going through right now.'

'Yeah, it looks tough, Mom,' I snapped. 'Nice tan, by the way. I know Orange County must have been a real hellhole. *How* did you manage?'

'Bianca Lynne Piper, I won't take that attitude from you!' she shouted. 'Despite what you think of me right now, I am still your mother, and I deserve a certain amount of respect.'

'Really?' I snorted. 'Like the respect you showed Dad by sending fucking divorce papers without warning him?

152

Or me! For God's sake, Mother, what the hell is the matter with you?'

More silence.

I knew this would get us nowhere. I knew I should listen to her, consider her side, and share my feelings reasonably. I'd seen enough *Dr Phil* to know we needed to compromise, but I didn't want to. Selfish, childish, immature . . . I might have been all of those things, but my father's face, the empty beer bottles I'd picked up last week, and the stupid divorce papers just kept popping into my mind. Listen? Consider? Be reasonable? How were those even options? She was just as childish and selfish as me. The only difference was that she hid it better.

Mom let out a slow breath before pulling the car over to the side of the road. She shut off the engine without saying a word, and I stared out my window at an empty field, which would be full of high cornstalks when summer finally showed up. The grey February sky said everything. Cold. Bleak. A wasted day. A wasted effort. But I wouldn't speak first. I would let her be the adult for once in her life.

Seconds ticked by. The only sound in the car was our breathing. Mom gave short, hesitant gasps, as if she were on the verge of speaking but changed her mind before the first word could escape her lips. I waited.

'Bianca,' she said eventually. We'd been quiet for at least five minutes. 'I'm . . . I'm sorry. I'm so . . . so sorry.'

I didn't say anything.

'I didn't want it to end like this.' The way her voice cracked made me wonder if she was crying, but I didn't turn my head. 'I haven't been happy for a long time, and after your grandma died, your dad suggested I take a trip. I thought it might help. Like I'd escape for a little while, give a few speeches in different towns, then come back and everything would be better. Go back to how it used to be when your dad and I first got married. But . . .'

Her long, thin fingers trembled as they closed around my hand. Reluctantly, I faced her. There were no tears on her cheeks, but I could see a misty glitter in her eyes. The dam just hadn't broken yet.

'But I was wrong,' she said. 'I thought I could escape from my problems, but I was so wrong, Bianca. No matter where you go or what you do to distract yourself, reality catches up with you eventually. I came home, and after a few days, I felt it again, so I'd leave on another trip. I'd stay away a little longer, book a few more places to speak, go a little farther away . . . until I couldn't go any farther at all. It caught up with me on the other side of the country, and I . . . I had to face it.'

'Face what?'

'That I don't want to be with your dad any more.' She looked down at our hands, still twined together. 'I love your dad very much, but I'm not *in* love with him . . . not the way he's in love with me. That's cliché as heck, but it's true. I can't keep lying and pretending things are OK with us. I'm sorry.'

'So you want a divorce?'

'Yes.'

I sighed and looked out the window again. Still grey. Still cold.

'You'll have to tell Dad,' I said. 'He thinks it was a mistake. He doesn't think you . . . you could ever do that to us.'

'Do you hate me?'

'No.'

The answer didn't really surprise me, even though the word just kind of flew out automatically. I wanted to hate her. Not so much for the divorce; as much as she'd been gone for the past few years, the idea of living with a single parent wasn't all that new or upsetting. And honestly, I'd been expecting them to separate for a while. Really, I'd wanted to hate her for Dad. For the pain I knew she was causing him. For that night he'd relapsed.

But it hit me then. She didn't cause that relapse. I

could blame her all I wanted, but that wouldn't do any good. She had to take responsibility for her own life, and Dad had to do the same. By staying married, letting things go on the way they had for the past three years, they'd both be living in denial.

My mother was finally facing reality. Dad would have to face it, too.

'I don't hate you, Mom.'

The sky had been black for hours by the time Mom dropped me off in the high school parking lot, where we'd left my car. We'd spent the afternoon just driving around Hamilton and talking about all that she'd missed. The same way we did every time she came back from a tour. Only this time, she wouldn't be coming home. At least not to stay.

'I'm gonna go see your dad now . . . I guess,' Mom said. 'Maybe you should spend the night with Casey, honey. I just don't know how he'll react . . . That's a lie. I do know how he'll react, and it won't be good.'

I nodded, hoping she was wrong – though our definitions of *not good* were different. I hadn't mentioned his relapse to her, mostly since it had passed without any significant drama. She was afraid of tears and yelling – the things that should be expected with a confrontation of this kind. I didn't want to make her worry about the drinking, too. Especially since it hadn't really been that big a deal in the end.

'God,' she whispered. 'I feel horrible. I'm telling my husband I want a divorce on Valentine's Day. I'm such a . . . a *bitch*. Maybe I should wait until tomorrow and—'

'You have to tell him, Mom. If you put it off now, you'll never do it.' I unfastened my seat belt. 'I'll call Casey and see if I can stay with her. You should go now . . . before it gets too late.'

'OK.' She took a deep breath and let it out slowly. 'OK, I will.'

I opened the door of the Mustang and climbed out. 'It'll be fine.'

Mom shook her head and fiddled with the keys dangling from the ignition. 'You shouldn't have to be the grown-up,' she murmured. 'I'm the mother. I should be comforting you, telling you it will be OK. This is so dysfunctional.'

'Functionality is overrated.' I gave her a reassuring smile. 'I'll talk to you tomorrow, Mom. Good luck.'

'Thanks,' she sighed. 'I love you, Bianca.'

'You, too.'

'Bye, baby.'

I shut the door and stepped away from the car. With

my smile still firmly intact, I waved and watched as the little red Mustang drifted out of the parking lot and turned onto the highway, where it hesitated as if debating whether or not to proceed. But my mother drove on. So I kept waving.

As soon as the taillights vanished, I allowed the smile to slip from my face. Yes, I knew things would be OK. Yes, I knew Mom was doing the right thing. Yes, I knew this was a step in the right direction for both my parents. But I knew Dad wouldn't see it that way . . . at least not at first. I'd smiled to reassure Mom, but for Dad I hung my head.

I pulled the car keys out of my back pocket and unlocked the door. After throwing my stuff onto the passenger's seat, I climbed inside and shut the door, putting a wall between my already shaking body and the February night. For several minutes, I just sat in the silent car, trying not to think or worry about my parents.

That was impossible, of course.

I reached a hand into my purse and began sifting through the clutter of gum wrappers and pens. Finally, I located my cell phone. I pulled it out and paused with my thumb poised over the keypad.

I didn't call Casey.

I waited through three rings before I got an answer.

'Hey. It's Bianca. Um, are you still busy?'

'Are you kidding me?'

I gawked at the giant flat-screen, feeling my face get hot. Again? Seriously? That was the tenth time in a row Wesley had beaten me since I'd arrived an hour earlier. I'd half expected to find some leggy blonde sneaking out of his bedroom when I walked up the steps, but the scene I found was quite different. Wesley was playing Soulcalibur IV. And because I'm a glutton for punishment, I'd challenged him.

My God, I had to find *something* I could beat him at!

And you know, something about beating the shit out of an animated character really made me feel better. Before I knew it, I wasn't even worried about Mom or Dad. Things would be OK. They had to be. I just had to be patient and let things happen. And in the meantime, I had to kick Wesley's ass . . . or try, at least.

'I told you, I'm awesome at everything,' he teased, putting the PS3 controller on the floor between us. 'That includes video games.'

I watched as the character Wesley had been operating moved across the screen, doing some sort of odd victory dance. 'Not fair,' I muttered. 'Your sword was bigger than mine.'

'My sword is bigger than everyone's.'

I lobbed my controller at his head, but of course he ducked and made me miss. Damn it. 'Perv.'

'Oh, come on,' he laughed. 'You walked right into that one, Duffy.'

I scowled at him for a moment, but I could feel the aggravation slipping away. Finally, I just shook my head . . . and smiled. 'OK you're right. I did leave that one wide open. But you know, boys that talk big never are.'

Wesley frowned. 'We both know that isn't true. I've proved it to you plenty of times.' He smirked, then leaned against me, letting his lips brush against my ear. 'But I can prove it again if you want me to . . . and you *know* you want me to.'

'I . . . I don't think that's necessary,' I managed. His lips were moving down my neck, sending an electric current up my spine.

'Oh,' he growled playfully. 'I do.'

I laughed as he shoved me to the floor, one of his hands perfectly catching the space above my left hip where I was most ticklish. He'd discovered that spot a couple of weeks ago, and I was furious with myself for letting him use it against me. Now he could make me squirm and laugh uncontrollably whenever he wanted, and I could tell that he totally got off on it. Jerk.

His fingers probed the sensitive spot over my hip as his mouth moved from my collarbone to my ear. I was laughing so hard I could barely breathe. Not fair. So not fair. I made a halfhearted attempt to kick him away, but he trapped my leg between his and proceeded to tickle me harder.

Just when I thought I might pass out from lack of oxygen, I felt something vibrate in my back pocket. 'Stop, stop!' I cried, shoving Wesley away. He rolled off me, and I stumbled to my feet, trying to catch my breath, and took my phone out of my pocket. I expected it to be Mom, letting me know how things had gone with Dad – putting any worries I might still have at ease – but when I glanced at the ID, my stomach lurched.

'Oh, shit. Casey.' I looked down at Wesley, still lying on the floor, his hands tucked behind his head. His T-shirt had ridden up a little, and I could just make out his hip bones, peeking out beneath the green fabric. 'Don't say anything,' I told him. 'She *cannot* know I'm here.' I flipped open the phone then and said, as smoothly as I could, 'Hello?'

'Hey.' She sounded pissed. 'What the hell happened to you tonight? Jess said the three of us were meeting for Valentine's Day, but you never showed.'

'Sorry,' I said. 'Something came up.'

'Bianca, you've been saying that a lot lately. Something is always coming up or you have plans or . . .'

Suddenly, I felt Wesley's breath hit the back of my neck. He'd gotten up from the floor and slid up behind me without me realizing it. His arms slid around my waist from behind, his fingers undoing the button of my jeans before I could stop him.

'. . . and Jess had her hopes up that we'd do something fun . . .'

I couldn't focus on a word Casey was saying as Wesley's hand slid beneath the waistband of my pants, his fingers moving lower and lower.

I couldn't say a word. I couldn't tell him to stop or show any reaction at all. If I did, Casey would know I wasn't alone. But, God, I could feel my whole body turning into a ball of fire. Wesley was laughing against my neck, knowing he was driving me crazy.

'. . . I just don't understand what's up with you.'

I bit my lip to keep from gasping as Wesley's fingers slipped to places that made my knees shake. I could feel the smirk on his lips as they moved to my ear. Asshole. He was trying to torture me. I couldn't handle it much longer.

'Bianca, are you there?'

Wesley bit my earlobe and pushed my jeans even lower with his free hand as the other continued to make me shiver.

'Casey, I have to go.'

'What? B, I—'

I snapped the phone shut and dropped it on the floor. I pushed Wesley's arms away from me and spun around to face him. Sure enough, he was grinning.

'You son of a—'

'Hey,' he said, raising his hands in surrender. 'You said not to say anything. You didn't say I couldn't—'

I dove for my abandoned video game controller and clicked the button that would restart the match, determined to teach him a lesson for messing with me like that. I'd already gotten in a few good blows before Wesley was able to retrieve his own controller and fight back.

'And you accuse me of being a cheater,' he said, blocking the punch my gladiator girl threw at him.

'Well, you deserve it,' I snapped, furiously tapping attack buttons.

It didn't matter. Even with my dramatic head start, he still beat me. Damn it.

'Happy Valentine's Day, Duffy.' Wesley turned to grin at me, his grey eyes sparkling with cocky triumph.

Why did he have to say that? I wondered as my thoughts drifted back to my parents. Had Mom broken the news to Dad yet? Were they fighting? Or crying?

'Bianca.'

I realized I'd been biting my lip a little too hard as the metallic taste of blood touched the tip of my tongue. I blinked at Wesley, who was watching me closely. He stared at me for a long moment, but instead of asking me what was wrong or if I'd be OK, he picked up his controller again. 'Come on,' he said. 'I'll take it easy on you this time.'

I forced a smile. Everything would work itself out. It had to. 'Don't be stupid,' I told Wesley. 'I'm going to kick your ass this time. I've just been holding back.'

He laughed, knowing I was full of shit. 'We'll see about that.'

And we started another game.

15

I'd never heard anything so freaking loud in my life. It sounded like a bomb was going off right next to my ear . . . a bomb that pulsed to the beat of Michael Jackson's 'Thriller.' Groggily I rolled over and picked my vibrating cell phone up off the nightstand, glancing at the time before I answered.

Five o'clock in the morning.

'Hello?' I groaned.

'Sorry to wake you up, honey,' Mom said through the speaker. 'I didn't wake Casey up too, did I?'

'Mm-mm. You're fine. What's up?'

'I left the house about two hours ago,' she said. 'Your dad and I had a long talk, but … he didn't handle it very well, Bianca. I knew he wouldn't. Anyway, I've just been driving around since then, trying to figure out what to do next. I've decided to check into a hotel in Oak Hill for a few days so that I can spend more time with you, and this weekend I'm gonna start moving down to Tennessee. Your granddad needs someone to look after him. It'll be a nice place to settle down. Don't you think?'

'Sure,' I murmured.

'I'm sorry,' Mom said. 'I should have told you all this later. Go back to sleep. Call me when you get out of school, and I'll tell you which hotel I'm in. Maybe we can go see a movie tonight?'

'Sounds good. Bye, Mom.'

'Bye, baby.'

I put my phone back on the nightstand and stretched my arms over my head, stifling a yawn. This bed, with its cushy mattress and expensive sheets, was way too damn comfortable. I'd never had such a hard time getting up in the morning, but I managed to plant my feet on the carpet eventually.

'Where are you going?' Wesley asked in a semi-sleepy voice.

'Home.' I pulled on my jeans. 'I've gotta take a shower and get ready for school.'

He pushed himself up on one elbow to look at me. His hair was a mess, brown curls falling into his eyes and sticking up in the back. 'You can shower here,' he offered. 'I might even join you if you're lucky.'

'No, thanks.' I grabbed my jacket off the floor and slung it over my shoulders. 'Will I wake your parents up if I go out the front door?'

'That would be difficult considering they're not here.'

'They didn't come home last night?'

'They won't be home for a week,' Wesley said. 'And God knows how long they'll stay then. A day. Maybe two.'

Now that I thought about it, I'd never seen another car in the almost-mansion's driveway. Wesley always seemed to be the only one here when I came over – which was pretty freaking often these days. 'Where are they?'

'I don't remember.' He shrugged and rolled onto his back again. 'Business trip. Caribbean vacation. I can never keep up with them.'

'What about your sister?'

'Amy stays with our grandmother when my parents are out of town,' he said. 'Which is essentially all the time.'

Slowly I moved back to the bed. 'So,' I said quietly, sitting on the edge of the mattress. 'Why don't you stay there, too? I bet your sister would like having you around.'

'She might,' Wesley agreed. 'My grandmother, however, is a different story. She detests me. She doesn't approve of my' – he made air quotes – '*lifestyle*. Apparently I'm a disgrace to the Rush name, and my father ought to be ashamed of me.' His laugh was hollow and cold. 'Because he and my mother are the staple of perfection, you know.'

'How does your grandmother know about your, uh, lifestyle?'

'She hears the gossip from her friends. Old hags hear their granddaughters swooning over me – and who can blame them? – and then they tell my grandmother all about it. She might actually *like* me if I'd date a girl seriously for a while, but part of me just doesn't want to give her the satisfaction. I shouldn't have to change my life to suit her or anyone else.'

'I understand what you mean.' And I did. Because I'd had that same thought a million times over the years. Recently, it had even pertained to him. It would be easy to change Wesley's opinion of me, to hang out with different people or bring another girl into my circle of friends – like that freshman from the basketball game – to avoid being the Duff. But why should I do anything just to fix what he or anyone else thought about me? I shouldn't have to.

And neither should he.

Somehow, though, his situation felt different. I glanced

168

around the room, feeling stupid for even comparing it to the Duff issue. Then, without meaning to, I found myself asking, 'But don't you get lonely? In this big house by yourself.'

Oh my God. Was I actually feeling *sorry* for Wesley? Wesley the womanizer? Filthy-rich Wesley? Wesley the jackass? Of all the emotions I'd felt for him, sympathy had never come up. What the hell was going on?

But if there was anything I could relate to, it was family drama. So it seemed like Wesley and I had some stuff in common. Ugh.

'You forget how rarely I'm alone.' He pushed himself into a sitting position and looked at me with a smirk. It didn't touch his eyes, though. 'You aren't the only one who finds me irresistible, Duffy. I usually have an endless flow of attractive houseguests.'

I bit my lip, not sure if I should say what was on my mind. Finally, I decided I might as well throw it out there. It wouldn't do any harm, after all. 'Listen, Wesley, this may sound weird coming from me, since I hate you and all, but you can tell me stuff if you want.' It sounded like something out of a cheesy G-rated movie. Great. 'I mean, I vented all of my shit about Jake to you, so if you want to do the same . . . well, I'm cool with that.'

The smirk slipped for a second. 'I'll keep that in mind.'

Then he cleared his throat and added stiffly, 'Didn't you say that you needed to go home? You don't want to be late for school.'

'Right.'

I started to stand, but his warm hand closed around my wrist. I turned around and found him looking at me. He leaned forward and pressed his lips against mine. Before I even realized what was happening, he pulled away and whispered, 'Thank you, Bianca.'

'Um . . . no problem.'

I didn't know what to make of it. Every other time Wesley and I had kissed, it had been a fierce, warlike make-out. A lead-in to sex. He'd never kissed me in such a gentle, greedless way, and it kind of freaked me out.

But I didn't have time to think about it as I ran down the stairs and through the foyer. Once I was in my car, I had to speed – which I really, really hate to do – all the way to my house, and I still didn't get there before six. That gave me only an hour and a half to shower, get dressed, and check on Dad. What a fantastic way to start the morning.

Even better was the fact that I could tell the living room lights were on when I pulled into my driveway. Not a good sign. Dad always – *always* – turned out every light in the house before bed. He treated it like a ritual. The fact that he'd left them on was definitely a bad omen.

I heard the snoring as soon as I tiptoed inside and instantly knew he'd bought more beer. Even before I saw the bottles on the coffee table or his unconscious form on the couch, I knew.

He'd gotten drunk enough to pass out.

I started to move forward but stopped myself. As much as I might want to, I didn't have time to clean up Dad's mess. I needed to go upstairs. I needed to go to school. And as I crept up to my bedroom, I told myself that he would be fine. He was just shocked, it would be fine, and this . . . episode would pass without incident. I could hardly hold a few drinks against the guy, considering the bombshell Mom dropped on him, could I?

I took a quick shower and blow-dried my hair (which always takes forever; seriously, maybe I should just hack all my hair off like Casey instead of wasting my time) before putting on some fresh clothes. After I brushed my teeth, I headed downstairs again and went into the kitchen to grab a Pop-Tart for the road. Then I took off, out the front door.

By the time I got to school, the student parking lot was almost full. I had to park in the very back row and jog – with my twenty-pound backpack – to the double doors. Of course that left me out of breath by the time I made it into the main hallway. *God*, I thought miserably as I lugged my fat ass toward Spanish, *no wonder I'm the Duff. I'm so fucking out of shape it's depressing.*

Well, at least the halls were pretty much empty. That meant no one had to witness my patheticness.

'Hey, where'd you go yesterday?' Jessica asked when I slumped into my desk only seconds before the bell rang. 'You weren't at lunch or in English. Casey and I were kind of worried.'

'I left school early.'

'I thought the three of us were gonna have a Valentine's Day thing to celebrate that we're all single.'

'That's kind of ironic, don't you think?' I sighed and shook my head, trying not to look into her big, hurt eyes. God, she was good at making me feel guilty. And I knew I was going to pay for hanging up on Casey last night. 'Sorry, Jessica. Something came up yesterday. I'll tell you about it after school, OK?'

Before she could say anything, Mrs Romali cleared her throat and shouted, '*Silencio! Buenos días, amigos.* Today we're going to get started on the present progressive tense, and I'll warn you now that it's pretty darn difficult.'

And it was. Mrs Romali passed out a worksheet that

kept us all busy until the end of the block. By the time the bell rang, I was really starting to question my affection for Spanish class, and I wasn't alone.

'Is it too late to switch classes for the semester?' Angela asked Jessica and me when we walked out of the classroom.

'About a month too late,' I told her.

'Damn it.'

'Bye, Bianca!' Jessica called as they ran toward their chemistry class. 'See you at lunch!'

I waved and started walking down the other hallway. Today, though, I was actually looking forward to AP government. Toby Tucker had asked me to sit near him. I wouldn't be the lonely girl in the back of the room anymore. I'd never thought that would change or that I would be so happy when it did. What can I say? The self-imposed isolation was finally beginning to bug me.

But Toby wasn't there. His seat was completely, one hundred percent empty when I walked into the classroom (for once I was way early, the way Mr Chaucer liked), and my heart kind of sank a little bit . . . or, you know, a lot. At least I didn't have to sit alone. Jeanine practically dragged me to the front of the room, apparently lost without Toby to keep her entertained. She must have been disappointed that I wasn't nearly as clever with political quips as her usual companion. All I could offer were a few sarcastic statements about the usefulness of the judicial system. God, I missed Toby.

So did Mr Chaucer. He seemed to get bored with his own uninterrupted lecture, and he dismissed the class only half-heartedly when the bell rang, his lower lip sticking out like a toddler's.

And they say teachers don't play favourites.

I was relieved to be out of that classroom, which seemed cold without Toby's enlightening commentaries, until I got into the cafeteria.

The lunch table wasn't exactly a warm, loving environment that afternoon. Casey glared at me all through lunch, obviously pissed that I'd hung up on her the night before. But apparently not pissed enough to skip out on meeting Jessica and me after school to hear my excuses.

I'd promised to explain things after class. Of course, that meant the second the last bell sounded, they dragged me into an empty bathroom and started making demands like 'Spill!' and 'Out with it!' before I could take a single freaking breath.

I groaned and slid down the cold concrete wall to land in a sitting position on the floor. I hugged my knees loosely and said, 'OK, OK. So Mom showed up here yesterday afternoon.'

'Is she back from her trip?' Jessica asked.

'Not exactly. She just came to talk to me. She and Dad are getting a divorce.'

Jessica clapped a hand over her mouth in shock, and Casey knelt down beside me, taking my hand. 'You OK, B?' she asked, abandoning her anger towards me.

'I'm fine,' I said. I knew they'd be more upset about it than I was. Casey, whose parents had gone through a long, bitter divorce, and Jessica, who could never imagine something so upsetting and unhappy.

'Is that why you skipped out on Valentine's Day last night?' Jessica asked.

'Yeah,' I said. 'Sorry. I just . . . didn't really feel like celebrating.'

'You should have called,' Casey said. 'Or said something to me on the phone last night. I would have listened, you know.'

'I know. But really, I'm fine. It was just a matter of time. I've been expecting it for a while now.' I shrugged. 'And, honestly, it doesn't really bother me. I mean, you know Mom hasn't been around much in the past few years, so it really won't change that much. But she's only in town a few days, which is why I need to be going right now.' I stood up.

'Where are you going?' Casey asked.

'I told Mom we'd see a movie together this afternoon.' I grabbed my backpack and glanced at my reflection in the mirror. 'Sorry. I know you guys want to talk about it or whatever, but Mom's leaving at the end of the week, so . . .'

'You sure you're OK?' Casey asked skeptically.

I hesitated, my hand raised to brush some auburn waves from my face. I could have told them then. I could have told them about Dad and the beer bottles and how confused I was. They were my best friends, after all. They cared about me.

But if I ratted Dad out, what would happen? What if word spread? What would people think of him then? I couldn't handle that. Even the thought of my best friends judging him made me uncomfortable. He was my dad, after all. And this was a small thing. He was just going through a rough patch. Nothing to worry about.

'Positive,' I said, turning away from the mirror with a forced smile. 'But I should get going. I don't want Mom to wait.'

'Have fun,' Jessica murmured, her eyes still wide with innocent shock. Maybe I should have given her the news a little more gently.

I was almost out the bathroom door when Casey called after me. 'Hey, B, wait a sec.'

'Yeah?'

'Let's go out this weekend,' she said. 'To make up for not hanging out on Valentine's Day. We could all go to the Nest. A Girl's Night Out. It'll be fun. We'll even buy you ice cream.'

'Sure. I'll call you later, but I really have to go.'

With a wave, I ran out of the bathroom. Yeah, I did want to see a movie with Mom, but that wasn't the reason for my hurry. There was something else I had to do first.

Once I made it to my car, I wasted no time in pulling out my cell phone. I dialled the familiar number and waited for the professional male voice to answer.

'You've reached Tech Plus. This is Ricky. How may I assist you?'

I wanted to talk to Dad. To make sure he was OK and let him know we'd get through this. Just, you know, be supportive. I knew he needed it. After the night he'd had, I knew he must be having a horrible day at work. Besides, if I was dealing with the news so well, I could at least help pull him through it. 'Good afternoon, Ricky,' I said. 'Is Mike Piper available?'

'I'm afraid not. Mr Piper didn't come in today.'

I sat there, stunned for a minute, knowing what that meant. But I shook off the worries creeping into my stomach. He was just having a bad hangover after a rough night. Probably more than enough to remind him why he'd quit drinking in the first place. He'd be fine tomorrow.

I hoped.

'Thank you, anyway,' I said. 'Have a nice day.'

I hung up the phone and started to dial another number. This time a woman with a clear, chirpy voice answered.

'Hello?'

'Hey, Mom.' I forced myself to sound at least semi-upbeat. If I was too happy, she'd know something was up. After all, I just wasn't the peppy type. 'Still want to go see a movie tonight?'

'Oh, hi, Bianca!' Mom exclaimed. 'Yeah, that sounds great. Listen, honey, have you talked to your dad today? Is he OK? He just got so upset last night, and he was crying when I left.' By the way she spoke, I could tell she had no idea he'd relapsed, that he'd touched a bottle. If she did, her voice would have been much more strained, full of concern. Maybe even on the verge of panic. But she sounded calm. Only slightly worried.

The fact that she was so blind really bothered me. I mean, he'd quit drinking almost eighteen years ago, but still. The thought should have crossed her mind.

But I didn't want to be the one to break the news to her.

'He's fine. I just got off the phone with him a second ago. He's going to be at work late tonight, so a movie works great for me.'

'Oh, OK. I'm glad to hear that,' Mom said. 'What do you want to see? I don't even know what's in theatres right now.'

'Me neither, but I was thinking a comedy would be good.'

16

Dad wasn't better the next day.

Or the day after that.

He went back to work at the end of the week, but I was sure I wasn't the only one who noticed the hangovers he took with him. It seemed like there was always beer or whiskey lying around the house now. He was always passed out on the couch or locked in his room. And he never mentioned it to me. As if I didn't notice. Was I supposed to ignore it? Pretend this wasn't a problem?

I wanted to say something. I wanted to tell him to stop. To tell him he was making a huge mistake. But how? How does a seventeen-year-old convince her father that she knows what's best? If I tried to stop him, he might get defensive. He might think I'd abandoned him, too. He might get angry with me.

Since Dad had stopped drinking before I was born, I

didn't really know much about the whole sobriety process. I knew that he'd had a sponsor once. Some tall, balding man from Oak Hill that Mom had always sent Christmas cards to when I was a kid. Dad didn't talk about him anymore, and I was sure that, even if I tried, I wouldn't have been able to locate his number. If I had, what would I say? How did that whole sponsor thing even work?

I felt powerless and useless and, more than anything, ashamed. I knew that, with Mom gone, it was my job to do something. I just didn't have a clue what that something was.

So in the weeks after Mom left for Tennessee, I spent most of my time at home avoiding Dad. I'd never really seen him drunk in my life, so I didn't know what to expect. All I had to go on were the little bits of conversations I'd overheard as a kid. He'd been an angry person once. He had a temper. I couldn't imagine this coming from my father, but I didn't want to start anytime soon. So I stayed in my bedroom, and he stayed in his.

I just kept telling myself it would pass. In the meantime, I'd keep his little secret to myself. Lucky for me, Mom was gullible enough to believe me whenever I told her everything was fine over the phone, despite my less than awesome acting abilities.

Honestly, I thought hiding my secrets from Casey

would be the hardest. She could always see right through me, after all. I tried avoiding her at first, ignoring her phone calls and making up excuses when she asked me to hang out. I never called her about that Girls' Night Out she'd suggested in the bathroom. I was sure she'd bombard me with questions the second she got me alone, so I always tried to use poor clueless Jessica as a buffer. But within a week, I got this strange feeling that *Casey* was steering clear of *me*.

She called less and less.

She stopped asking if I wanted to go to the Nest on weekends.

She even switched seats with Jeanine at lunch, putting herself all the way across the table – as far away from me as possible. Once or twice, I even caught her giving me dirty looks.

I wanted to know what the hell her problem was, but I was scared to confront her. I knew that if we actually talked about it, I wouldn't be able to keep lying about Dad. Not to her. But it was his secret, his shame, not mine to tell. I wouldn't let anyone, not even Casey, find out.

So I had to let her supreme weirdness slide for the time.

Wesley was really the only thing getting me through

those weeks. Some part of me was appalled at myself, but what could I say? I needed that escape – that high – more than ever, and he was always just a short drive away. A fix three or four times a week was all it took to keep me sane.

God, I was like a fucking druggie. Maybe my sanity was long gone already.

'What would you do without me?' he asked one night. We were tangled in the silky sheets of his gigantic bed. My heart was still pounding as I came down from the high of what we'd just done, and he wasn't helping matters by putting his lips so close to my ear.

'Live a happy . . . happy life,' I murmured. 'I might even . . . be an optimist . . . if you weren't around.'

'Liar.' He bit my earlobe playfully. 'You'd be absolutely miserable. Admit it, Duffy. I'm the wind beneath your wings.'

I bit my lip, but I still couldn't hold back the laughter – and just as I was finally catching my breath, too. 'You just referenced Bette Midler . . . in bed. I'm starting to question your sexuality, Wesley.'

Wesley looked at me with a defiant glint in his eye. 'Oh, really?' He grinned before moving his mouth back to my ear and whispering, 'We both know that my manhood has never been in question . . . I think you're just changing the subject because you know it's true. I'm the light of your life.'

'You . . .' I struggled for words as Wesley pressed his mouth into the crook of my neck. The tip of his tongue moved down to my shoulder and made my brain get all fuzzy. How was I supposed to argue under these conditions? 'You wish. I'm just using you, remember?'

His laughter was muffled against my skin. 'That's amusing,' he said, his lips still grazing my collarbone. 'Because I'm pretty sure your ex is out of town by now.' One of his hands slid between my knees. 'Yet you're still here, aren't you?' His fingers began gliding up and down my inner thigh, making it difficult for me to think of a retort. He seemed to like this, because he laughed again. 'I don't think you hate me, Duffy. I think you like me a lot.'

I squirmed uncontrollably as Wesley's fingertips danced along the inside of my leg. I wanted so badly to argue, but he was sending electric currents up my spine.

Finally, when I thought I might explode, his hand moved to my hip and he pulled his mouth away from my shoulder. 'Oh, thank God,' I whispered as he reached for a condom in the nightstand drawer, knowing what came next.

'I suppose it's a good thing I don't mind having

you around,' he said with that cocky grin. 'Now, let me answer all of those questions you claim to have about my sexuality.'

And my head filled with clouds again.

But I couldn't deny things were getting way out of hand. It became painfully clear to me one Friday afternoon in English that something wasn't right.

Mrs Perkins was passing out old papers she'd graded and chattering away about some Nora Roberts book she'd just finished – totally unaware that no one was listening to her – when she stopped at my desk. She gave me this big, goofy smile, like the smile of a proud grandmother. 'Your essay was wonderful,' she whispered to me. 'Such an interesting take on Hester. You and Mr Rush are an excellent team.' Then she handed me a tan folder and patted my shoulder.

I opened the folder as she walked away, a little confused about what she'd said. Inside was a paper that I instantly recognized. *Hester's Escape: An Analysis by Bianca Piper and Wesley Rush.* In the top-left corner, Mrs Perkins had scribbled our grade in bright red ink. A ninety-eight. An A.

I couldn't help but beam at the paper. Had it really been only a month and a half since we'd written this in Wesley's bedroom? Since the first time we'd slept together?

It felt like decades had passed. Millennia even. I looked across the room at him, and my smile vanished.

He was talking to Louisa Farr. No, not just *talking*. Talking just involves the vibration of vocal cords, and there was way more than that going on. His hand was on her knee. Her cheeks were getting red. He was giving her his cute, cocky grin.

No! *Repulsive* grin. Since when did I think that display of arrogance was cute? And what was this weird twinge I felt in my stomach?

I looked away as Louisa started to play with her necklace, a definite sign of flirting.

Whore.

I shook myself, surprised and a little worried. What was wrong with me? Louisa Farr wasn't a whore. Sure, she was a preppy cheerleader – co-captain of the Skinny Squad – but Casey had never had bad things to say about her. The girl was just talking with a cute guy. We'd all done the same. And it wasn't as if Wesley was taken or anything. It wasn't like he was committed to anyone.

Like me . . .

Oh God! I thought, realizing what that twinge in my gut must mean. *Oh God, I'm jealous. I'm seriously fucking jealous! Oh, shit!*

I decided I was sick. I had a fever or PMS or something

was severely impairing my mental stability, because there was no way in hell I'd be jealous that a man-whore like Wesley was hitting on someone else. I mean, that was his nature. The world might have actually stopped spinning if Wesley didn't flirt with poor, naive girls. Why should I be jealous? That was ridiculous. So I must be sick. I had to be.

'Are you OK, Bianca?' Jessica asked. She swivelled around in her desk to look at me. 'You look p.o.'ed. Are you mad or something?'

'I'm fine.' But my words came out through gritted teeth.

'OK,' Jessica said. She was just as gullible as my mom. 'Listen, Bianca, I really think you should talk to Casey. She's kind of upset, and I think you two really need to have a heart-to-heart. Maybe today? After class?'

'Yeah . . . whatever.' But I wasn't listening. I was too busy coming up with ways to mutilate Louisa's perfect little face.

PMS. This was definitely just a bad case of PMS.

I got my ass out of that classroom the second the bell rang. My head would explode if I had to hear Louisa's girly, oh-I'm-so-happy-you're-flirting-with-me-Wesley giggle one more fucking time. So what if she was as thin as my pinkie and had boobs the size of basketballs!

187

I bet she had an IQ of twenty-seven.

Stop it, I told myself. *Louisa has never done anything to me. I have no right to think those things about her . . . even if she might be a moron.*

I threw my stuff into my locker and ran towards the cafeteria, eager to escape the school building. I was so focussed on not thinking about my PMS-induced jealousy that I didn't even see Toby until I skidded to a stop about six inches from him.

'In a hurry?' he asked me.

'Sort of,' I sighed. 'Sorry for almost running into you.'

'It's not a problem.' He nervously played with his glasses. 'But do you think you'd mind slowing down the pace? I'd like to talk to you.'

I wasn't all that surprised. Toby and I had kind of gotten to be friends over the past couple weeks. We mostly talked in AP government, but you know, that was a definite improvement. Actually, I'd even become somewhat comfortable around him. While my heart still fluttered a little when he walked into the room, I no longer worried about losing my voice.

'Sure,' I said. At least it would give me something else to think about for a few minutes.

He smiled and fell into step with me. 'Can you keep a secret?' he asked as we reached the cafeteria, where the student body congregated, waiting for the final bell that would dismiss them for the afternoon.

'Most of the time. Why?'

'Do you remember when I missed school a few weeks ago? The day after Valentine's Day?'

'Uh-huh. I believe that was the worst day of Mr Chaucer's life,' I said. 'I thought the guy was going to cry when he realized no one was there to do most of his job for him.'

Toby laughed – but only a small laugh – and said, 'I was skipping school . . . well, for an interview.' He pulled a large envelope from the inside of his blazer and whispered, 'I applied to Harvard. I just got my letter in the mail this morning.'

'Why is that a secret?'

His cheeks went pink in the cutest possible way. 'I don't want to be humiliated if I don't get in,' he said.

'You'll get in.'

'I don't know that.'

'I do.'

'I wish I had as much confidence in me as you do.'

'Oh, come on, Toby,' I said seriously. 'All great politicians – like senators and presidents – go to awesome colleges. You're going to be a great politician, so they have to let you in. Besides, you're one of the smartest kids in the senior class. You're valedictorian, aren't you?'

'I am,' Toby agreed, frowning at his envelope. 'But . . . but it's *Harvard*.'

'And you're *Toby*.' I shrugged. 'Even if you didn't get in, there are a million other schools that would kill to have you. That doesn't matter, though, because I *know* you got in. Do yourself a favour and open the letter.'

Toby stopped in the middle of the cafeteria and smiled at me. 'See,' he said, 'this is why I wanted you to be the one with me when I open it. I knew you'd be—'

I cut him off. 'While I'm sure the next few words out of your mouth are going to be incredibly sweet, I'm one hundred per cent aware that you're stalling. Open the letter, Toby. Even a rejection is better than putting yourself through this hell. You'll feel better if you just read it.'

'I know. I—'

'Now.'

He ripped open the envelope, and I realized just how odd this was. He was coming to *me* with this very personal thing. For support. For encouragement. Back in January, I never would have imagined commanding Toby Tucker to open his acceptance letter. I never would have imagined *speaking* to him, period.

My, oh my, how things can change.

In the best ways possible, of course.

He slid the paper from the torn envelope with shaking fingers and began to read. I watched his eyes scan the page and widen. Was that joy or heartbreak? Shock, maybe? Surprise that he got in or surprise that he hadn't?

'Well?'

'I . . . I was accepted.' Toby dropped the paper and let it float gracefully to the floor. 'Bianca, I got in!' He grabbed me by the shoulders and pulled me into him, wrapping his arms around me.

That was something else I never would have expected to happen back in January.

'I told you that you would,' I said, returning the hug.

Over his shoulder, I spotted Casey and Jessica walking across the cafeteria. They were looking at me as they moved through the crowd of students; they saw me wrapped in Toby's arms. But for some reason the expressions on their faces didn't mirror the happiness I felt. Jessica looked kind of sad, but Casey . . . well, she looked downright furious.

Why? What was going on with her? With both of them.

Toby squeezed me before letting go and kneeling down to scoop up his fallen letter. 'I can't believe it. My parents will never believe it.'

I pulled my eyes away from my friends as they vanished behind a group of freshmen and turned my attention back to the beaming boy in front of me. 'If they know you at all, Toby, they'll totally believe it,' I said. 'We've all known that you're destined for great things for a long time. I mean, I've known for years.'

Toby looked surprised. 'Years? But we really didn't start talking until just a few weeks ago.'

'But we've had classes together since we were freshmen,' I reminded him. 'We didn't have to talk for me to know you were awesome.' I grinned and clapped him on the back. 'And you just proved me right.' The bell rang, and I turned towards the doors that led to the student parking lot. 'See you later, Toby. Congratulations!'

'Yeah. Thanks, Bianca.'

As I walked to the double doors, I wondered if I'd said too much. Did I give myself away as a semi-stalker? God, I hoped not. The last thing I wanted was to scare the poor guy away after less than a month of actual human contact. That would really make me a loser.

I was about to push open the door that led to the student parking lot when a loud 'Ahem' caught my attention. I turned around and saw Casey leaning against the school's nearly empty trophy case, her arms crossed over her chest. The way her eyes were narrowed annoyed me right away.

'What?' I asked.

She scowled and let her arms fall heavily to her sides. 'Nothing,' she grumbled. 'Forget it!'

'Casey, what are you—?'

'Not now, B.' She turned around and started stomping away from me. 'I have cheer practice.'

My hands flew automatically to my hips. 'What the fuck is wrong with you?' I demanded. 'You sound like a total bitch.'

She stopped and looked over her shoulder at me. '*I'm* the bitch? *You* ignore *me*, and I'm the bitch? WTF, Bianca!' She shook her head. 'Whatever. I'm not having this conversation right now. Not when we were *supposed* to have it ten minutes ago, like you told Jess we would. I guess you were too busy hanging all over that geek to—'

'Criticizing Toby sounds pretty damn bitchy to me, Casey,' I snapped. How dare she! She knew I liked him. She knew that having him pay any attention to me was a big deal! She knew, and yet she was bitching at me for it? 'You're acting like a preppy cheerleader snob.'

Her eyes flashed, and for a second it looked like she might pounce on me. I seriously thought I was going to get into an all-out, hair-pulling, reality-show girl fight with my best friend right in front of the parking lot doors.

But she walked away. Not a word. Not even a sound. She just drifted towards the gymnasium, leaving me pissed off and totally confused.

I'd fought with Casey before; it's bound to happen when you've been friends as long as we had. But this argument really unnerved me, mostly because I didn't know what her deal was. I stormed across the parking lot, trying to figure out what I could have done to deserve that drama. Clearly I'd set her off somehow.

And of course things just had to get better and better.

My car wouldn't start. I tried and tried again, but still got nothing. The battery was completely dead.

'Fuck!' I yelled, slamming my fist into the steering wheel. This was *not* what I needed. Hadn't my day been bad enough? Hadn't my *life* been had enough? It was like nothing ever went right. 'Shit! Damn! Hell! Start, you piece of—'

'Having car problems, Duffy?'

I paused mid-rant to glare at the offending shadow. I opened the door and told Wesley, 'My fucking car won't turn on.' Then I saw the girl standing next to him.

Skinny. Big boobs. It wasn't Louisa Farr. This girl was cuter. She had a round, sweet face with curly brown hair that bounced around her shoulders and large grey eyes. Way prettier than me, of course. Probably some freshman who only had to take one look at Wesley's sexy smile and pretty, shiny car before she put out. Again, that twinge of jealousy overpowered me. Just PMS.

'Would you like me to give you a ride?' he asked.

'No,' I said quickly. 'I'll just call . . .' But who would I call? Mom was in Tennessee. Dad was at work. Casey had cheer practice. Not that it mattered. She was mad at me anyway, and she and Jess both relied on their parents – or me – to drive them around. Who would come get me?

'Come on, Duffy,' Wesley said, grinning at me. 'You know you want to ride with me.' He bent down to look me in the eyes. 'What's the worst that could happen?'

'That's OK.' There was no way I was riding in the same car as Wesley and his latest conquest. Nope. Not a chance.

'Don't be ridiculous. You can call someone later. There's no point staying in the parking lot until dark. I just have to drop Amy off, and then I can take you home.'

Amy, I thought. *So that's the bimbo's name.*

Then something in the back of my mind clicked.

Oh my God! Amy! Amy was his *sister!* I looked at the girl again, wondering how I'd missed it. Curly brown hair, dark grey eyes, very attractive. Duh. The resemblance was obvious. I was an unbelievable dumbass.

Wesley reached past me and pulled my keys out of the ignition.

'Fine,' I said, feeling significantly better. I snatched back my keys and dropped them into my purse. 'Let me get my stuff.' Once I had everything I needed, I locked the doors and followed Wesley to his car, which was easy to spot since it was the only Porsche in the parking lot.

'Now, Duffy,' Wesley said as he climbed into the driver's seat. I slid into the back so that Amy, who was apparently the quiet type, could sit with her brother. 'This means you'll actually have to admit that I do nice things for people on occasion.'

'I never said you don't do nice things,' I told him as I attempted to situate myself in the cramped backseat. God, for being such fancy cars, Porsches had zero legroom. I had to sit sideways with my knees pulled up to my chest. So not comfortable. 'You do. But only when it benefits you in some way.'

Wesley scoffed. 'Did you hear that, Amy? Can you believe what she thinks of me?'

'I'm sure Amy knows what you're like.'

Wesley went silent.

Amy laughed but she seemed kind of nervous.

She didn't say much during the ride, though Wesley made several attempts to coax her into our conversation. At first I wondered if maybe it was because of me, but it didn't take long to figure out that she was just shy. When we pulled into the driveway of the large, old-fashioned house, which I knew must belong to Wesley's grandmother, Amy looked into the backseat and said quietly, 'Bye. It was nice to meet you,' before ducking out of the car.

'She's sweet,' I said.

'She needs to break out of her shell.' Wesley sighed as he watched her hurry up to the front porch. Once she'd disappeared into the big house (it was no almost-mansion, but clearly his grandma had money, too), he looked back at me. 'You can take the front seat if you want.'

I nodded and got out of the car. I opened the passenger's door and eased myself into the seat Amy had just abandoned. Right around the time I got my seat belt fastened, I heard Wesley let out a low groan. 'What's your problem?' I asked, looking up. But I figured out the answer before he said a word.

A woman in her sixties had just come out of the house, and she was walking towards the car. Wesley's grandma, no doubt. Wesley's grandma who *hated* him. No wonder he looked like he wanted to hide. I felt a little anxious as

I watched the woman, who was very well dressed in an expensive-looking salmon sweater and perfectly creased slacks, stride toward the car.

Wesley rolled down his window when she got close enough to hear him. 'Hi, Grandma Rush. How are you?'

'Don't play with me, Wesley Benjamin. I'm furious with you at the moment.' But she didn't sound furious. Her voice was high-pitched and soft. Silky. She sounded like the sweetest woman ever, but her words didn't fit the part.

'What did I do this time?' Wesley asked with a sigh. 'Wear the wrong shoes? Or is it that the car isn't clean enough today? What mild imperfection are you going to throw at me this afternoon?'

'I would suggest you refrain from using that tone with me,' she said in the least intimidating voice imaginable. This would have been funny if Wesley didn't look so unhappy. 'Live your life how you like, but leave little Amy out of it.'

'Amy? What did I do to Amy?'

'Honestly, Wesley,' his grandma said with a dramatic sigh. 'Why don't you just let Amy take the bus? I don't approve of you driving her around with your' – she paused – '*friends* in the backseat.' She looked across

198

Wesley, her eyes locking with mine for an instant before shifting back to her grandson. 'I wouldn't want them to be a negative influence on your sister.'

For a second I was confused. I was a straight-A student. I'd never been in any trouble in my life. Yet this woman thought I would somehow damage her precious granddaughter.

And then it hit me.

She thought I was one of Wesley's tramps. She thought I was a slutty chick he screwed around with. Wesley had told me that his grandmother disapproved of his 'lifestyle'. She hated the way he slept around. And seeing me in the backseat, she'd just assumed I was another floozy he'd picked up.

I looked away, staring out my window to avoid seeing the expression of disgust on the old woman's face. I felt hurt and angry.

Mostly because I knew it was true.

'That is none of your business,' Wesley growled. I'd never heard him sound so pissed before. 'You have no right to disrespect my friend, and it certainly isn't your place to decide what I do with my own sister. You should know me well enough to know that I wouldn't do anything to harm her, despite what you've convinced her of. I'm not the monster you tell her I am, you know.'

'I think I should drive Amy home from school after today.'

'Go ahead,' he said. 'But you won't keep me away from her. She's my sister, and Mom and Dad will have a fit if I tell them that you're trying to break apart our family, Grandmother.'

'I'm afraid your family is already broken, my dear.'

There was a buzz, indicating that Wesley had rolled his window back up, and the engine revved. I watched as the old woman walked back towards her house. Then, with squealing tyres, Wesley backed out of the driveway and sped down the street. I glanced over at him, worried and unsure of what to say. Luckily, he spoke first.

'I'm sorry. I didn't know she was coming outside. She shouldn't have treated you that way.'

'It's OK,' I said.

'No, it's not. She's a shrew.'

'I gathered that much.'

'And the worst part is that she's right.'

'About what?' I asked.

'About our family,' he said. 'She's right. It is broken. It has been for a long time. Mom and Dad are always gone, and Grandma's managed to come between Amy and me.'

'Amy still loves you.'

'Maybe,' he murmured. 'But she thinks less of me. Grandma has her convinced that I'm some no-good son of a bitch. I've seen the way Amy looks at me now. She looks at me like she's sad. Like she's disappointed in me. She thinks I'm a horrible person.'

'I'm sorry,' I said quietly. 'If I'd known, I wouldn't have made the joke about you only doing nice things for . . . for benefits.'

'It's fine.' The car was slowing down a little. 'Honestly, you're right. And Grandma is, too. I just never wanted Amy to see me that way.'

I couldn't resist the urge to reach over to the gearshift and put my hand over Wesley's. His skin was warm and soft, and I could feel his pulse throbbing steadily beneath my palm. I forgot about my stupid car and my fight with Casey. I just wanted Wesley to smile again. Even that cocky grin would have worked. I hated that he was so hurt by the possibility of losing his sister's respect. I wanted to comfort him. I cared about him.

Oh my God. I actually *cared*?

17

Ten minutes later, the Porsche pulled into my driveway. I grabbed my stuff and reached for the door handle. 'Thanks for the ride.' A glance back over my shoulder showed me that Wesley was still sulky. Well, hell! Why not? 'You can come inside if you want. My dad isn't home yet.'

Wesley grinned at me as he cut the engine. 'You're a dirty-minded little girl, Duffy. It would appear that you're trying to corrupt me.'

'You're way past corruption,' I assured him.

We got out of the car and walked up the driveway together. I dug the keys out of my purse and unlocked the front door, allowing Wesley to walk inside ahead of me. I watched his eyes move around the living room, and I couldn't help feeling a little self-conscious. He must have been comparing the place to his almost-mansion.

Obviously there was *no* comparison. I didn't even live in a coatrack house like Jessica.

'I like it,' Wesley said. He looked back at me. 'It's cosy.'

'That's nice for *small*, isn't it?'

'No. I'm serious. It's comfortable. My house is too big, even for four people, and since I'm the only one in it most of the time . . . I like yours better. Cosy, like I said.'

'Thanks.' I was flattered. Not that I cared what he thought, but . . .

'Where's your room?' he asked, winking at me.

'I knew that was coming. Now who's corrupting whom?' I took him by the elbow and led him up the stairs. 'Right here.' I gestured to the first door. 'I warn you, it's about the size of a Cracker Jack box.'

He opened the door and peered inside. Then he looked back at me with that familiar smirk. 'We'll have enough room.'

'Enough room for what?'

Before I knew what was happening, Wesley had grabbed me by the hips and was pushing me into my bedroom. He kicked the door shut behind us, spun me around, and slammed me against the wall, where he began kissing me so hard that I thought my head might pop off. I was surprised, but once that wore off, I joined in. I wrapped my arms around his neck and kissed him back. He tightened his grip on my waist and shoved my jeans down as low as they would go without unbuttoning. Then he slid his hands under the elastic band of my underwear and rubbed his fingers along my hot, tingling skin.

After a few minutes, he pulled his mouth away from mine. 'Bianca, can I ask you something?'

'No,' I said quickly. 'I am *not* giving you a blow job. No fucking way. Just the thought of it is disgusting and degrading and . . . No. Never.'

'While that's a little disappointing,' Wesley said, 'it's not what I was planning to ask you.'

'Oh.' That was a little embarrassing. 'Well, then what?'

He took his hands out of my pants and placed them gently on my shoulders. 'What are you escaping from now?'

'Excuse me?'

'I know your ex-boyfriend left town weeks ago,' he said. 'But I can tell there is still something bothering you. As much as I'd like to believe it's just me – you can't get enough of me – I know there's more to it. What are you running from, Bianca?'

'Nothing.'

'Don't lie.'

'It's none of your business, OK?' I pushed him away from me and yanked my jeans back up where they belonged. Automatically, I knelt down by the pile of clean clothes at the foot of my bed and started folding them. 'Let's just talk about something else.'

Wesley sat down on the floor beside me. 'Fine,' he said. I could tell he was using that I'll-be-patient-until-you-decide-to-tell-me voice. The one you use with little kids. Too bad for him. That would never happen. He was just my sex toy, after all, not my psychiatrist.

We talked about school while I folded my clothes. When they were all in neat stacks, I stood up and moved to sit on my bed.

'Aren't you going to put them away?' Wesley asked.

'No,' I said.

'Then what was the point in folding them?'

I sighed and stretched out on my back, kicking off my Converses. 'I don't know,' I admitted, resting my head on the pillow and staring at the ceiling. 'I guess it's a habit or whatever. I fold the clothes every night, and it makes me feel better. It's relaxing and it clears my head. Then the next morning, I dig through the stacks for what I'm gonna wear, and they all get messed up, so I get to fold them again that night. Like a cycle.'

My bed creaked as Wesley climbed on top of me,

wedging himself between my knees. 'You know,' he said, looking down at me. 'That's pretty strange. Neurotic, really.'

'Me?' I laughed. 'You're the one who's trying to get in my pants again, like, ten seconds after a failed attempt at a heart-to-heart. I'd say we're both pretty fucked up.'

'Very true.'

We started kissing again. This time his hands moved up my shirt and unhooked my bra. There wasn't much room in my little twin bed, but Wesley still managed to get my top off and my jeans unzipped in record time. I started to undo his pants, too, but he stopped me.

'No,' he said, moving my hand away. 'You might not agree with blow jobs, but I have a feeling you'll enjoy this.'

I opened my mouth to argue but shut it quickly as he started kissing down my stomach. His hands began moving my jeans and underwear down toward my knees, one of them pausing briefly to squeeze the ticklish place above my hip, causing me to jerk once with a giggle. His lips moved lower and lower, and I was surprised by how much I was anticipating their final destination.

I'd heard Vikki and even Casey talk about their boyfriends going down on them and how good it felt. I'd heard, but I didn't entirely believe it. Jake and I had never done that, and I'd always just assumed it was gross and weird.

It was kind of weird at first, but then it wasn't anymore. It felt . . . strange – but in a good way. Dirty, wrong, *amazing*. My fingers curled in the sheets, gripping the cloth tightly, and my knees shook. I was feeling things I'd never felt before. 'Ah . . . oh,' I gasped with pleasure and surprise and—

'Oh, shit.'

Wesley jumped away from me. He'd heard the car door slam, too. That meant my dad was home.

I pulled up my underwear and fastened my jeans quickly, but it took me a minute to find my bra. Once I was completely dressed, I flattened my hair and did my best not to look like a kid with her hand caught in the cookie jar.

'Should I leave?' Wesley asked.

'No,' I said breathlessly. I could tell he didn't want to go back to the empty almost-mansion. 'Stay a little while. It's fine. Dad won't care. We just can't . . . do *that*.'

'What else is there to do?'

So, like complete losers, we played Scrabble for the next four and a half hours. There was barely enough space in the floor of my tiny room for someone as tall as Wesley to stretch out on his stomach, but he managed, and I sat across from him, the board between us as we spelled out words like *quixotic* and *hegemony*. Not exactly the most exciting Friday night, but I enjoyed it way more than I would have if I'd gone to the Nest or some lame party in Oak Hill.

Around nine, after I'd kicked his ass three times – finally, something I could beat him at! – Wesley got to his feet. 'I guess I should go home,' he sighed.

'OK.' I stood up. 'I'll walk you downstairs.'

I was in such a good mood that I'd managed to forget all about Dad . . . until we ran into him in the living room. I smelled the whiskey before I saw the bottle on the coffee table, and my cheeks burned with embarrassment. *Please don't notice*, I thought to myself as I walked Wesley toward the front door. I guess I should've started worrying when he hadn't checked upstairs to see whose Porsche was in our driveway. I mean, it wasn't like having a car that shiny in front of our house was a common occurrence. Maybe Wesley hadn't thought about that either. It was a Friday night, after all. Dads could drink whiskey on weekends . . . well, ones that weren't recovering alcoholics, but Wesley didn't know that side of the story. As long as my father acted normal, this might slide by as nothing out of the ordinary.

But, of course, I never had that kind of good luck.

'Bumblebee!' Dad said, and I could tell he was already smashed. Great. Just fucking fantastic. He stumbled to his feet and looked over at the front door, where Wesley and I stood. 'Hey, Bumblebee. I didn't even know you were home. Who's this?' His eyes narrowed at Wesley. 'A boy?'

'Um, Dad, this is Wesley Rush,' I said, trying to stay calm. 'He's a friend of mine.'

'A "friend" . . . I bet.' He grabbed the whiskey bottle before taking a few unsteady steps toward us, his eyes squinting at Wesley. 'Did you have fun up in my little girl's bedroom, boy?'

'I sure did,' Wesley said, clearly trying to sound like one of those innocent oh-gee-whiz! boys from fifties TV shows. 'We played three games of Scrabble. Your daughter is really good with words, sir.'

'Scrabble? I'm not an idiot. That must be some new code for . . . for oral sex!' Dad snarled.

I must have turned scarlet. How did he know? Could he see right into my mind? No, of course he couldn't. He was just drunk and making accusations, and looking guilty would only make things worse. So I laughed as if it were ridiculous. As if it were a joke. Wesley, following my lead, did the same.

'Sure, Dad,' I said. 'And intercourse is Yahtzee, right?'

'I'm not being funny!' Dad snapped, swinging his bottle and sloshing whiskey onto the carpet. Wonderful. I'd be the one cleaning that up. 'I know what's up. I've seen the way your slutty friends dress, Bianca. They're rubbing off on you, aren't they?'

I couldn't force the laughter any longer. 'My friends aren't slutty,' I whispered. 'You're drunk off your ass, and you don't know what you're saying.' With a surge of bravery, I reached forward and swiped the bottle from his hand. 'You shouldn't have any more, Dad.'

For a second, I felt good. That was what I should have done all along. Just taken things into my own hands and removed the bottle. I felt empowered. Like I could fix things.

'I should go,' Wesley said behind me.

I started to turn around and say bye, but the words never left my mouth. I felt the bottle slip from my hand and heard it smash on the floor beside me. I was knocked to the ground, but for a second I didn't understand what had happened. Then the delayed pain in my temple stunned me. It was like I'd been hit by something. Something hard. Something blunt. Something like the palm of my father's hand. I reached up and rubbed my head in shock, barely feeling the actual pain.

'See!' Dad yelled. 'Boys don't stay with whores, Bianca.

They leave them. And I'm not going to let you turn into a whore. Not my daughter. This is for your own good.'

I looked up as he reached a hand down to grab my arm. I squeezed my eyes shut, waiting to feel his fingers clamp around my forearm.

But they never did.

I heard a loud *thud*, and Dad grunted in pain. My eyes flew open. Wesley moved away from Dad, who was massaging his jaw with a shocked look on his face. 'Why, you little shithead!'

'Are you all right?' Wesley asked, kneeling in front of me.

'Did you just punch my dad?' I couldn't help but wonder if I was delirious. Had all of this really just happened? Totally bizarre.

'Yes,' Wesley admitted.

'How dare you touch me!' Dad screamed, but he was having trouble balancing enough to approach us again. 'How dare you fuck my daughter, then hit me, you son of a bitch!'

I'd never heard my father swear like that before.

'Come on,' Wesley said, helping me to my feet. 'Let's get out of here. You're coming with me.' He wrapped an arm around me, pulling me close against his warm body, and ushered me out the open door.

'Bianca!' Dad yelled behind us. 'You better not get in that damn car! You better not leave this house! You hear me, you little whore!'

The ride to Wesley's house passed in silence. Several times I saw him open his mouth like he wanted to speak, but he always shut it again. I was in too much shock to say anything. My head didn't hurt that much. I just couldn't wrap my head around what Dad had done. But worse was the embarrassment. Why? Why did Wesley have to see that? What did he think of me now? What did he think of Dad?

'That's never happened before,' I said, breaking the silence when we pulled into the driveway of the almost-mansion. Wesley cut the engine and looked over at me. 'Dad's never hit me . . . or even yelled at me like that before.'

'All right.'

'I just want you to know that wasn't normal for us,' I explained. 'I don't live in an abusive house or anything. I don't want you to think my dad is some kind of psychopath.'

'I was under the impression that you didn't care what people thought,' he said.

'About me. I don't care what they think *about me*.' I

didn't know that was a lie until the words had left my mouth. 'But my family and friends are different . . . My dad isn't a psychopath. He's just having a rough time right now.' I could feel the lump rising in my throat, and I tried to gulp it down. I needed to explain. He needed to know. 'My mom just filed for a divorce, and . . . and he just can't handle it.'

The lump wasn't going away. It just kept growing. All of my worries and fears had been leading up to this moment, and I couldn't fight them back anymore. I couldn't keep them bottled up. Tears started gushing down my cheeks, and before I knew it I was sobbing.

How had this happened? It felt like a bad dream. My father was the sweetest, nicest man I knew. He was naive and fragile. This wasn't him. Even though I'd heard his reasons for sobriety before – even though I knew, in the back of my head, that his drinking was dangerous – it still didn't seem real. It didn't seem possible.

I felt like my world was finally spinning out of control. And this time, I couldn't deny it. I couldn't ignore it. And I definitely couldn't escape it.

Wesley didn't say anything. He just sat with me in silence. I didn't even realize he was holding my hand until after the tears had stopped. Once I'd caught my breath and wiped away the few salty drops from my eyes, he opened his door and walked around to open mine. He helped me out of the car – not that I needed it, but it was still nice – and led me up to the porch with his arm tight around me, like the way he'd guided me out of my house, keeping me close. As if he was afraid I might slip away in the darkness between his car and the front door.

Once we were inside, Wesley offered me a drink. I shook my head, and we went upstairs like we always did. I sat on the bed, and he sat down next to me. He wasn't looking at me, but he seemed to be deep in thought. I couldn't help wondering what horrible things were on his mind. I didn't ask. I didn't want to know.

'Are you all right?' he asked, turning to face me finally. 'Do you need an ice pack or anything?'

'No,' I said. My throat was sore from crying, and my words came out kind of croaky. 'It doesn't hurt anymore.'

He reached over and brushed the hair away from my face, his fingers barely grazing my temple. 'Well,' he said quietly. 'At least now I know.'

'Know what?'

'What you're trying to escape from.'

I didn't respond.

'Why didn't you tell me that your father has a drinking problem?' he asked.

'Because it's not my place to tell,' I said. 'And it'll pass. He's just going through a hard time right now. He hasn't had a drink in eighteen years. Just since the divorce papers came in . . . He'll get better.'

'You should talk to him. When he's sober, you should tell him that it's getting out of hand.'

'Yeah,' I scoffed. 'And make him think I'm against him, too? When my mom has just handed him the divorce papers?'

'You're not against him, Bianca.'

'Tell me, Wesley, why don't you talk to *your* parents?' I asked. He was being a hell of a hypocrite, wasn't he? 'Why don't you tell them that you're lonely? That you want them to come home? It's because you don't want to upset them, right? You don't want them to blame you for their misery? If I tell Dad he has a problem, he'll think I hate him. How can I hurt him more? He just lost everything.'

Wesley shook his head. 'Not everything. He didn't lose *you*,' he said. 'At least not yet. If you don't talk to him, he'll just end up driving you away, and then he will be in far worse pain.'

'Maybe.'

Wesley's fingers continued to rub soothingly against my temple. 'This doesn't hurt, does it?'

'Not at all.' Actually, the way he was massaging my skull felt pretty good. I sighed and leaned into his hand. 'The things he said hurt way more,' I murmured. I bit my lower lip. 'You know,' I said to Wesley, 'I've never been called a whore in my life, and today two different people have implied that I am. What's funny is, I'm pretty sure they're right.'

'That's not funny,' Wesley muttered. 'You're not a whore, Bianca.'

'Then, what am I?' I demanded, feeling suddenly angry. I pushed his hand away from my head and stood up. 'What am I? I'm screwing a guy who isn't my boyfriend and lying about it to my friends . . . if they're even my friends anymore. I don't even think about it now, whether this is right or wrong! I'm a whore. Your grandma and my dad both think so, and they're right.'

Wesley stood up, his face hard and serious. He grabbed me by the shoulders and held me firmly, forcing me to look up at him. 'Listen to me,' he said. 'You are *not* a whore. Are you listening, Bianca? What you are is an intelligent, sassy, sarcastic, cynical, neurotic, loyal, compassionate girl. That's what you are, OK? You're not a slut or a whore or anything remotely similar. Just because you have some secrets and some screwups . . . You're just confused . . . like the rest of us.'

216

I stared at him, stunned. Was he right? Was the rest of the world just as lost as I was? Did everyone have their secrets and screwups? They must. I knew Wesley was just as messed up as me, so surely the rest of the world had its imperfections, too.

'Bianca, *whore* is just a cheap word people use to cut each other down,' he said, his voice softer. 'It makes them feel better about their own mistakes. Using words like that is easier than really looking into the situation. I promise you, you're not a whore.'

I looked at him, into his warm grey eyes, and suddenly understood what he was trying to tell me. The message hidden beneath the words.

You're not alone.

Because he understood. He understood how it felt to be abandoned. He understood the insults. Understood *me*.

I pushed myself onto my tiptoes and kissed him – really kissed him. It was more than just a precursor to sex. There was no war between our mouths. My hips rested lightly beneath his, not pressed tightly. Our lips moved in soft, perfect harmony with each other. This time it meant something. What that something was, I didn't know at the time, but I knew that there was a real connection between us. His hands stroked gently through my hair, his thumb grazing my cheek – still damp from crying earlier. And it didn't feel sick or twisted or unnatural. Actually, it felt like the most natural thing in the world.

I slid off his shirt, and he pulled mine over my head. Then he laid me down on the bed. No rush. This time things were slow and earnest. This time I wasn't looking for an escape. This time it was about him. About me. About honesty and compassion and everything I'd never expected to find in Wesley Rush.

This time, when our bodies connected, it didn't feel dirty or wrong.

It felt horrifyingly right.

18

I knew something was wrong the instant I opened my eyes the next morning.

The sky looked dull and cold outside Wesley's window, but I felt warm. So warm. Wesley's arm was draped over me, holding me against his chest, and his soft, rhythmic breathing heated the back of my neck. It was so peaceful. So perfect. I felt safe and content.

And that was the problem.

I caught sight of a pink sweater lying forgotten in the corner of the room. It had been there for weeks. Property of some nameless girl. One of many Wesley had brought up to his bedroom. Seeing it, I suddenly remembered exactly whose bed I was in. Who was holding me.

I shouldn't have felt *safe* or *content*. Not here. Not with Wesley. It was wrong. I should have been disgusted. I should have been repulsed. I should have wanted nothing more than to push him away from me. What the hell was going on? What was wrong with me?

And just as I asked myself the questions, the answers hit me like a tidal wave. An icy tidal wave that left me wide-eyed and shocked.

I was jealous of the other girls he talked to.

I was willing to do anything to make him smile.

I felt safe and content in his arms.

Oh my God, I thought, half-panicked. *I'm in love with him.*

I had to shake myself then. No, no, no. Not love. *Love* was a big word. Too big. Love took years upon years to develop … right? I was *not* in love with Wesley Rush.

But I had feelings for him. Feelings other than hatred and disgust. It was more than a crush. More than anything I'd felt for Toby Tucker over the past three years. Maybe even more than I'd felt for Jake Gaither all those years ago. It was real. It was powerful.

And it was terrifying.

I had to get out of there. I couldn't stay. I couldn't let myself fall into this trap. No matter how I felt about Wesley, he would never feel the same.

Because he was Wesley Rush.

And I was the Duff.

There was no way in hell I was going to torture myself

that way. I'd learned my lesson with Jake. Getting too close just led to getting hurt, and Wesley had plenty to hurt me with. Last night he'd seen me at my weakest. I'd let him in. I'd opened up. And if I didn't leave now, I'd pay the price.

No matter where you go or what you do to distract yourself, reality catches up with you eventually. Mom had said that about herself and Dad.

A bitter smile spread across my face as I reluctantly crawled out of Wesley's arms. Mom had been right. Wesley was my distraction. He was supposed to be my escape from emotions. From all the drama. And here I was . . . feeling nothing *but* emotions.

I crept around the room, trying to get dressed without making any noise. After yanking on my sweater and jeans, I grabbed my cell phone and slipped out onto the balcony.

Before I could talk myself out of it, or convince myself that she wouldn't answer, I dialled Casey's cell phone number. I knew she'd still be pissed off with me, but I couldn't think of any other options. No matter how mad she was, I knew Casey would help me. She'd help anyone. It was just part of her nature.

'H'lo?' she grunted sleepily after two rings.

Damn, a little voice murmured in the back of my head.

After all this time, I couldn't believe this was how Casey would find out my secret. But I knew it was for the best. I knew if I didn't leave then, I never would. I knew, but I didn't want to go. I didn't want to feel what I felt. And I *really* didn't want Casey – or anybody, for that matter – to know about it.

'Hello? Bianca?'

Too bad I never got what I wanted.

'Hey, Casey, I'm sorry to wake you up, but can you do me a big favour? Please.'

'B, are you OK?' she demanded, her drowsiness vanishing. 'What's up? What's wrong?'

'Can you get your mom's keys and come pick me up? I really need a ride home.'

'Home?' She sounded confused. Not a good thing when combined with fear. God, I was going to give the poor girl ulcers one day. 'You mean you aren't at home? You didn't stay at your place last night?'

'Chill out, Casey. I'm fine,' I said.

'Don't fucking tell me to chill out, Bianca,' she snapped. 'You've been acting weird for weeks and totally ignoring me every time I tried to talk to you. Now you're calling me early in the morning and telling me to pick you up, but I should chill out? God, where the hell are you?'

This was the part I'd been dreading, so I took a deep

breath before answering her question. 'I'm at Wesley's. ...
You know the giant house on—'

'Yeah,' Casey said. 'Wesley *Rush's* place? I know where
it is.' She was curious, but she tried to hide it behind her
anger. Her acting skills were no better than mine. 'Fine,
I'll be there in ten minutes.' And she hung up.

I shut the phone and shoved it into my back pocket.

Ten minutes. Just ten short minutes.

I sighed and leaned against the railing of the balcony.
From here, boring-ass Hamilton looked like a creepy
ghost town. The streets were empty this early in the
morning (they were never really busy, to be honest), and
all the little grey-roofed shops were closed. The image
wasn't helped by the dull, sunless sky that left everything
under a layer of gloom.

Sunless gloom. Go figure, right?

'You may not be aware of this, but humans tend to
sleep in on Saturdays.'

I turned around and found Wesley standing at the
balcony entrance, rubbing his eyes sleepily with a
little smile on his face. Despite the chilly wind, he was
wearing nothing but his black boxers. Damn, he had an
amazing body . . . but I couldn't think about that. I had
to end this.

'We need to talk.' I tried to find something to look at

besides his hot, half-naked body. My feet seemed like the best option.

'Hmm,' Wesley mused, running a hand through his messy curls. 'You know, my father says those are the four most frightening words a woman can say. He claims that nothing good ever begins with "We need to talk." You're worrying me a little here, Duffy.'

'We should go inside.'

'That's not promising.'

I followed him into his bedroom, wringing my hands uncontrollably. (Sweaty palms are *so* attractive.) He flopped onto his bed and waited for me to do the same, but I remained standing. I couldn't get too comfortable. Casey would be there to pick me up in about eight and a half minutes – I was counting – so I had to keep this short and sweet.

Or just short. Nothing about this felt sweet to me.

Anxiously, I reached up and scratched the back of my neck. 'Listen,' I said. 'You're a great guy, and I appreciate everything you've done for me.'

Why did this sound so much like a breakup? Didn't you actually have to be dating someone to dump them?

'Really?' Wesley asked. 'Since when? You've never referred to me as anything better than a scumbag. I knew

I'd grow on you eventually . . . but something tells me I should be suspicious.'

'But,' I went on, ignoring him as best I could. 'I can't do this anymore. I think we should stop, um, sleeping together.'

Yep. Definitely seemed breakup-ish to me. All I needed to do was throw in an 'It's not you; it's me,' and it would be perfect.

'Why?' He didn't sound hurt. Just surprised.

It hurt me that he didn't sound hurt.

'Because this isn't working for me anymore,' I said, sticking with the traditional lines I'd heard in movies. They were classics for a reason, after all. 'I just don't think this' – I gestured between us – 'is in my, uh … *either of our* best interests.'

Wesley narrowed his eyes at me. 'Bianca, does this have something to do with what happened last night?' he asked seriously. 'If so, I want you to know that you don't have to worry about—'

'That's not it.'

'What, then? You're not making sense.'

I stared at my shoes. The rubber edges were starting to peel, but the bright red fabric of the Converses hadn't faded at all. *Bright red.* 'I'm like Hester,' I whispered, more to myself than to Wesley.

'What?'

I looked up at him, surprised he'd heard me. 'I'm like . . .' I shook my head. 'Nothing. We're done. I'm done.'

'Bianca—'

Two quick honks from the driveway saved me.

'I – I have to go.'

I was so focused on getting the hell out of that house that I didn't hear the words Wesley yelled after me. His voice simply faded into the distance, where I hoped to leave him forever.

19

Casey revved the engine as I climbed into her mother's ancient pickup truck. Miss Waller (formerly Mrs Blithe; she went back to her maiden name after the divorce) could have had a much nicer vehicle. Back when she was married to Casey's dad, they'd had plenty of money. Mr Blithe had offered to buy her a Lexus, but she'd refused. She loved the rickety old Chevy, which she'd gotten her junior year of high school. Her daughter, on the other hand, despised it. Especially since it was the only vehicle she got to drive.

Casey definitely wouldn't have turned her dad's Lexus down. Unfortunately, Mr Blithe had lost what generosity he ever possessed after the divorce was finalized.

She was gazing through her windshield at the almost-mansion while I pulled on my seat belt. She had pink pajamas decorated with green frogs on under her jacket, and her short hair stuck up in every direction. Unlike me, Casey could make looking like crap seem cute and sexy. She didn't even have to try.

'Hi,' I said.

She looked over at me. Her eyes swept across my face – already searching for telltale signs of trouble – and her forehead wrinkled. After a short staring contest, she turned away and put the truck into drive, struggling a little with the stick shift. 'OK,' she said as we pulled out of the driveway. 'What's going on? And don't tell me things are fine, because I got my ass up at seven a.m. and I might just wring your neck if you don't give me a real answer.'

'Oh, yes, because resorting to threats always gets me talking.'

'Don't give me that bullshit,' Casey growled. 'You're just avoiding the subject, which you do a lot. That might work with Jess, but you should know damn well by now that it won't throw me off one bit. Now explain. Start with why I just picked you up at Wesley's house.'

'Because I stayed the night.'

'Yeah, I figured that much out on my own.'

I bit my lip, not completely sure why I was still hiding the truth. I mean, it wasn't as if I could keep the truth from her for much longer. She'd have it pieced together soon enough, so why not just spill it now? Now that Wesley and I were over, anyway. Was lying – or withholding, really – just instinctive now? After all these weeks of secrecy, had I developed a habit?

And if I had, wasn't it about time to break it?

She sighed and the truck slowed a little. 'Tell me the truth, Bianca, because I'm pretty confused right now. Confused and annoyed. Last time I checked, you *hated* Wesley Rush. And I mean *hated*.'

'I did,' I said. 'I still do . . . sort of.'

' "Sort of"? Jesus, stop dancing around the answers. Look, you've been ditching Jess and me for weeks. We barely see you anymore because you don't do shit with us. Jess won't say it, but she seriously thinks you don't like us anymore. She's upset, and I'm pissed because you've totally abandoned us. You're always distracted and zoning out. And you dance around our fucking questions! Damn it, Bianca, give me some answers here . . . please.' The anger in her voice broke into a small plea of desperation. She lowered her voice. 'Please, tell me what's going on with you.'

My heart ached as guilt wrapped around my chest like a boa constrictor. I let out a long breath, knowing I couldn't lie anymore. At least not about this. 'We've been sleeping together.'

'Who? You and Wesley?'

'Yeah.'

'Since when?'

'End of January.'

Casey was quiet for a long moment. Then, after it sank in, she asked, 'If you hate him, why have you been hooking up with him?'

'Because . . . it made me feel better. With all of the drama with my parents and then Jake showing up and all . . . I just needed to distract myself. I wanted to escape from it all . . . you know, in a non-suicidal way. Sleeping with Wesley just seemed like a decent idea at the time.' I stared out the window, not wanting to see the expression on her face. I was sure she'd be disappointed in me. Or, in a sick way, maybe even proud of me.

'So . . . is that where you've been for the past month?' she asked. 'Is that why you've been bailing on us? You've been with Wesley?'

'Yeah,' I murmured. 'Every time things got to be too much, he was just there. I could relieve the stress without freaking you or Jessica out. It seemed like a decent idea. Then I was addicted . . . but it all caught up with me, and now things suck worse than ever.'

'OMG, are you pregnant?'

I gritted my teeth and turned around to face her. 'No,

Casey, I'm not fucking pregnant.' Was she serious? 'God, I'm smart enough to use a condom, and I've been on birth control for, like, three freaking years, OK?'

'OK, OK,' Casey said. 'You're not pregnant . . . thank God. But if that's not the problem, why do things suck worse?'

'Well, for one, you're pissed at me . . . and I like Wesley.'

'Well, duh, you are screwing him.'

'No, I mean . . .' I shook my head and turned to look out the window again. The little suburban houses of Hamilton sped past us, simple and clean. Surrounded by their innocent picket fences. I would have killed to be simple and clean like these little houses. Instead, I felt complicated and dirty and tainted. 'I don't like him,' I explained. 'He annoys the hell out of me ninety-six percent of the time, and sometimes I'd like nothing better than to strangle him to death. But at the same time I . . . I want him to be happy. I think about him way more than I should, and I—'

'You love him.'

'No!' I shouted, spinning around to face her. 'No, no, no! I do *not* love him, OK? Love is rare and hard to find and takes years upon years to develop. Teenagers don't fall in love. I don't *love* Wesley.'

231

'Fine,' Casey said. 'But you have feelings for him, right?'

'Yeah.'

She glanced at me before turning back to the road, half grinning. 'I knew it. I mean . . . all those jokes I made about it were just teasing, but I knew something would happen after you kissed him.'

'Shut up,' I muttered. 'This sucks.'

'Why?'

'Why what?'

'Why is it a bad thing? So what if you have feelings for him. Isn't that supposed to be great and exciting and give you butterflies in your tummy or whatever?'

'No,' I said. 'It's not great or exciting. It's terrible. It's excruciating.'

'But why?'

'Because he'll never like me back!' God, wasn't it obvious? Couldn't she put two and two together? 'He'll never care about me that way, Casey. I'm wasting my time even thinking that it's possible.'

'Why won't he like you back?' she asked.

Did she have a million questions or what? 'Stop.'

'No, I'm being serious, B,' Casey pushed. 'I'm pretty sure you can't read minds or see into the future, so I don't see how you know that he won't ever like you. Why wouldn't he?'

'You don't like me very much right now,' I pointed out.

'I'll get over it,' she said. 'Well, eventually. But seriously, what's stopping Wesley from liking you back?'

'I'm the Duff.'

'Sorry. The what?'

'Duff.'

'Is that even a word?'

'The designated ugly fat friend,' I sighed. 'The unattractive girl in the group. That's me.'

'That's stupid.'

'Is it?' I snapped. 'Is it really that stupid, Casey? Look at you. Look at Jessica. You two look like you jumped out of an issue of *Teen Vogue*. I can't compete with that. So, yeah, I'm the fucking Duff.'

'You are not. Who told you that?'

'Wesley.'

'You're shitting me!'

'Nope.'

'Before or after you fucked him?'

'Before.'

'Well, then, he didn't mean it,' Casey said. 'He's been sleeping with you, right? So he must find you attractive.'

I snorted. 'Look who you're talking about, Casey.

Wesley isn't particularly picky when it comes to sex. I could look like a gorilla, and he still wouldn't hesitate to fuck me, but dating me is a totally different situation. He wouldn't even date a girl on the Skinny Squad—'

'I really hate it when you call us that.'

'—but me? He would never be the boyfriend of a Duff.'

'Seriously, Bianca,' Casey said. 'You are *not* the Duff. If any of us is the Duff, it's me.'

'Funny.'

'I'm not joking,' she insisted. 'I'm still mad at you, so why would I go out of my way to be nice? I mean, I'm like freaking Bigfoot. I'm six one now! Most guys have to look up to see my face, and no guy likes being shorter than a chick. At least you're cute and petite. I'd *kill* to be your height . . . and to have your eyes. You have way prettier eyes than me.'

I didn't say anything. I was sure she'd gone insane. How the hell could she be the Duff? Even in her frog pajamas she looked like she'd just stepped off the set of *America's Next Top Model*.

'If Wesley can't see how adorable you are, he doesn't deserve you,' she said. 'You just need to move on. Put Wesley out of your mind.'

Yeah, right. Move on to who? Who would want me?

Nobody.

But I couldn't say that to Casey. It would probably just start another stupid fight, and we hadn't really finished the first one yet, so I just nodded.

'So . . . what about the Tucker kid?'

I looked at her, surprised. 'Toby? What about him?'

'You've had a crush on him forever,' she reminded me. 'And I saw you all over him in the cafeteria yesterday—'

'He hugged me,' I interjected. 'That is hardly me being *all over* him.'

She rolled her eyes. God, I was really rubbing off on her. 'Whatever. The point is, you were getting cosy with Toby, but now you're suddenly in—'

I shot her a warning glare.

'—you suddenly *like* Wesley,' she finished.

'What's your point?' I asked.

'I don't know,' she sighed. 'It's just . . . I feel like you've kept so much from me. Like so much has changed so fast with you. I feel really in the dark right now.'

More guilt. Great. She was laying it on thick today, but I guess I deserved it.

'Not that much has changed,' I assured her. 'I still have a crush on Toby . . . not that it matters. We're just friends. He hugged me yesterday because he got into the college he wanted and was really happy. I wish it had been more, but it wasn't. And the thing with Wesley is just . . . it's stupid. It's over. We can pretend it never happened. I'd prefer that, actually.'

'What about your parents? The divorce? You haven't even brought it up since the day after Valentine's.'

'Everything's fine,' I lied. 'The divorce is still happening. My parents are fine.'

She gave me a skeptical look before turning back to the road. She knew I was full of shit, but for once she didn't push it. Finally, after a long moment, she spoke again. Luckily, she changed the subject.

'OK. So where the hell is your car?'

'At school,' I said. 'The battery's dead.'

'That blows. I guess you'll have to get your dad to go fix it.'

'Yeah,' I muttered. *If I can get him sober for more than ten seconds.*

There was a long silence. After a few minutes, I decided to swallow the little pride I had left. 'I'm sorry I called you a bitch yesterday.'

'You should be. You also called me a preppy cheerleader snob.'

'Sorry. Are you still mad at me?'

'Yeah,' she said. 'I mean, not as much as I was yesterday, but . . . it really hurt, Bianca. Jess and I have been so worried about you, and you barely talk to either of us anymore. I kept asking and asking if you wanted to go out, and you totally blew me off. Then I saw you talking to Toby when you were supposed to be talking to me, and . . . I was kind of jealous. Not in a creepy way, but . . . I'm supposed to be your best friend, you know? It felt like you just tossed me aside. And now it really bothers me that you started sleeping with Wesley instead of just talking to me.'

'Sorry,' I mumbled.

'Stop saying that. Don't just be sorry,' she said. 'Sorry doesn't change the future. Next time, think about me. And Jess, too. We need you, B. And just remember that we're here for you, and we care about you . . . for some ungodly reason.'

I cracked a little smile. 'I'll remember.'

'Just don't abandon me again, OK?' The words came out in a weak murmur. 'Even with Jess, I was really lonely without you . . . and I didn't have anyone cool to drive me around. Do you know how much it sucks to have Vikki as your chauffeur? She almost hit some poor old dude on a bike the other day. Did I tell you that story?'

We drove around Hamilton for a while, just wasting gas and catching up on what we'd missed. Casey had a crush on a basketball player. I was acing English. Nothing too personal. Casey knew my secret now – or part of it – and she wasn't mad at me anymore . . . well, not *that* mad at me. She assured me I had a lot of grovelling to do before we were totally good again.

We drove around until her mom called at ten, demanding to know where her truck was, and Casey had to take me home.

'Are you going to tell Jessica about this?' she asked quietly as she turned onto my street. 'About Wesley?'

'I don't know.' I took a deep breath, deciding that keeping secrets wasn't the best idea. It had only fucked things up so far. 'Look, you can tell her. Tell her everything if you want. But I don't want to talk about it. I just kind of want to forget about this if I can.'

'I understand,' Casey said. 'I think she should know. I mean, she is our best friend . . . but I'll tell her you're moving on. Because that's what you're doing, right?'

'Right,' I murmured.

I couldn't help feeling anxious when she pulled into my driveway. I stared at the oak front door, at the shuttered windows that looked in on my living room, and at our simple, clean, picket-fenced yard. I'd never realized what a mask my family lived behind.

Then I thought of Dad.

'I'll see you Monday,' I said, looking away so she

couldn't see the worry on my face.

Then I slid out of the truck and started walking toward my house.

20

I was standing on the porch before I realized I didn't have my keys. Wesley had pulled me from the house so quickly the night before that I hadn't been able to grab my purse. So I found myself knocking on my own front door, hoping Dad was awake to let me in.

Fearing, dreading, remembering.

I took a step back as the knob turned and the door swung open. There stood Dad, his eyes red and deeply circled behind his glasses. He looked really pale, like he'd been sick, and I could see his hand shaking on the doorknob. 'Bianca.'

He didn't smell like whiskey.

I let out a breath I hadn't realized I was holding. 'Hi, Dad. I, um, left my keys inside last night, so . . .'

He moved slowly forward, like he was afraid I might run away. Then he wrapped his arms around me, pulled me into his chest, and buried his face in my hair. We stood there together for a long moment, and when he finally spoke, I could tell the words came through sobs. 'I'm so, so sorry.'

'I know,' I murmured into his shirt.

And I was crying, too.

Dad and I talked more that day than we had in seventeen years. Not that we weren't close before. It's just that neither of us is very expressive. We didn't share our thoughts or feelings or do any of that stuff they tell you is important on those public service announcements you see on Nickelodeon. When we ate dinner together, we were always in front of the TV, and there was no way either of us would interrupt the programme with lame small talk. That's just how we were.

But that day we talked.

We talked about his work.

We talked about my grades.

We talked about Mom.

'She's really not coming back, is she?' Dad took off his glasses and rubbed his face with both hands. We were sitting on the couch. For once, the television was off. Ours were the only voices that filled the room. It was a good kind of semi-silence, yet scary at the same time.

'No, Daddy,' I said, bravely reaching out to squeeze his hand. 'She's not. This just isn't the right place for her anymore.'

He nodded. 'I know. I've known for a long time that she wasn't happy . . . maybe even before she knew. I just hoped—'

'That she'd change her mind?' I offered. 'I think she wanted to. That's why she kept leaving and coming back, you know? She didn't want to face the truth. She didn't want to admit that she wanted a' – I paused at the next word – 'divorce.'

Divorce was just so final. More than a fight. More than a separation or a long speaking tour. It meant their marriage – their life together – was really and truly finished.

'Well,' he sighed, squeezing my hand back. 'I guess we were both running away in different ways.'

'What do you mean?'

Dad shook his head. 'Your mother took a Mustang. I took a whiskey bottle.' He reached up and readjusted his glasses, an unconscious habit – he always did it when he was making a point. 'I was so devastated by what your mother did to me that I forgot how horrible drinking is. I forgot to look on the bright side.'

'Dad,' I said, 'I don't think there is a bright side to

divorce. It's a pretty sucky thing all around.'

He nodded. 'Maybe that's true, but there are a lot of bright sides to my life. I have a job I like, a nice house in a good neighbourhood, and a wonderful daughter.'

I rolled my eyes. 'Oh God,' I muttered. 'Don't go all *Lifetime* movie on me. Seriously.'

'I'm sorry,' he said, smiling. 'But I mean it. A lot of people would kill for my life, but I didn't even consider that. I took it – and you – for granted. I'm so, so sorry for that, Bumblebee.'

I wanted to look away when I saw the tears glistening at the corners of his eyes, but I forced myself to focus only on him. I'd been turning away from the truth for too long.

He apologized multiple times for everything that had happened over the past few weeks. He promised me he'd start going to weekly Alcoholics Anonymous meetings again, to go back on the wagon, to call his sponsor again. And then we poured every single bottle of whiskey and beer down the drain together, both of us eager for a clean slate.

'Is your head all right?' he asked me about a million times that day.

'It's fine,' I kept telling him.

He always shook his head and murmured more

243

apologies for slapping me. For saying what he had. Then he'd hug me.

Seriously, a million times that day.

Around midnight, I joined him in his nightly ritual of turning out the lights. 'Bumblebee,' he said as the kitchen went dark. 'I want you to thank your friend next time you see him.'

'My friend?'

'Yeah. The boy who was with you last night. What's his name?'

'Wesley,' I muttered.

'Right,' Dad said. 'Well, I deserved it. He was brave to do what he did. I don't know what's going on between you two, but I'm glad you have a friend who's willing to stand up for you. So please tell him I said thanks.'

'Sure.' I turned and walked up the stairs to my bedroom, praying that wouldn't be anytime soon.

'But, Bianca?' He winced and rubbed his jaw. 'Next time tell him he should feel free to write a strongly worded letter first. Hell of an arm on that kid.'

I smiled in spite of myself. 'There won't be a next time,' I told him, taking the last few steps and heading to my bedroom.

Both my parents were facing reality, giving up their distractions. Now it was my turn, and that meant quitting

Wesley. Unfortunately, there were no weekly meetings, no sponsors, or twelve-step programmes for what I was addicted to.

21

I was pretty sure Wesley wouldn't approach me at school. Why would he? It wasn't like he'd miss me . . . even if I really, really wanted him to. He wasn't losing anything. He had plenty of replacement girls ready and willing to fill any gaps I might have left in his schedule. So there was no need for an avoidance plan on Monday morning.

Except that I didn't even want to *see* him. If I had to look at him day after day, I could never hope to forget about him. I could never hope to move on. For this situation, I did need a plan, and I had one all lined up.

Step one: keep distracted in the hallway in case he passed me.

Step two: stay busy in English and never look over at his side of the classroom.

Step three: speed out of the parking lot in the afternoon so I didn't run into him.

Dad made step three possible by fixing my car Sunday, so I was sure I could keep from seeing Wesley. In a matter of weeks, I'd be able to put our relationship – or lack thereof – out of my mind. If not, well, we'd graduate in May and I'd never have to look at that cocky smirk ever again.

That was the theory, anyway.

But by the time the final bell rang on Monday, I knew my plan sucked ass. Not looking at Wesley didn't necessarily equal not thinking of Wesley. In fact, I spent most of my day thinking about not looking at him. Then I just thought about all the reasons I shouldn't be thinking of him. It never freaking ended! Nothing seemed to distract me.

Until Tuesday afternoon.

I was on my way to lunch after an unbearably long AP government class when something happened that gave me just the distraction I needed. Something unbelievable and shocking. Something pretty damn awesome.

Toby fell into step with me in the hallway. 'Hey,' he said.

'Hi.' I did my best to sound at least halfway pleasant. 'What's up, Harvard Boy?'

Toby grinned and looked down, shuffling his feet. 'Not much,' he said. 'Just trying to decide what to write about for the editorial assignment. Mr Chaucer wasn't very specific. What are you going to write yours about?'

'I'm not sure,' I admitted. 'I'm thinking of doing it on gay marriage.'

'Supporting or opposing?'

'Oh, definitely supporting. I mean, the government has no right to dictate who can and can't publicly declare their love for each other.'

'How romantic of you,' Toby said.

I snorted. 'Hardly. I'm not romantic at all, but it's basic logic. Denying homosexuals the right to marriage infringes on their liberty *and* equality. Pretty screwed up.'

'My thoughts exactly,' Toby agreed. 'It seems we have a lot in common.'

'I guess we do.'

We walked for a couple of seconds in silence before he asked, 'So, do you have any plans for prom?'

'No,' I told him. 'I'm not going. Why pay two hundred bucks for a dress, thirty for a ticket, forty for hair and makeup, and a handful more for dinner, where all you can have is a salad with no dressing because you have to avoid getting gunk on the poufy dress? It's kind of ridiculous.'

'I see,' Toby said. 'That's a little unfortunate . . . I was kind of hoping you'd go with me.'

OK, so I hadn't seen that coming. At all. *Ever*. Toby Tucker, the boy I'd crushed on for years, wanted to ask me to prom? Oh my God. *Oh my God*. And I'd totally bashed the whole institution of high school dances like an opinionated idiot. I'd practically rejected him without even meaning to. Oh, shit. I was a moron. A *complete* moron. And now I was at a loss for words. What did I say? Did I apologize or take it back or—

'But it's fine if you feel that way,' Toby said. 'I've always thought prom was a pointless rite of passage, so we're on the same page.'

'Uh, yeah,' I said lamely.

Oh, someone fucking shoot me right now!

'But,' Toby pressed, 'are you opposed to regular dates? Ones without poufy dresses or crappy salads?'

'No. I don't have a problem with those.'

My head was spinning. Toby wanted me to go on a date with him. A date! I hadn't been on a real date since . . . Hell, I'd *never* been on a real date. Unless you counted making out with Jake in the back of a movie theatre a date.

I didn't.

But why? Why would Toby want to go on a date with *me?* I was the Duff. Duffs don't get dates. Not real ones. Yet Toby was defying the odds. Maybe he was a bigger man than most. Just like how I'd always imagined him in my stupid, girly, midclass daydreams. Not shallow. Not conceited. Not cocky or vain. A perfect gentleman.

'That's good,' he said. 'In that case . . .' I could tell he was nervous. His cheeks were turning pink, and he was staring at his shoes and playing with his glasses. 'Friday? Would you like to go out with me on Friday night?'

'I'd like . . .'

Then the inevitable happened. I thought of the douche bag. The playboy. The womanizer. The one person who could ruin this moment for me. Yes, I had a crush on Toby Tucker. How could I not? He was sweet and charming and smart . . . but my feelings for Wesley were way beyond that. I'd skipped the crush kiddie pool and jumped right into the deep, shark-infested ocean of emotions. And, if you'll forgive the dramatic metaphor, I was a lousy swimmer.

But Casey had told me to move on, and here Toby was, tossing me a float and offering to save me from drowning. I'd be stupid not to accept. God only knew how long it might be before another rescue party came along.

And, come on, Toby was adorable.

'I'd like that,' I said, hoping my pause hadn't freaked him out too much.

'Great.' He sounded relieved. 'I'll pick you up at seven Friday night.'

'Cool.'

We separated in the cafeteria, and I think I skipped – yeah, skipped like a little kid – to the lunch table, my bad mood totally forgotten.

And it stayed forgotten.

For the rest of that week, I didn't think about how I shouldn't be thinking of Wesley. I didn't think of Wesley at all. Not once. My brain was too full of things like *What should I wear?* and *How should I fix my hair?* All the stuff I'd never worried about before. Talk about surreal.

But those were the things that Casey and Jessica were experts on, so they came home with me on Friday afternoon, and they were eager to make me their own personal Barbie doll. If I hadn't been so nervous about this date, I would have been horrified, my feminist sensibilities offended at their preening and squealing.

They forced me into, like, twenty different outfits (all of which I hated) before deciding on one. I wound up in a knee-length black skirt and a low-cut turquoise blouse, cut just low enough that you could make out the curve of my tiny boobs. Then they spent the rest of the time using a flatiron on my unwilling hair. It took them two hours – that's no exaggeration, by the way – to get it all straight.

It was already six-fifty when they placed me in front of the mirror to examine their work.

'Perfect,' Casey announced.

'Cute!' Jessica agreed.

'See, B,' Casey said. 'All of that Duff shit is ridiculous. You look freaking smoking right now.'

'What Duff shi— uh, *stuff*?' Jessica asked.

'Nothing,' I said.

'B thinks she's the ugly one.'

'What?' Jessica cried. 'Bianca, do you really think that?'

'It's not a big deal.'

'She does,' Casey said. 'She told me so.'

'But you're not, Bianca,' Jessica insisted. 'How could you think that?'

'Jessica, don't worry about it,' I said. 'It's no big—'

'I know,' Casey said. 'Isn't it stupid? Isn't she hot, Jess?'

'She's super-hot.'

'See, B. You're super-hot.'

I sighed. 'Thanks, guys.' Time for a subject change. 'So, um, how are you getting home? I can't take you if Toby is picking me up in ten minutes. Are your parents coming to get you?'

'Oh, no,' Jessica said. 'We aren't leaving.'

'What?'

'We'll be here when you get back from your date,' Casey informed me. 'Then we're having an ultra-girly, tell-all slumber party in honour of our B's first big date.'

'Yep,' Jessica chirped.

I gawked at them. 'You're not serious.'

'Do we look like we're kidding?' Casey asked.

'But what will you do while I'm gone? Won't you be bored or whatever?'

'You have TV,' Jessica reminded me.

'And that's all we really need,' Casey said. 'We already called your dad. You don't have a choice.'

The doorbell rang before I could argue any further, and my friends practically pushed me down the stairs. Once we were in the living room, they started straightening my skirt and adjusting the collar of my shirt, attempting to maximize the amount of cleavage I was showing.

'You're going to have such a good time,' Casey sighed happily, pushing some hair behind my ear. 'You'll be over Wesley in no time.'

My stomach clenched.

'Shh . . . Casey . . .' Jessica murmured. I knew Casey had told her the whole story by now, but she hadn't said anything to me about it, which I appreciated. I really just wanted to keep my mind as far from Wesley as possible.

I hadn't spoken to him since the morning I'd left his house. He'd tried to talk to me once or twice after English, though. I just avoided him, starting up conversations with Jessica or Casey and rushing out of the class as fast as I could.

'OMG, sorry,' Casey said, biting her lip. 'I didn't think.' She cleared her throat awkwardly and scratched the back of her head, ruffling her short hair.

'Have fun!' Jessica chimed, forcing the uncomfortable pause away. 'But, you know, not *too* much fun. My parents might not like you so much if I have to bail you out of jail.'

I laughed. Only Jessica could save us from these awkward moments with such bubbly grace.

I looked at Casey, and I could see a spark of fear in her eye. She wanted me to move on after Wesley, but I knew she was worried. Worried I'd leave her behind again. Worried Toby would replace her.

But she had nothing to be afraid of. This was totally different from my relationship with Wesley. I wasn't running anymore. Not from reality. Not from my friends. Not from anything.

I smiled to reassure her.

'Go! Go!' Jessica squealed, her blond ponytail swinging as she bounced excitedly.

'Yeah,' Casey said, smiling back at me. 'Don't keep the boy waiting.'

They shoved me forward and disappeared back upstairs in a fit of giggles and whispers.

'Freaks,' I muttered, shaking my head and fighting a small giggle. I took a deep breath and pulled open the door. 'Hey, Toby.'

He stood on my front porch, looking as cute as always in his navy blazer and khaki pants. He looked like a Kennedy. With a bowl cut. He gave me a big boyish smile that showed off all his ivory teeth. 'Hi,' he said, shifting to stand in front of me. He'd been waiting off to one side of the door. 'Sorry. I decided to wait. I heard giggling.'

'Oh.' I glanced over my shoulder. 'Yeah. Sorry about that.'

'Wow. You look beautiful, Bianca.'

'No, I don't,' I said, totally embarrassed. No guy but my dad had ever said that to me before.

'Of course you do,' he said. 'Why would I lie?'

'I don't know.' Oh, wow, I was lame. Why couldn't I just take a compliment? What if I sent him running before we even started the date? God, that would be shitty. I cleared my throat and tried to look like I wasn't inwardly slapping myself.

'So are you ready to go?' Toby asked.

'Yeah.'

I stepped outside and shut the door behind me. Toby took my arm and led me down the sidewalk to his silver Taurus. He even opened the passenger door for me, like boys do in those old movies. Very classy. I couldn't help wondering, *again*, why on earth he was interested in me. He put the key in the ignition and turned to smile at me. His smile was definitely his best feature. So I smiled back, feeling the little butterflies flutter around in the pit of my stomach.

'I hope you're hungry,' he said.

'Starved,' I lied, knowing very well that I was way too nervous to eat.

By the time we left Giovanni's, a tiny Italian restaurant in Oak Hill, I'd become a little more comfortable. My nerves were dying down, and I'd even managed to eat a small bowl of meatless spaghetti. We were laughing and talking, and I was enjoying myself so much that I didn't want the date to be over when Toby paid the bill. Lucky for me, he felt the same way.

'You know,' he said as the bells on the door jingled behind us. 'It's only nine-thirty. I don't have to take you home yet . . . unless you want to go home, which is fine, of course.'

'No,' I said. 'I'm not in a hurry to go home. But what do you want to do?'

'Well, we can walk,' Toby suggested. He gestured down the sidewalk that ran alongside the busy street. 'It's not very exciting, but we can window-shop or talk or—'

I smiled at him. 'Walking sounds fun.'

'Wonderful.'

He looped his arm in mine, and we began to stroll down the well-lit sidewalk. We'd passed a couple of small shops before either of us spoke. Thank God he opened his mouth first because, even though I wasn't that nervous anymore, I had no clue what I could say that wouldn't make me sound like a complete goofball.

'Well, since you know all about my college situation, I want to know about yours. Have you applied anywhere yet?' he asked.

'Yeah. I've applied to a couple, but I haven't picked one yet. I guess I'm kind of procrastinating.'

'Do you know what you'll major in?'

'Probably journalism,' I said. 'I don't know, though. I've always wanted to be a reporter for the *New York Times*. So I applied to a couple of schools in Manhattan.'

'The Big Apple,' he said, nodding. 'Ambitious.'

'Yeah, well, watch me end up like that girl in *The Devil Wears Prada*,' I said. 'A complete loser working at some stupid fashion magazine when all I really want to do is write about world events or interview revolutionary congressmen . . . like you'll be.'

He beamed at me. 'Oh, you wouldn't be a complete loser.'

'Whatever,' I laughed. 'Can you imagine me writing about fashion? An industry where size fours are considered fat? No way. I'd wind up committing suicide.'

'Something tells me you'd be good at anything you tried,' he said.

'Something tells me you're kissing my ass a little bit there, Toby.'

He shrugged. 'Maybe, but not much. You're pretty great, Bianca. You tell it like it is, you don't seem like you're afraid to be yourself, and you're a Democrat. That makes you awesome in my book.'

OK, so I blushed. Can you blame me?

'Thank you, Toby.'

'There's nothing to thank me for.'

Wow. Was he perfect or what? Cute, polite, funny . . . and he liked me for some unknown reason. It was like we were made for each other. Like he had the puzzle piece that fit with mine. Could I get any luckier?

A cold March breeze was blowing, and I began regretting that I'd let Casey and Jessica dress me. They'd never been seasonably sensible when it came to clothing. My bare legs were freezing (they hadn't let me wear panty hose), and the thin material of my blouse definitely didn't shield me from the wind. I shivered and wrapped my arms around myself in an effort to warm up.

'Oh, here,' Toby said. He pulled off his blazer, just like boys are supposed to do, and held it out for me. 'You should have told me you were cold.'

'I'm fine.'

'Don't be silly.' He helped me slide into the sleeves. 'Honestly, I'd rather not be dating a Popsicle.'

Dating? I mean, this was a date, but were we *dating* now? I'd never dated anyone, so I wasn't really sure. Either way, hearing him say that made me very happy . . . and strangely nervous at the same time.

Toby turned me around and adjusted the blazer around my neck and shoulders.

'Thanks,' I murmured.

We were standing in front of an old antiques store, its windows illuminated by the light of fancy, old-fashioned lamps, like the ones my grandpa had in his living room. The glow spilled onto Toby's angular face, glinting off the rims of his glasses and highlighting his almond-shaped eyes . . . which were staring down at me.

His fingers still lingered on the collar of the blazer.

259

Then his hand slid up from my shoulder to my jaw. His thumb grazed my cheek, stroking it over and over again. He leaned toward me slowly, giving me plenty of time to stop him if I wanted to. Yeah, right! As if I would dream of it.

And he kissed me. Not a make-out kiss, but not just a peck either. It was a real kiss. Gentle and sweet and long. The kind of kiss I'd wanted to share with Toby Tucker since I was fifteen years old, and it felt exactly like I'd always imagined it would. His lips were soft and warm, and the way they moved against mine made the butterflies in my belly go berserk.

OK. I know, I know. I think PDAs are gross and immature, but *come on*. I was a little too distracted to care who might be watching. So, yeah, I put my usual values aside for a second and wrapped my arms around his neck. I mean, I could always go back to my crusade against public make-outs in the morning.

I slipped into the house around eleven o'clock that night and found Dad waiting for me on the sofa. He smiled at me and muted the TV. 'Hey, Bumblebee.'

'Hi, Dad.' I shut and locked the front door. 'How was your AA meeting?'

'Strange,' Dad admitted. 'It's weird being back

again . . . but I'll get used to it. What about you? How was your date?'

'Amazing,' I sighed. God, I couldn't stop smiling. Dad was probably going to think I'd had a lobotomy or something.

'That's good,' Dad said. 'Tell me again, who did you go out with? Sorry. I can't remember his name.'

'Toby Tucker.'

'Tucker?' Dad repeated. 'You mean Chaz Tucker's son? Oh, that's great, Bumblebee. Chaz is a good guy. He's the technology director for a company downtown, so he comes into the store all the time. Wonderful family. I'm glad to hear his son's a nice kid, too.'

'He is,' I said.

The sound of shuffling came from upstairs, and we both glanced up at the ceiling. 'Oh.' Dad shook his head and looked back at me. 'I almost forgot about them. They've been suspiciously quiet all night.'

'Yeah,' I said. 'I should get up there before Casey has an aneurysm. See you in the morning, Dad.'

'OK,' Dad said. He reached for the remote and turned up the volume on the television. 'Good night, Bumblebee.'

I'd danced halfway up the stairs before Dad called out to me again. 'Hey, Bumblebee?'

I paused and leaned against the banister, looking down at the living room. 'Yeah?'

'Whatever happened to Wesley?'

I froze, feeling myself choke a little. 'W-What?'

'Your friend. The one who, um . . . was with you that night.' He looked up at me from the couch, readjusting his glasses. 'You don't talk about him much.'

'We don't hang out anymore,' I told him, using that voice that made it clear he shouldn't ask questions. All teenage girls know that voice and use it on their fathers frequently. Usually, the unspoken order is followed. My father loved me, but he knew better than to delve into the drama of my high school experience.

Smart Dad.

'Oh . . . I was just wondering.'

'Bianca!' My bedroom door flew open, and Jessica, dressed in neon orange pajamas, leapt out of my room. She sprinted halfway down the stairs and grabbed me by the arm. 'Stop making us wait! Come tell us everything.'

The way Jessica was beaming almost pushed Dad's mention of Wesley from my mind.

Almost.

'Goodnight, Mr Piper!' Jessica yelled as she dragged me to my bedroom.

After a few steps, my feet picked up again and I

reminded myself that I'd just had the best date ever with the guy of my dreams. I felt myself succumbing to the giddy joy my best friends expressed as soon as I walked into the room. Squealing, jumping, cheering . . .

I had the right to be happy about this. Even we cynics deserved a night off once in a while, right?

22

My good mood lasted all the way through to Monday afternoon. I mean, what was there to be irritated about? Nothing. Things were back to normal at home. My friends hadn't dragged me to the Nest in weeks. Oh, yeah, and I'd just gone on a date with the perfect boy. Who could complain?

'I don't think I've ever seen you this happy,' Casey observed as we pulled out of the student parking lot. Her voice was full of pep, an unfortunate side effect of cheerleading practice, and she bounced up and down in her seat. 'It's so refreshing!'

'God, Casey, you make me sound suicidal or something.'

'It's not that,' she said. 'It's just that you haven't been as bitter as usual lately. It's a nice change.'

'I'm not bitter.'

'You are so.' She reached over and patted my knee. 'But that's OK, B. It's just part of your personality. We accept it. But you *aren't* bitter now, and that's freaking awesome. Don't take it as an insult.'

'Whatever.' But I broke into a smile.

'See there!' Casey cried. 'You're grinning. You can't stop, can you? Like I said, you're happier than I've ever seen you.'

'OK, maybe you're kind of right,' I admitted. It was sort of true. I had Casey and Jessica back. Things were normal again with Dad. Why complain?

'I always am.' She leaned forward and changed the radio to some shitty Top 40 station. 'So, what's up with you and *Toby*? Anything gossip-worthy?'

'Not really. He's coming over this afternoon.'

'Ooh!' She sat back in her seat and winked at me. 'Sounds gossip-worthy to me. You've picked up some extra-large condoms, right?'

'Shut up,' I said. 'It's not that kind of thing, and you know it. He's just coming over to work on our editorials for AP government. It's—'

I was cut off when my cell phone, which was lying in the cup holder, started vibrating and playing loud music. My fingers instantly clinched around the steering wheel. I knew who I'd set that ringtone for, and those few chords were all it took to derail my entire afternoon.

'Britney Spears? You have "Womanizer" as a ringtone, seriously? OMG, B, that song is so, like, 2008,' Casey laughed.

I didn't say anything.

'Aren't you gonna answer it?'

'No.'

'Why not?'

'Because I don't wanna talk to him.'

'Who?'

I didn't respond, so Casey picked up my cell phone and checked the ID. I heard her let out a knowing sigh. A few seconds later, the music stopped playing, but I couldn't force my body to relax again. I felt stiff and anxious, and it didn't help that Casey had her eyes glued on me.

'You haven't talked to him?'

'No,' I muttered.

'Since the day I picked you up from his house?'

'Mm-mm.'

'Oh, B,' she sighed.

The car became quiet – well, except for the annoying sound of an untalented pop singer on the radio, but she was too busy whining about her cheating boyfriend to care about my issues.

'What do you think he wants?' Casey asked when the song ended. She sounded a little bitter.

'Knowing Wesley . . . probably a booty call,' I grumbled. 'It's never anything more than that.'

'Well, then, it's a good thing you didn't answer.' She tossed my phone back into the cup holder and folded her arms over her chest. 'Because he doesn't deserve you, B. And you're with Toby now, and he's perfect for you and treats you the way you should be treated . . . unlike the douche bag.'

Part of me wanted to stop her. To defend Wesley. He hadn't really treated me badly. I mean, yeah, he'd called me Duffy to no end, which was annoying and hurtful, but overall, Wesley had been good to me.

I didn't tell Casey this, though. I didn't say anything at all. She didn't know about that last night with Wesley, how he had been my friend for about twelve solid hours. She didn't know about Dad's relapse, or the way Wesley had stood up for me. Those were things I could never tell her.

She was getting pissed at him only because she was scared. Scared I'd run back to him and forget about her and Jessica again. Defending Wesley wouldn't have helped put that worry to rest.

Toby had gone from geek to hero in Casey's mind in a

matter of days. Simply because he hadn't taken me from her. I wasn't spending every afternoon with him the way I had with Wesley. I didn't really want to. Sometimes that scared me, but I figured that that was normal. This was a healthy, nonescapist relationship, unlike what I'd had with Wesley. And at the moment, I was really happy to be spending some time with my friends.

I turned into Casey's driveway and hit the automatic unlock button on my door. 'Don't worry about me. You're right. Toby is awesome, and he's made it so much easier to move on. I already have. Things are going well for me, so don't worry.'

'OK,' she said. 'Good. Well, I'll see you tomorrow, B.'

'Bye.'

She climbed out of the car, and I drove away, wondering whether I'd just lied to her. Honestly, I wasn't sure.

On the way home, Wesley called again.

I ignored him.

Because things were going well for me.

Because I was moving on.

Because talking on a cell phone and driving at the same time just isn't safe.

I pushed Wesley out of my mind when I saw Toby's car already parked in my driveway. Dad wasn't home from work yet, so he sat on the front porch steps with a book. The sun glinted off the rims of his glasses, making them look extra sparkly. Like he was a trophy.

I got out of the car and hurried up the sidewalk toward him. 'Hey,' I said. 'Sorry. I had to take Casey home.'

He looked up at me with a smile.

Not a crooked grin . . .

I had to shake myself. I wasn't going to think about Wesley. I wasn't going to let myself miss him. Not when I had Toby. Sweet, normal, sparkly-smiling Toby.

'It's fine,' he said. 'I'm enjoying the weather. It's so unpredictable in the spring.' He stuck his bookmark in the pages of his novel. 'It's nice to have a little bit of sunlight.'

'Brontë?' I asked, seeing the cover of his book. '*Wuthering Heights*? Isn't that a little girly, Toby?'

'Have you read it?'

'Well, no,' I admitted. 'I've read *Jane Eyre*, which was definitely full of early feminism. I'm not saying that's a problem. Personally, I'm a total feminist, but it's a little sketchy for a teenage boy.'

Toby shook his head. '*Jane Eyre* is Charlotte Brontë. *Wuthering Heights* is Emily. The sisters are very, very different. Yes, *Wuthering Heights* is usually considered a love story, but I disagree with that. It's almost a ghost story, and there's more hate than romance. Every character is atrocious and spoiled and selfish . . . It's kind of like watching an episode of *Gossip Girl* in the 1800s. Except, of course, much less ridiculous.'

'Interesting,' I muttered, chagrined that I secretly watched *Gossip Girl* on a regular basis.

'It isn't a favourite of most boys my age, I admit,' he said. 'But it's a page-turner. You should read it.'

'I might.'

'You should.'

I smiled and shook my head. 'Are you ready to go in or what?'

'Absolutely.' He snapped the book shut and got to his feet. 'Lead the way.'

I unlocked the door and let him walk inside ahead of me, where he immediately took his shoes off. Not that we live like pigs or anything, but no one *ever* does that in our house. I couldn't help being impressed.

'Where will we be working?' he asked.

I realized suddenly that I was watching him and looked away. 'Oh,' I said casually. 'Um . . . my room? Is that OK?' *God, I hope he doesn't think I'm a stalker freak for staring at him like that.*

'If it doesn't bother you,' Toby said.

'No, it's cool. Come on.'

He followed me up the stairs. When we reached my bedroom, I pushed the door open a crack, checking quickly for embarrassing items (bras, panties, et cetera) that might be lying on the floor. Sure the coast was clear – and praying I hadn't been too obvious – I swung the door the rest of the way open and gestured for Toby to walk inside.

'Sorry it's a little messy,' I said, looking down at the pile of unfolded, clean clothes that always stayed on the floor at the foot of my bed and trying not to think about the last time I'd had a boy in my room and how he'd laughed at my neurotic clothes folding. What would Toby think of it?

'It's fine.' Toby moved a stack of overdue library books out of my chair and placed them on the desk. Then he sat down. 'We're seventeen. Our rooms are supposed to be messy. It wouldn't be natural if they weren't.'

'I guess not.' I climbed onto my bed and sat with my legs crisscrossed. 'I just didn't want it to bug you.'

'Nothing about you could bug me, Bianca.'

It took everything I had to ignore how cheesy that sounded. I smiled anyway and looked down at my purple comforter. I'd never received so many compliments from one person, and I wasn't very good at accepting them. Mostly because I was always too busy mocking how

271

mushy they were. But I was working on that.

And the truth was, I was kind of blushing.

I didn't even notice Toby had moved until he was sitting beside me. 'Sorry,' he said. 'Did I embarrass you?'

'No . . . well, yeah, but in a good way.'

'As long as it's in a good way.'

He leaned forward and kissed me on the cheek, but I didn't let him stop there. I turned my head and pressed my lips against his, just as he started to pull back. It didn't go quite as smoothly as I'd hoped. I mean, his glasses kind of knocked me in the face for a second, but I pretended I hadn't noticed.

His lips were so soft that I wondered if he used ChapStick. Seriously, nobody has lips that perfect naturally, do they? He must have been disgusted by mine, which probably felt rough and scaly to him.

But if he was, he didn't show it. His hand moved up my arm and rested on my shoulder, pulling me a little closer. We sat on my bed and kissed for a few minutes, but the sound of my cell phone broke the moment. *Damn it!*

And of course, it was that same Britney Spears ringtone – the one I wanted *least* to hear at that exact moment – that seemed to scream at me. Toby pulled away and looked down at the floor where I'd dropped my purse. When I didn't move, he turned back to me with raised eyebrows.

'Ignoring someone?' he asked.

'Well . . . um, yeah.'

'Are you sure you don't need to answer it?'

'Positive.'

Before he could ask any more questions, I kissed him again. Hard this time. And even though he hesitated for an instant, he returned it. I fumbled to take off his glasses and placed them on the nightstand beside my bed before our arms twisted around each other, the kiss deepening.

I pulled him down onto the pillows with me. There wasn't quite enough room for both of us on my twin bed, so he had to lie partially on top of me. One of his hands was in my hair, and the other rested near my elbow.

He wasn't trying to grab my boob, he hadn't slid his hand up my shirt, and he didn't attempt to unzip my jeans.

Actually, Toby didn't try *anything* risky. I had the feeling I was going to have to make all of the big moves, like loosening the buttons on his shirt, which I did.

For an instant, I wondered if he was hesitating because of me. Because I was the Duff. Because he didn't really find me attractive. Despite all those compliments he paid me, it didn't feel like he wanted me. Not the way Wesley had.

No. I knew that wasn't right. It wasn't that Toby didn't want the big things – he was a teenage boy, after all – but he was a gentleman. A patient, respectful boy who didn't want to cross any lines. And we'd only been dating for a couple of days.

Did that make me a slut? The fact that we'd only been dating for, like, four days and I was already rolling around with him in my teeny-tiny bed? Had my thing with Wesley totally twisted my perception of sex?

Or did every girl do it?

Vikki slept with most of her boyfriends on the first date.

The whole school thought Vikki was a whore, though.

Casey had slept with Zack only a week after they'd started going out.

Casey had been fifteen at the time, and Zack was her first real boyfriend. She was naive and stupid, and she didn't hesitate to admit that it was a major mistake.

But I knew I wouldn't feel that way about Toby. I mean, I was the one pushing this forward. I *wanted* to go farther with him. Because I liked him. Because he was cute and sweet. Because he wasn't ashamed to date me. I couldn't think of one good reason *not* to sleep with him.

God, I just wanted to stop thinking. I kissed him harder, pulled him closer, trying to re-create that mind-numbing feeling I'd had before . . . with Wesley. But it wasn't working. I couldn't stop thinking.

I undid the rest of the buttons on Toby's shirt and helped him throw it onto the floor. He was kind of scrawny with hardly any muscle – Casey would have called him 'skinny chic' or something. Tentatively, his hands began to lift the hem of my T-shirt. He moved slowly in case I wanted to stop him. Just like how he kissed me, always worried he might have crossed the line. I hooked my leg around his waist and ground my body against his. No lines. Maybe there were no lines. Maybe I'd never had any to begin with.

God knows how long we spent making out on my bed, pieces of clothing being removed at a snail's pace. I was already breathless by the time he had the nerve to pull my T-shirt over my head and toss it to the carpet. While part of me appreciated his patience, I couldn't help thinking, *Took you long enough.*

I could feel his right hand inching – like a turtle – toward the clasp of my bra. At this rate, it would have been midnight before he got it off, and for some reason, I felt urgent and anxious. I wanted him to get it off. I wanted to feel attractive and desired. I wanted to *stop thinking*. So I pushed him away and sat up, my legs still wrapped around him. We both breathed heavily, gazing at each other.

'Are you sure about this?' Toby whispered.

'Very.'

I reached around to undo the clasp, but right when my fingers grazed the hook, there was a knock on my bedroom door.

'Bianca?'

Toby and I jumped. Both our necks snapped around just as the door swung open.

Wesley Rush stared back at us, frozen in the doorway.

23

'Oh God,' I muttered as Toby and I made a frantic effort to untangle ourselves. He scrambled off my bed and grabbed his shirt off the floor, his face glowing scarlet. I reached down and picked up my T-shirt. 'Wesley, how did you get in here?' I demanded.

'The door was unlocked,' he said. 'You didn't answer when I knocked . . . Now I can see why.' His dark grey eyes were big with what I could only guess was shock, dissolving quickly into disgust, and they stared directly at Toby.

Why was he shocked?

Because he didn't think anyone else would fool around with the Duff?

'But *what* are you doing here?' I asked, feeling a sudden surge of anger rush through my veins. I yanked my T-shirt over my head and stood up.

'You weren't answering your phone,' Wesley muttered. 'I was worried, but it looks like you're just fine.' He glared at Toby for a moment before looking back at me. 'My mistake.'

Now he was the one who looked angry.

Angry and *hurt*.

I didn't get it.

I looked over at Toby. His shirt was on and buttoned, and he was staring awkwardly at his feet. 'Hey,' I said. He looked up at me. 'I'll be right back, OK?'

He nodded.

I pushed Wesley into the hallway with one hand and shut my bedroom door behind me with the other. 'God, Wesley,' I hissed, irritated as I ushered him down the stairs. 'I always knew you were a perv, but watching me? That's a whole new level of creepy.'

I assumed he'd say something to that. Something arrogant and cocky. Or maybe just tease me, the way he always did. But he just stared at me, a serious expression on his face. Not at all what I'd expected from Wesley.

Silence.

'So,' he said at last. 'You and Tucker are together now?'

'Yes,' I answered uneasily. 'We are.'

'When did that happen?'

278

'Last week . . . not that it's any of your business.' Another jab. Another attempt to make this conversation normal.

But he didn't take the bait. 'Right. Sorry.' He sounded so awkward. So different from the smooth, confident Wesley I was used to.

Another uncomfortable silence.

'Why are you here, Wesley?'

'I told you,' he said. 'I got worried. You've been avoiding me for the past week at school, and when I called you today, you didn't answer. I thought something might have happened with your dad. So I came to make sure you were OK.'

I bit my lower lip, a wave of guilt washing over me. 'That's sweet,' I murmured. 'But I'm fine. Dad apologized for the other night, and he's going to AA meetings now, so . . .'

'So you weren't going to tell me?'

'Why would I?'

'Because I care!' Wesley yelled. His words crashed into me, stunning me for a second. 'I've been worried about you since you left my house a week ago! You didn't even say why you left, Bianca. What was I supposed to do? Just assume you would be all right?'

'God,' I whispered. 'I'm sorry. I didn't—'

279

'I'm worrying about you, and you're fucking that pretentious little—!'

'Hey!' I shouted. 'Don't bring Toby into this.'

'Why have you been avoiding me?' he asked.

'I haven't been avoiding you.'

'Don't lie,' Wesley said. 'You've been doing everything you can to stay away from me. You won't even look at me in class, and you practically sprint down the hallway if you see me coming. Even when you hated me, you didn't act like that. You might threaten to stab me, but you *never*—'

'I still hate you,' I snarled up at him. 'You're infuriating! You act like I owe you something. I'm sorry I made you worry, Wesley, but I just can't be around you anymore. You helped me escape from my problems for a while, and I appreciate that, but I have to face reality. I can't keep running away.'

'But that is exactly what you're doing right now,' Wesley hissed. 'You're running away.'

'Excuse me?'

'Don't pretend, Bianca,' he said. 'You're smarter than that, and so am I. I finally figured out what you meant when you left. You said you were like Hester. I get it now. The first time you came to my house, when we wrote that paper, you said Hester was trying to escape.

280

But everything caught up with Hester in the end, didn't it? Well, something finally caught up with you, but you're just running away again. Only, he' – Wesley pointed to my bedroom door – 'is your escape this time.' He took a step toward me, forcing me to crane my neck even more to see his face. 'Admit it, Duffy.'

'Admit what?'

'That you're running away from *me*,' he said. 'You realized you're in love with me and you bailed because it scared the shit out of you.'

I scoffed as if it were ridiculous – *wishing* it were ridiculous – and rolled my eyes, stepping back to show he couldn't intimidate me, that he wasn't right. 'Oh my God. Get over yourself. You're so fucking dramatic, Wesley. This isn't a damn soap opera.'

'You know it's true.'

'Even if it is,' I cried, 'what does it matter? You could sleep with anybody, Wesley. So what if I walk away? So what if I have feelings for you? I was just a screw to you! You would never actually commit to me. You could never commit to *anyone*, but especially not to Duffy. You don't even find me attractive.'

'Bullshit,' he growled, his eyes on my face as he moved closer to me again.

He was so close. My back was pressed to the wall, and

Wesley stood only inches away. It had only been a week, but it felt like ages since we'd been in this kind of proximity. A shiver ran up my spine as I remembered the way his hands felt on me. The way he'd always made me feel wanted, even if he had called me the Duff. Did he? Did he find me attractive despite the nickname? How? Why?

'Then why would you call me that?' I whispered. 'Do you know how much it hurts? Every time you call me Duffy, do you know how shitty it makes me feel?'

Wesley looked surprised. 'What?'

'Every time you call me that,' I said, 'you're telling me how little you think of me. How ugly I am. God, how can you possibly find me attractive when you put me down *all the time*.' I hissed the last words through gritted teeth.

'I didn't—' His eyes fell, staring at his shoes for a moment. I could tell he felt guilty. 'Bianca, I'm sorry.' He looked into my eyes again. 'I didn't mean—' His hand reached out to touch me.

'Don't,' I snapped, shrugging away from him. I slid to the side and stepped away from the wall. I wasn't going to be cornered. I wasn't going to let him have the power here. 'Just stop, Wesley.'

It didn't matter if some part of him found me attractive.

That didn't change things. I was just another girl he'd slept with. One among many.

'I didn't mean anything to you,' I told him.

'Then why am I here?' he demanded, turning to face me again. 'Why the hell am I here, Bianca?'

I glared up at his hardened face. 'I'll tell you why. Your parents leave you by yourself, so you fill your life with meaningless flings. With girls you'll never have anything serious with – girls who practically worship you – so that they don't abandon you. The only reason you're here is because you can't take the thought that someone else walked away from you. Your sensitive ego can't handle that, and it's easier to make me miss you than to make your parents come home.'

He was speechless, just staring at me with his jaw visibly clenching for a few seconds.

'Did I hit the mark, Wesley?' I spat. 'Do I get you as well as you think you get me?'

He glared at me for a few minutes – *long* minutes – before stepping back. 'Fine,' he muttered. 'If that's how you want it, I'll go.'

'Yeah,' I said. 'You should.'

He turned and stormed out of the house. I heard the front door slam, and I knew he was gone. For good. I took a few deep, slow breaths to clear my head and walked back up to my bedroom, where Toby waited for me.

'Hey,' I sighed, sitting down on the bed beside him. 'I'm so sorry about that.'

'What happened?' he asked. 'I wasn't eavesdropping, but there was a lot of yelling. Are you OK?'

'I'm fine,' I said. 'It's a long, complicated story.'

'Well, if you ever want to talk about it' – Toby adjusted his glasses and gave me a nervous smile – 'I've got the time to listen.'

'Thanks,' I said. 'But I'm OK. Everyone has dirty laundry, right?' *Well, everyone except you, Toby.*

'Right,' he agreed. He leaned over and kissed me gently. 'Sorry we were interrupted earlier.'

'Me, too.'

He pressed his lips to mine again, but I couldn't enjoy it. I just kept thinking of Wesley. He had looked so hurt. But that's what I had wanted when I left him, just a little, wasn't it? For him to miss me? I tried to push it down, wanting so badly to lose myself in Toby's arms. But I couldn't.

Not the way I'd been able to lose myself with Wesley.

I pulled away, disgusted with myself. How could I think of Wesley when I was kissing a guy like Toby Tucker? What was the matter with me?

'Is something wrong?' Toby asked.

'It's nothing,' I lied. 'Just . . . we should probably start doing research for our editorials.'

'You're right.' He didn't seem irritated or offended or dejected at all. Perfect manners. A perfect smile. The perfect boy.

So why wasn't I *perfectly* happy?

24

Wesley stayed on my mind for the next couple of days, which put me in a really pissy mood – pissier than usual, that is.

I didn't want to think about him. I wanted to think about Toby, who was obviously way too good for me. He could tell I was grumpy, but instead of harassing me about the cause, he just squeezed my hand, kissed me on the cheek, and bought me candy in hopes of making me smile again. How could I be thinking of another guy – an annoying, egotistical, womanizing guy – when such a wonderful one stood right in front of me? Maybe someone needed to slap me or put me through shock treatments like they give crazy people in the movies. That might have brought me to my senses.

But Wesley seemed to be everywhere. He was always climbing into his car just as I walked out to the student parking lot or standing two feet ahead of me in the lunch line. Do you know how hard it is to forget someone exists when they're constantly in your sight? Pretty damn hard. For a second, I actually wondered if he might be doing this on purpose, like stalking me or something, but I ditched that idea when I noticed that he didn't even look at me anymore. Like he was too mad about the things I'd said to acknowledge me.

It should have been a relief not to have his creepy eyes crawling all over me, but it wasn't at all. It hurt.

Every time I saw Wesley, I was overcome with a flood of emotions. Anger, sadness, pain, irritation, regret, lust, and, worst of all, guilt. I knew I shouldn't have said those things about his attachment issues – even if they were totally true. And despite my urge to apologize, I kept my mouth shut tight. Honestly, I would rather have dealt with the knowledge that I was a terrible person than suffer through another uncomfortable conversation with him.

Though I couldn't avoid the conversation with his sister.

I was in the library one morning, trying to find a book that didn't contain romantic vampires or kids flying on dragons, when Amy walked up to me. I swear, she was so freaking quiet that I didn't have a chance to run. One minute I was alone, the next she was right beside me. I was ambushed.

'B-Bianca,' she stammered. She was wringing her hands and staring at the ground, as if talking to me was actually going to kill her.

'Oh. Um, hey, Amy.' I shoved the book I was examining back onto the shelf. 'What's going on?' I kept my face pointed away from her, pretending I was still scanning the titles in front of me.

I didn't want to look at her. For one, she looked too much like her brother, and I was trying – and failing miserably – to forget about him. For another, I couldn't stand to meet her eyes when she tore into me, which I just knew she was about to do. Not that I could blame her.

Well, OK, so I couldn't really imagine timid little Amy *tearing into* anything, but still.

'I, um . . . I have something to say to you,' she said, trying to sound determined.

Or maybe Amy was upset at me for facilitating Wesley's 'lifestyle'. Maybe she wanted to blame me for the distance between them.

If that was the case, I wanted to defend him. To tell her that her grandmother was misrepresenting Wesley. That he wasn't a bad guy – and definitely not a bad brother. But I knew not to get involved. It wasn't my place to fix his family issues. He wasn't even part of my life anymore.

'OK. Go ahead.'

Here it comes, I thought. *Whatever she says, don't cry.*

'I . . . I want to . . .' She took a deep breath. 'Thank you.'

'Huh?' I turned around to face her. Surely I hadn't heard her right. There was just no way.

'Thank you,' she repeated. 'For Wesley. He . . . he's a lot different, and I know it has to be because of you. I . . . I appreciate it, so thank you.'

Before I could ask for a detailed explanation – spoken slowly so that I could follow – Amy turned around and hurried away, her brown curls bouncing behind her.

I was left standing in the middle of the library, totally confused.

And it got worse later that day.

When Wesley rounded the corner after lunch while I was pulling notebooks out of my locker, I wasn't really surprised. Like I said, he was *everywhere*. Vikki was with him, clinging to his arm and flipping her hair like the girl in a shampoo commercial. She was laughing, but I could have bet money that whatever Wesley had said wasn't all that funny. She just wanted to inflate his ego . . . as if it needed to get any bigger.

'Over here,' she giggled, pulling him into the alcove ten feet away from me. 'I wanna talk to you.'

Talk? I thought. *Yeah, not likely.*

I swear, I tried not to listen. I knew hearing them flirt would only get me worked up, but Vikki's squeaky voice carries, and they were standing really close to me, and yeah, a masochistic little part of me couldn't stop myself. I started arranging the textbooks in the bottom of my locker, trying to make enough noise that I wouldn't be able to hear their conversation.

'What are you doing for prom?' Vikki asked.

'I don't have any plans,' Wesley answered.

I shuffled my papers loudly, hoping that, even if I couldn't drown out their words, they would notice me and take the make-out session elsewhere. I mean, they weren't groping each other yet, but I knew both of them well enough to be sure it wouldn't take long.

'Well,' Vikki said, either not hearing me or just not caring. 'I thought maybe we could go together.' I didn't have to look to know she was scraping her long, polished fingernails lightly down Wesley's arm. Vikki used the same moves on every guy. 'I thought maybe after the dance we could have a little time alone . . . at your place, maybe?'

290

I had the serious desire to puke. I grabbed my books, slammed my locker shut, and prepared to bolt toward my next class before I had to hear Wesley say yes. *Let them have each other!* I thought bitterly. *STDs all around! To hell with it.* But he answered before I could even take a step.

'I don't think so, Vikki.'

I froze.

What? *What?* Rewind for a second, please. Did Wesley really turn down a girl? A girl who was perfectly willing to fuck his brains out? I had to be dreaming.

Vikki seemed to be experiencing a similar reaction. 'What? What do you mean?'

'I'm just not interested,' Wesley said. 'But I'm sure you have plenty of other boys who would love to join you. Sorry.'

'Oh.' Vikki stumbled out of the alcove with a look of hurt surprise. 'It's, um, OK. Not a problem. Just thought I'd offer.' She hesitated for a second. 'I guess I'll see you later? Gotta go to class. Bye.' And she took off down the hall, obviously confused.

She wasn't the only one.

Was this the difference Amy had been talking about? Was Wesley suddenly inclined to be less man-whorish? If so, how was that because of me?

I stared as Wesley walked out of the alcove. Then, for the first time in days, he looked at me. His eyes locked with mine. A weak smile tugged at the corners of his mouth, but the expression in his eyes was unreadable. I could tell he wasn't angry, though. That fact sent instant relief through my tense muscles.

Knowing he wasn't pissed at me made the guilt ebb a little . . . but not entirely. I'd still said some cold things to him, and in that second, as I held his gaze, I thought of speaking, of apologizing. I thought about it, but I didn't say a word.

Wesley took a step toward me, and I suddenly remembered who I was – who *he* was. While Wesley's rejecting Vikki was undeniably surprising, it didn't change the fact that I didn't have a chance with him; he would never want a real relationship . . . especially not with me. And then there was the fact that I was dating Toby. Plus, I knew that communicating with Wesley would just make my steadily improving life complicated again. I wouldn't punish myself that way.

I spun around and started running down the hallway, pretending I didn't hear him call after me.

I slowed when I turned down another hallway and saw Toby (my boyfriend? I wasn't sure how this worked) waiting for me by the old, out-of-order snack machines.

He smiled and adjusted his glasses, and I could tell he was genuinely pleased to see me. Was I equally happy to see him? I was. Of course I was, but the smile on my face felt artificial.

Toby's arm wrapped around my shoulders when I got close enough. 'Hey.'

'Hi,' I sighed.

He leaned down and kissed me on the lips before asking, 'Is it OK if I walk you to class?'

I glanced over my shoulder at the emptying hallway. 'Sure,' I murmured, facing forward again. I leaned my head on his shoulder. 'That sounds . . . perfect.'

A few days later, I found Jessica waiting for me outside my third-block calculus class. 'Can we talk on the way to English?' she asked without the usual bob in her step or swing to her hair. I could tell something was up by the way she bit her lower lip.

'Um, sure,' I said, shifting my books under my right arm. Seeing my perpetually perky friend looking so solemn made me uneasy. 'Is something wrong?'

'Kinda . . . not really.'

We shoved our way through the packed halls together, trying not to step on too many people's toes. I waited for Jessica to speak, my curiosity and anxiety rising. I really wanted to say, 'Hurry up! Out with it!' Luckily, though, she started talking before my legendary low patience ran out.

'It's about you and Toby. I just don't think you're right together.' She said it so fast that I wasn't sure if I'd heard her at first. 'I'm sorry, Bianca,' she moaned. 'It's not any of my business, but I don't see a spark there, you know? And Casey totally disagrees with me. She says you're better with Toby, and she might be right, but . . . I don't know. You don't seem like yourself when you're with him. Please don't be mad.'

I shook my head, trying to fight my sudden urge to laugh. That was it? That was what she was worried about? I'd seriously thought someone was dying or, at the least, her mom had forbidden her going to prom. Instead, it turned out that she was worried about *me*. 'Jessica, I'm not mad at you at all.'

'Oh, good,' she breathed. 'I was really scared you would get p.o.'ed at me.'

Ouch. Was I *that* bitchy? So horrible that one of my best friends was afraid to tell me her opinion because I might go into a rage or something? God, that made me feel like shit.

'It's not that I don't like Toby,' Jessica continued. 'I do. He's sweet, and he's nice to you, and I know you need that after . . . after my brother.'

My heart may have actually stopped beating for a second there. I stopped right where I was and, after a stunned pause, whirled around to stare at Jessica. 'How do you . . . ?' I managed to whisper.

'Jake told me,' she said. 'I was telling him about my friends when your name came up, and he told me about your thing a few years ago. He feels horrible about it now, and he wanted me to apologize for him, but I didn't want to bring it up. I'm sorry, Bianca. It must be really hard for you to be my friend after what Jake did.'

'That's not your fault.'

'I just can't believe you didn't say anything. It must have been on your mind when Jake came to visit. Why didn't you tell me?'

'I didn't want you to think less of your brother,' I said. 'I know you think a lot of him, and I didn't want to ruin that.'

Jessica didn't say anything. She stepped forward and wrapped her arms around me, hugging me as close to her as humanly possible. It was a little awkward at first, especially considering the fact that Jessica's giant boobs were practically smothering me, but I gradually fell into her embrace. My arms slid around her waist, returning the hug. Knowing I had someone who would hold me like this, with nothing to gain, made me feel like one of the luckiest people in the world.

'I love you, Bianca.'

'Um, what was that?'

Jessica released me and took a step back. 'I love you,' she said. 'You and Casey both. You're the best friends I've ever had, and I don't know where I'd be if you two hadn't come along my sophomore year. I'd probably still be letting those preppy girls walk all over me.' She looked down at her feet. 'You two always try to protect me, like not telling me about what an a-hole my brother was. And I want to do the same thing for you.'

'Jessica, that's sweet.'

'That's why I'm telling you this,' she went on. 'I know Toby is nice and he likes you, but I don't see a connection. I mean, I'm glad you're spending time with me and Casey again, and I think it's cool that he hangs out with us sometimes, but what I care about is that you're happy. You might look happy, but I don't think you are.' She took a deep breath and tugged at the hem of her floral-print skirt. 'I don't want to bring this up, but . . . I've heard some rumours about Wesley lately.'

I bit my lip. 'Oh.'

'He hasn't been as flirty lately,' she said. 'I haven't seen him with any girls, and I thought' – she looked at me with wide chocolate eyes – 'I thought maybe you'd want to know. I mean, I know you have feelings for him, and—'

I shook my head. 'No,' I said, 'it's not that simple.'

She nodded. 'OK,' she said. 'I just thought I'd throw it out there. Sorry.'

I sighed and smiled, reaching out to take her hand and pulling her towards the English classroom. 'It's OK. I appreciate you being concerned – I really, really do. And you might be right . . . about me and Toby, I mean. But this is just high school. We're only dating. It's not like I'm looking for a husband or whatever. I don't think you need to worry about me yet. I'm fine.'

'Casey says you're usually lying when you say that,' Jessica informed me.

'She does, huh?'

I released Jessica's hand as we walked into English class, determined to avoid answering her accusation. That proved to be pretty easy, really. I was able to feign distraction – well, it wasn't entirely fake – when I noticed the folded piece of paper lying on my desk. I sat down and picked it up, assuming it was from Casey. Who else would be writing me a note?

But Casey always drew a smiley face over the *i* in my name, and the handwriting on the outside of this paper was small, cursive, and faceless.

Confused, I unfolded the paper and read the single sentence that was scrawled across the top.

Wesley Rush doesn't chase girls, but I'm chasing you.

25

At one time, I thought being the Duff meant no boy drama. Clearly, I was wrong. How did this happen? How did I, the ugly girl, end up in the middle of a love triangle? I wasn't a romantic. I didn't really even *want* to date. But there I was, torn between two attractive guys that, by all means, I shouldn't have had a shot with. (Trust me, not as glamorous as it sounds.)

On one side, I had Toby. Smart, cute, funny, polite, sensitive, and practical. Toby was perfect in every conceivable way. I mean, he was a little dorky, but that was what made him so adorable. I liked being with him, and he always put me first. He respected me and never seemed to lose his patience. There was absolutely nothing to complain about with Toby Tucker.

On the other side, there was Wesley. A jerk. An asshole. An arrogant, womanizing rich boy who put sex before everything else. Sure, he was incredibly hot, but he could annoy the hell out of me. He was irritatingly charming, and his cute little grin could really get under my skin. But he had a way of making my heart race and my head spin. I wasn't afraid to be a bitch around him. I hated to admit it, but Wesley understood me. I felt like myself when I was with him, whereas I was always trying to hide my neuroses around Toby.

God, life had been so much easier when no one noticed me.

The note from Wesley weighed half a tonne in my back pocket as I headed out to the student parking lot that afternoon. To say I was confused would have been a massive understatement. I mean, that single sentence left me with a million different questions, but there was one in particular:

Why the hell does Wesley want me?

Seriously. The guy had dozens of girls who would kill to be with him. Why me? Wasn't he the one who had called me the Duff in the first place? What the fuck?

But when I got home, it just got worse.

On Toby's suggestion, I'd started reading *Wuthering Heights* in my spare time. Honestly, the main characters pissed me off so much that it was hard to push through the book. I was considering putting it down for good that day, but a line of dialogue caught my attention.

'My love for Linton is like the foliage in the woods.
Time will change it, I'm well aware, as winter changes
the trees – my love for Heathcliff resembles the eternal
rocks beneath – a source of little visible delight, but
necessary.'

As stupid as it sounds, that little excerpt really got in my head, like a song you hate but can't stop singing. I tried to read on, but the words kept bouncing around in my brain. I turned back the page and read the lines again and again. I was trying to figure out why they bugged me so much when I was interrupted by the sound of the doorbell.

'Thank God,' I muttered, relieved to have a reason to slam the book shut. I jumped off my bed and ran downstairs. 'Coming!' I yelled. 'Just a second!'

I pulled open the front door, expecting to find Toby, who'd said he might drop by later. But the man on my front porch was a chubby redhead in his fifties. Definitely not my boyfriend. He wore a shabby green uniform and a hat that didn't quite fit. The name tag on his jacket read *JIMMY*. He was holding a bouquet of flowers in his right hand, and a clipboard was wedged under his arm.

'Are you Miss Bianca Piper?' he asked.

'Um . . . yeah.'

His squinty eyes lighted with a smile. 'Sign this, please,' he said, giving me the clipboard and a pen. 'Congratulations.'

'Er, thanks,' I said, handing the clipboard back to him.

He passed me the bouquet, which I now saw was full of *real* red roses, and produced a white envelope from his back pocket. 'This is for you, too,' he said. 'You're a lucky girl. It's not often I get to make a delivery like this to someone your age.' He smiled. 'Young love.'

Young love? God, I had to fight the urge to correct him. To give him my long speech about how teenagers don't fall in love. But he was still talking.

'Your boyfriend must really be a keeper. Not many boys are so thoughtful at that age.'

I stared down at the roses and said, 'You're probably right.' Was Toby still trying to cheer me up? God, he was so nice. Too bad I didn't deserve all of the kindness.

After thanking the delivery guy, I closed the door. I felt guilty for considering my situation a love triangle. It was just me and Toby, and Wesley danced along the outskirts, far away from us . . . or that's how it should have been. That's how Toby deserved for it to be.

I put the bouquet on the kitchen table and opened the envelope, expecting to find a sappy but perfectly worded letter from my flawless boyfriend. It was the kind of thing I'd normally scoff at, but I'd let Toby get away with it. He really did have a way with words sometimes. That would help when he became a famous politician.

But the handwriting on the letter was the same as in the note in my back pocket. This time, however, there was much more to absorb.

Bianca,

Since you keep running away from me at school, and, if I remember correctly, the sound of my voice causes you to have suicidal thoughts, I decided a letter might be the best way to tell you how I feel. Just hear me out.

I'm not going to deny that you were right. Everything you said the other day was true. But my fear of being alone is *not* the reason I'm pursuing you. I know how cynical you are, and you're probably going to come up with some snarky reply when you read this, but the truth is, I'm chasing you because I really think I am falling in love with you.

You are the first girl who has ever seen right through me. You're the only girl who has ever called me on my bullshit. You put me in my place, but, at the same time, you understand me better than anyone ever has. You are the only person brave enough to criticize me. Maybe the only person who looks close enough to find my faults – and, clearly, you've found many.

I called my parents. They're coming home this weekend to talk to Amy and me. I was afraid to do this at first, but you inspired me. Without you, I never could have done that.

I think about you much more than any self-respecting man would like to admit, and I'm insanely jealous of Tucker – something I never thought I'd say. Moving on after you is impossible. No other girl can keep me on my toes the way you can. No one else makes me WANT to embarrass myself by writing sappy letters like this one.

Only you.

But I know that I'm right, too. I know you're in love with me, even if you are dating Tucker. You can lie to yourself if you want, but reality is going to catch up with you. I'll be waiting when it does . . . whether you like it or not.

Love,

Wesley

P.S.: I know you're rolling your eyes right now, but I don't care. Honestly, it's always been kind of a turn-on.

I stared down at the letter for a long moment, finally understanding what Amy had been thanking me for. Wesley was trying to fix things . . . because of me. Because of what I'd said. I'd actually managed to get through that thick skull of his. That was absolutely shocking to me.

It took a second for the other surprises to sink in. Words like *love* and *only* leapt off the page at me. It was my first love letter – not that I'd ever wanted one, but still – and it wasn't even from my boyfriend. The wrong guy had given it to me. The wrong guy wanted me. Wesley was the wrong guy.

Or was he exactly the right guy?

I was so consumed with my thoughts that I jumped when the phone rang, and I scurried across the linoleum in an effort to answer it. 'Hello?'

'Hi, Bianca,' Toby said.

My heart sped up and pumped shame through my veins. Wesley's letter, which I still held, burned the fingers of my right hand, but I managed to sound normal when I said, 'Hey, Toby. Are you on your way over?'

'No,' he sighed. 'Dad has errands for me to run, so I can't come by this afternoon. I'm really sorry.'

'That's OK.' I shouldn't have felt relieved, but I was. Seeing Toby would have meant hiding the flowers and entering a potential web of lies, and we all know what a shitty liar I am. 'Don't worry about it.'

'Thanks for being so understanding. But I was really looking forward to spending a little time with you. We just don't get much time together at school.' He paused. 'Do you have plans tomorrow night?'

'Nope.'

'Then do you want to go on a date? A band is playing at the Nest, and I thought we could go. Of course your friends can come, too. Would you like that?'

'Sounds great.' See, little lies like that I could pull off. I hated live music, and I despised the Nest, but pretending the opposite would make Toby happy, and Casey would be thrilled to be invited along. So why not? White lies were easy enough, but anything bigger and I was screwed.

'Cool,' Toby said. 'I'll pick you up at eight.'

'OK. Bye, Toby.'

'I'll see you tomorrow, Bianca.'

I hung up the phone, but my feet refused to move. The letter still blazed against my skin, and I found myself staring down at the tempting words. Why wasn't this easier? Why did Wesley have to come along and make me question everything? I felt like I was betraying Toby with every sentence I read. Like I was cheating on him.

But now I knew that every time I kissed Toby, I was hurting Wesley.

'Arrrrrgh!' With a scream that exploded in my chest and clawed its way through my lungs, I wadded the letter into a tight ball and hurled it across the room as hard as I could. It moved through the air slowly before bouncing delicately off the floral wallpaper and landing on the floor.

Finally, with my throat aching, I sank to the floor, buried my face in my hands, and – I admit it – cried. I cried out of frustration and confusion, but mostly for myself, for being caught in such a position, like the selfish little girl I was.

I thought of Cathy Earnshaw, the spoiled, selfish heroine in *Wuthering Heights*, and I remembered the passage I'd been reading before the doorbell rang. But when the words drifted through my brain, they were slightly different.

'My love for Toby is like the foliage in the woods. Time will change it, I'm well aware, as winter changes the trees – my love for Wesley resembles the eternal rocks beneath – a source of little visible delight, but necessary.'

My head shook back and forth feverishly. *Like*, I corrected myself. *My like for Wesley is blah, blah, blah*. I wiped my eyes and got to my feet, trying to calm my ragged breathing. Then I turned and walked back upstairs.

All of a sudden I wanted to know how the book ended.

26

After staying up all night to read – and folding my clothes at least ten times – I discovered that *Wuthering Heights* doesn't have a happy ending. Because of stupid, spoiled, selfish Cathy (yeah, I have no room to talk, but still), everyone winds up miserable. Her choice ruins the lives of the people she cares most about. Because she picked propriety over passion. Head over heart. Linton over Heathcliff.

Toby over Wesley.

This, I decided as I dragged my tired ass to school the next morning, was *not* a good omen. Normally, I don't believe in omens or signs or any of that destiny crap, but the similarities between my and Cathy Earnshaw's situations were too eerie to ignore. I couldn't help but wonder if the book was trying to tell me something.

I was dully aware that I was reading way too much

into it, but my lack of sleep coupled with the stress of everything else made my mind go to some interesting places. Interesting, but not productive.

I was pretty much a zombie all day, but during the middle of calculus, something finally woke me up.

'Did you hear about Vikki McPhee?'

'About how she's totally knocked up? Yep. Heard this morning.'

My head snapped up from the problem I was half-heartedly attempting to solve. Two girls sat side by side in the row ahead of me. I recognized one of them as a junior cheerleader.

'God, what a slut,' the cheerleader said. 'No telling who the father is. She sleeps with everyone.'

I hate to admit it, but my first reaction to this was pure selfish fear. I thought of Wesley. Sure, he'd rejected Vikki in the hallway a few days ago, but what if something had changed? What if that letter had been a joke? A game to mess with my head? What if he and Vikki had . . .

I forced the thought away. Wesley was careful. He always used a condom. Besides, it was like that girl had said – Vikki slept with everyone. The chances of Wesley being the father were slim. And I didn't have a right to worry about that, anyway. He wasn't my boyfriend. Even if he had pretty much professed his love for me in a letter.

I was with Toby, and whatever Wesley decided to do wasn't any of my business.

My second thought was of Vikki. Seventeen, on the verge of graduation, and, if the rumours were true, pregnant. What a nightmare. And everyone knew. I could hear people buzzing about it in the hallway when I left calculus. In a school the size of Hamilton, it didn't take long for gossip to spread. Vikki McPhee was the girl on everyone's mind.

Including mine.

So when I walked out of a bathroom stall a few minutes before English and found Vikki standing at the sink, reapplying her dark pink lipstick, I had to make an effort to avert my eyes.

But I had to say *something*. I mean, we weren't close or anything, but we did eat lunch together every day. 'Hey,' I mumbled.

'Hey,' she replied, still tracing the lipstick across her lower lip.

I turned on the faucet and stared at my reflection in the mirror, trying hard not to sneak a peek at her. How far along was she? Had her parents found out yet?

'It's not true, you know.'

'What?'

Vikki capped her lipstick and dropped it into her

purse. She was watching me in the mirror, and I could see now that her eyes were a little red.

'I'm not pregnant,' she said. 'I mean, I thought I was, but the test was negative. I took it two days ago. But I guess someone overheard me telling Jeanine and Angela and . . . whatever. But I'm not pregnant.'

'Oh. Well, that's good.' Yeah, probably not exactly the right thing to say, but I was kind of caught off guard.

Vikki nodded and tugged at one of her strawberry-blond curls a little. 'I was relieved. I don't know how I would have told my parents. And the guy never would have made a good father.'

'Who?'

That was such a selfish question.

'Just this guy . . . Eric.'

Thank God, I thought. Then, of course, I felt incredibly guilty. This wasn't the time to be thinking about myself.

'He's just this stupid frat boy who gets a kick out of fucking high school girls.' She looked down, so I couldn't see her eyes in the mirror anymore. 'And I didn't even give a shit. I just let him use me, and I never thought . . . even when the condom broke . . .' She trailed off, shaking her head. 'Anyway, I'm glad it was negative.'

'Right.'

'It is scary, though,' she said. 'I freaked out when I was

waiting for the test. I just couldn't believe I was in that situation, you know?'

'I'm sure,' I said, but I didn't find it all that surprising. It was Vikki, after all. Hadn't she been setting herself up for that kind of thing for a while? Sleeping with people she didn't care about. Forgetting about the consequences.

Just like I did . . .

OK, so it hadn't been *people*. Wesley was the only guy. And I did care about him . . . now, after I'd stopped sleeping with him. But that was just . . . well, I didn't know what you'd call it. Not quite luck. Maybe coincidence? Either way, I was smart enough to know that it didn't happen often.

But I *had* forgotten about the consequences. And it suddenly hit me how easily Vikki and I could trade places. I could have been the girl everyone was talking about. I could have had a pregnancy scare. Or worse. I mean, I was on birth control, and Wesley and I were always safe, but these things fail sometimes. It could easily have failed for us. And yet there I was, judging Vikki for pretty much the same thing. I was a hell of a hypocrite.

'*You are not a whore.*' I had a sudden flash of Wesley that last night in his bedroom, telling me exactly who I was. Telling me that the rest of the world was just as confused as me. That I wasn't a whore, and I wasn't alone.

I didn't know Vikki that well. I didn't know what her home life was like or anything that personal aside from her boy issues. And standing there in the bathroom, listening as she told me her story, I couldn't help but wonder if she'd been running away from something, too. If I'd been judging her, thinking of her as a slut all this time when, in reality, we were living scarily similar lives.

Calling Vikki a slut or a whore was just like calling someone the Duff. It was insulting and hurtful, and it was one of those titles that just fed off of an inner fear every girl must have from time to time. Slut, bitch, prude, tease, ditz. They were all the same. Every girl felt like one of these sexist labels described her at some point.

So, maybe, every girl felt like the Duff, too?

'God, I'm late,' Vikki said as the tardy bell rang. 'I should go.'

I watched as she gathered her purse and textbooks off the counter, wondering what was going through her head. Had all of this made her realize the consequences of her choices?

Our choices.

'See you around, Bianca,' she said, moving toward the door.

'Bye,' I said. Then, without meaning to, I added, 'And, Vikki . . . I'm sorry. It's really messed up the way people are talking about you. Just remember that what they say doesn't matter.' Again, I thought of Wesley and what he'd said to me in his bedroom. 'The people who call you names are just trying to make themselves feel better. They've fucked up before, too. You're not the only one.'

Vikki looked surprised. 'Thanks,' she said. She opened her mouth like she might say something else, but then closed it again. Without another word, she left the bathroom.

For all I knew, Vikki might go out and hook up with another guy that same night. She might not have learned anything from this experience. Or maybe she'd change her behaviour altogether – at the very least, she might be more careful. I might never know. That was her choice. Her life. And it wasn't my place to judge.

It was never my place to judge.

And as I walked down the hall, five minutes late for English, I decided that I'd think twice before calling Vikki – or anyone else for that matter – a whore again.

Because she was just like me.

Just like everyone else.

That was something we all had in common. We were all sluts or bitches or prudes or Duffs.

I was the Duff. And that was a good thing. Because anyone who didn't feel like the Duff must not have friends. Every girl feels unattractive sometimes. Why had it taken me so long to figure that out? Why had I been stressing over that dumb word for so long when it was so simple? I should be proud to be the Duff. Proud to have great friends who, in their minds, were *my* Duffs.

'Bianca,' Mrs Perkins greeted me as I walked into the classroom and took my seat. 'Well, better late than never, I suppose.'

'Yeah,' I said. 'Sorry it took me so long.'

When I got home that afternoon, I was too exhausted to climb the stairs, so I collapsed on the couch and fell into a nice doze. I'd forgotten how good it felt to take a nap in the middle of the day. I mean, Europeans have the right idea with their siestas. Americans should consider adding them to their daily schedule because they're incredibly refreshing, especially after a dramatic day like I'd had.

It was almost seven when I woke up, which didn't give me much time to get ready for my date. My hair, which looked like a haystack after snoozing on the couch, would take almost the entire hour to repair. Just great.

Since I'd started dating Toby, I'd been paying more attention to how I looked. Not that he cared about that kind of thing. The guy probably would have said I was pretty in a clown suit – rainbow wig and all. But I felt this constant need to impress him. So I straightened my hair and pulled it into a high ponytail, put on a pair of silver clip-on earrings (I'm too chicken to get any piercings), and found the shirt Casey had given me for my seventeenth birthday. The silky material was white patterned with intricate silver designs, and it fit me tight in the chest, which made my ittybitty boobies appear somewhat bigger.

It was almost eight o'clock by the time I struggled down the stairs in my platform wedge sandals, risking my safety for the sake of looking taller. I was careful to avert my eyes when I walked past the kitchen because Dad, obviously thinking the roses were from Toby, had put the bouquet in an antique vase on the dining table last night. It was a sweet gesture, but seeing the bright red flowers only brought back the annoying questions. So I stumbled into the living room and plopped down on the couch to wait for my date, promising myself that I'd figure out my romantic mess sometime over the weekend.

For lack of anything better to do, I picked up the copy

of *TV Guide* that was lying on the coffee table and began scanning the TV schedule. A yellow Post-it note wedged between the pages caught my attention, and I flipped to the section it was marking. Dad had highlighted a *Family Ties* marathon for the following Sunday night, using the little slip of paper as a bookmark. I smiled and pulled a pen out of my purse, scribbling, '*I'll make popcorn*,' on the Post-it. Dad would see it when he got home from his meeting.

Just when I put the magazine back on the table, the doorbell rang. I stood up as quickly as I could without falling and walked over to the door, expecting to be greeted by a big undeserved Toby smile. But the smile that flashed in front of me, while sparkly and white, belonged to someone quite different.

'Mom?' I practically gasped the word, sounding like some chick in a soap opera who's just learned her evil twin is still alive or something. Embarrassed, I cleared my throat and said, 'What are you doing here? I thought you were in Tennessee.'

'I was, but I came to visit you, of course,' my mother replied, cocking her head to the side in her movie-star fashion. Her platinum blond hair was pulled into a neat clip at the back of her head, and she was wearing a red-and-black knee-length dress. Typical Mom.

'But it's, like, a seven-hour drive,' I said.

'Oh, believe me, I know.' She sighed dramatically. 'Seven and a half in bad traffic. So . . . are you going to invite me in or not?' I could tell by the way her hands twisted around the strap of her handbag that she was nervous to be back in this house.

'Um, yeah,' I said, stepping aside. 'Come in. Sorry. But, uh, Dad's not here.'

'I know.' She was looking around the living room in a way that made me feel anxious for her. She eyed the armchair and couch that had once belonged to her as if debating whether she was allowed to sit there now. 'He has his AA meetings on Fridays. He told me.'

'You talked to him?' This was news to me. As far as I'd known, my parents had been avoiding contact since Mom's reappearance last month.

'We've spoken on the phone twice.' She pulled her eyes away from the furniture and focused them on me. They felt like heavy weights on my shoulders. 'Bianca, sweetie . . .' Her voice was soft and sad. Painful to hear. 'Why didn't you tell me he was drinking again?'

I shifted, trying to slide out from under her gaze. 'I don't know,' I mumbled. 'I guess I just hoped it would pass. I didn't want to worry you over nothing.'

'I understand, but, Bianca, this is a serious issue,' she

said. 'You know that now, I hope. If it ever happens again, you don't get to keep it to yourself. You have to tell me. Do you understand?'

I nodded.

'Good.' She sighed, looking immensely relieved. 'Anyway, that's not why I'm here.'

'Why *are* you here?'

'Because your dad also told me something else,' she teased. 'Something about a boy named Toby Tucker.'

'You drove seven and a half hours because I have a date?'

'I have other reasons to be in Hamilton,' she said. 'But this is the most important. So, is it true my baby has a boyfriend?'

'Um, yeah,' I said, shrugging. 'I guess.'

'Well, tell me about him,' Mom urged, finally deciding to sit down on the sofa. 'What's he like?'

'He's nice,' I said. 'How's Grandpa?'

Her eyes narrowed suspiciously. 'He's fine. What's wrong? You're taking your birth control, aren't you?'

'God, Mother, yes,' I groaned. 'That's not the issue.'

'Thank the Lord. I'm too young and hot to be a nana.'

No kidding, I thought, remembering Vikki.

'Then, what's the problem?' she pressed. 'I came because I heard you had a hot date tonight, and I wanted

320

to have that special Mommy moment. But if you're having problems, I get to spill out some Mommy advice, too. It's like a two-for-one visit, isn't it? Makes the travel time worth it.'

'Thanks,' I grumbled.

'Oh, honey, I'm kidding. What's wrong? What's the matter with this boy?'

'Nothing. He's absolutely perfect. He's smart and nice and totally right for me. Only there's another guy . . .' I shook my head. 'It's stupid. I'm being an idiot. I just need a little time to think things over. That's all.'

'Well,' Mom said, standing up. 'Just remember to do what makes you happy, OK? Don't lie to yourself because you think it's safer. Reality doesn't work like that . . . I think I told you that before.'

She had.

But I'd been running for so long I wasn't sure what I wanted anymore.

'Though,' Mom continued, 'I brought you a little something for your date, and it might help you out while you're thinking everything over.'

I watched with mild horror as she pulled a pink-and-yellow box from her handbag. Any object that came wrapped in those colors couldn't be a good thing. 'What is it?' I asked as she placed the box in my outstretched hand.

'Open it and find out, silly.'

Sighing, I pulled the hideous bow off the box and flicked open the lid. Inside was a small silver chain with a little white metal charm in the shape of a B. Like the ones girls wear in middle school, as if they'll forget their own name or something.

Mom reached forward and removed the necklace from the box. 'I saw it and thought of you,' she said.

'Thanks, Mom.'

She put down her handbag and moved around to stand behind me, pushing my hair aside so that she could fasten the chain around my neck. 'It's gonna sound corny, so try not to roll your eyes at me, OK? But maybe this will help you remember who you are while you're figuring things out.' She moved my hair back into place and stepped in front of me again. 'Perfect,' she said. 'You look wonderful, sweetie.'

'Thank you,' I said, and this time I really meant it. Seeing her made me realize just how much I'd missed my mother.

At that moment, the doorbell rang, and I knew it had to be Toby. As I reached for the knob, I felt Mom slide into place behind me, ready to observe.

Oh, great.

'Hey,' I said, opening the door and glancing away from Toby's blinding smile.

'Hi,' he said. 'Wow. You look beautiful.'

'Of course she does,' Mom interjected. 'What did you expect?'

'Mother,' I hissed, shooting her a dirty look over my shoulder.

She shrugged. 'Hello, Toby,' she said, waving. 'I'm Gina, Bianca's mother. I know, I look more like her sister, right?'

I gritted my teeth. Toby laughed.

'Have a good time,' Mom said, kissing me on the cheek. 'I'm going to pack up some of my things that are still here, but I'm talking at a retirement centre in Oak Hill Sunday, so I'll be staying at a hotel for the weekend. We'll have lunch tomorrow so I can get all the details.'

She pushed me out the door before I could argue with this, and then I was alone with Toby on the porch.

'She's funny,' he said.

'She's insane,' I muttered.

'What kind of talks does she give? She said she was going to a retirement home?'

'Oh. She wrote a self-esteem book.' I glanced back at the house, watching through the window as Mom moved past, headed for the bedroom she used to sleep in, prepared to pack up the last few things she'd left behind. I'd never realized the irony until that moment. For the past couple of months, I'd been struggling with my own self-esteem while my mother coached others on how to improve theirs. Maybe if I'd talked to her, it wouldn't have taken me so long to figure things out. 'She talks to people around the country about learning to accept themselves.'

'Sounds like a fun job,' Toby said.

'Maybe.'

He smiled, wrapping his arm around my waist and leading me off the porch.

I sighed and danced out of his grip as I let myself into the car.

27

Casey and Jessica were waiting in the backseat of the Taurus. Both of them grinned mischievously at me when I climbed into the passenger's seat. 'Someone's dressing sexy,' Casey teased. 'I gave you that shirt nine months ago. Is this the first time you've worn it?'

'Um . . . yeah.'

'Well, it looks good on you,' she said. 'Looks like I'm the Duff tonight. Thanks a lot, B.' She winked at me, and I couldn't help but smile. Casey had recently taken to using *Duff* as a word of her own, moulding it into our casual conversations. At first I'd found it kind of unsettling. I mean, the word was an insult. It was horrible. But after the revelation I'd had that day in the bathroom with Vikki, I appreciated what Casey was doing. The word was ours now, and as long as we held on to it, we could control the hurt it inflicted.

'It's a messy job,' I teased. 'But, hey, someone's gotta do it. I promise to be the Duff next weekend.'

She laughed.

'Are you wearing a padded bra?' Jessica blurted out, apparently unaware of our conversation. 'Your boobs look bigger.'

There was a long moment of silence, and I suddenly realized that I would have been safer with my mother.

Casey burst into a fit of laughter as I buried my face in my hands, completely mortified. Toby didn't show any reaction. Thank God. If he had, I might have committed suicide right there in the car. Banged my head against the window until my brain was flattened like a pancake. Instead of snickering or glancing at my chest to see if Jessica was right, Toby acted like boobs hadn't even been mentioned. He just stuck the key in the ignition and pulled out of my driveway.

Note to self, I thought. *Murder Jessica when there are no witnesses.*

Though, in a weird way, Toby's lack of reaction bugged me. Wesley would have made a joke. He would have looked at my chest, of course, but then he would have said something. He would have made me laugh. He wouldn't have just ignored it like Toby.

God! Of all things, this should *not* have been

something that bothered me.

'You know,' Casey said when she was finally able to stop laughing. 'It was pretty cool of you guys to invite us along.' She smiled at me, and I knew she was glad to be included. 'But you realize this is totally going to ruin your date, right?'

'How so?' Toby asked.

'Because we get to be your chaperones!' Jessica declared with way too much enthusiasm.

'Which makes it our job to put a stop to all forms of hanky-panky,' Casey added. 'And we'll enjoy doing it.'

'Yep.'

But Toby and I had no need to worry. The minute we got inside the Nest, my friends took off for the dance floor, flipping their hair and shaking their butts in the usual fashion.

'It looks like they're the ones who need to be chaperoned,' Toby chuckled as he led me to an empty booth.

'That's usually my job,' I said.

'Do you think they can survive if you take a night off?'

'We'll see.'

He smiled and touched my earring with his fingertips. 'The band won't start for half an hour,' he said, moving his hand down my neck to rest on my shoulder. It didn't do anything for me. But if Wesley had done this, trailed his fingers across my skin that way, I would have . . .

'Do you want me to get us some drinks before the bar gets too crowded?'

'Sure,' I said, choking back the thought of Wesley. 'I'll have a Cher— *Diet* Coke.'

'OK,' he said. 'I'll be right back.' He kissed me on the cheek and left for the bar.

People were spilling through the doors of the club. There was always a bigger crowd on nights when a band played. A few eighth-grade girls took the booth behind me, bragging loudly about how they'd pretended to be in high school to get in. A junior and one of his friends sidled past me, a poorly concealed beer bottle hanging out of his baggy jacket, and, for a split second, I caught a glimpse of the dark-haired freshman Jessica and I had watched at the basketball game weeks ago. She walked through the door, hand in hand with a cute boy I didn't recognize. Even from my distance, I could see the smile on her face. She looked beautiful, and I knew one of her preppy blond friends was being forced to fill in as the Duff in her absence. Then she and her date were gone, swept away by the crowd, leaving me with an inexplicable smile on my lips.

I didn't know what kind of band was supposed to be performing, but based on the number of kids with purple hair and lip rings who were walking in, I figured I'd be hearing Emo music.

There went my smile.

Great. Whiny boys with guitars. So my style, right?

I was absentmindedly watching the flood of people when *he* appeared among the crowd. At first I didn't even notice. He was with Harrison Carlyle, talking casually as they pushed their way toward the bar. It was easy to track his movement. He stood a few inches taller than everyone around him, he glanced around the crowd with more confidence than the rest of our classmates, he walked through the swarms with more grace than any normal teenager could manage, and my eyes followed him without my brain's consent.

Halfway to the bar, Wesley turned his head in my direction. His dark eyes locked with mine for an instant. *Shit.* I looked away, praying he hadn't noticed me, even though I was sure he had.

'God,' I muttered, clenching my fist under the table. 'It's like he's everywhere.'

'Who's everywhere?' Toby asked, taking his seat across from me and sliding my glass along the smooth surface of the table.

'No one.' I took a sip of the Diet Coke and tried not to make a face. The lack of sugar left a bad taste in my mouth. I swallowed and asked, 'What's the name of the band that's playing again?'

'Black Tears,' he answered.

Yep. That sounded like Emo shit to me.

'Cool.'

'I've never heard their music,' Toby admitted, running a hand over his bowl-cut blond hair. 'But people have told me they're good. Plus, they're about the only band in Hamilton. It seems like everyone else who plays here is from Oak Hill.'

'Uh-huh.'

I shifted uncomfortably in my seat, conscious of Wesley's eyes on me. The way they crept along my skin made me insane, and I hoped that Toby wouldn't notice me twitching. He'd probably think I was on crack or something.

'I finished *Wuthering Heights*,' I said, desperate to start a conversation that would get my thoughts off Wesley. It took me a minute to realize this was definitely not the best subject for that task.

'Did you like it?' Toby asked.

'Well, it gave me a lot to think about.' I could have slapped myself. Wasn't it that damn book that had me so freaked out in the first place? Why did I have to bring it up? But it was too late to change the topic now. Toby had jumped into a full-on book critique.

'I know. I've always wondered what made Emily Brontë choose to write such unpleasant characters. I mean, throughout the whole book, I just thought that both Heathcliff and Linton were such bastards, and Cathy . . .'

I swirled my straw in my drink, only half listening. Every time Toby said *Heathcliff*, my eyes automatically darted over his shoulder to glance at Wesley. As always, he looked gorgeous, wearing jeans and a tight white T-shirt beneath a slightly too large black jacket. He was sitting alone at the bar, stretched out and casually leaning back with both elbows on the bar moulding. Alone. Not a single girl clinging to him. Hell, even Harrison had disappeared. Joe was the only person close enough to keep him company, and he seemed to be busy with a herd of thirsty Goth kids.

Wesley's eyes stayed fixed on me the entire time. From where I sat, it was hard to read their expression, but they never wavered for a second. Yeah, it was unnerving, but I knew that I would've been disappointed, maybe even hurt, if I'd found that he'd turned away. I actually caught myself checking every few minutes to see if he was still watching me.

'Bianca?'

Startled, I focused on Toby again. 'Hmm?'

'Are you all right?' he asked.

My fingers had been toying with the little *B* charm around my neck without my realizing it. Immediately I dropped my hand to my side. 'I'm fine.'

'Casey warned me that you're probably lying when you say that,' he said.

I gritted my teeth and searched the dance floor for my so-called friend. She was being added to my hit list.

'And I think she's right,' Toby sighed.

'What?'

'Bianca, I can see what's going on.' He glanced over his shoulder at Wesley before turning back to me with a little nod. 'He's been staring at you since he got here.'

'Has he?'

'I can see him in the mirrors over there. And you've been staring back,' Toby said. 'It's not just tonight either. I've seen the way he looks at you during school. In the hallways. He likes you, doesn't he?'

'I . . . I don't know. I guess.' Oh God, this was uncomfortable. I just kept spinning my straw between my fingers and watching the little waves that appeared on the surface of my drink. I couldn't meet Toby's gaze.

'I don't have to guess,' he said. 'It's pretty obvious. And the way you look at him makes me think you're in love with him, too.'

'No!' I cried, releasing my straw and glaring up at Toby. 'No, no, *no*. I am not in love with him, OK?'

Toby gave me a small smile and said, 'But you do have feelings for him.'

I couldn't see any sign of pain in his eyes, just a touch of amusement. That made it a lot easier to give him an answer. 'Um . . . yeah.'

'Then go to him.'

I rolled my eyes without meaning to. It was just so automatic. 'Jesus, Toby,' I said, 'that sounds like a line out of a bad movie.'

Toby shrugged. 'Maybe, but I'm serious, Bianca. If you feel that way about him, you should go over there.'

'But what about—?'

'Don't worry about me,' he said. 'If you want Wesley, that's who you should be with right now. Dating me won't make your feelings for him go away . . . I should know. Definitely don't worry about me, Bianca. The truth is, I'm in the same situation as you. I just didn't want to admit it.'

'How?'

Now Toby was the one staring at his drink, nervously

333

adjusting his glasses. 'I'm not over Nina.'

'Nina? Your ex?'

He nodded. 'We broke up over a month ago, but I still think about her a lot. I really do like you, so I thought that if we dated, maybe I'd forget about her. For a while I did, but . . .'

'Well, then, you should call her,' I said. 'Instead of just sitting here pouting, you should call Nina and tell her how you feel. Tonight.'

He brought his eyes back up to meet mine. 'You're not angry? You don't feel used?'

'That would make me a huge hypocrite since I was kind of using you, too. Even though I really didn't mean to.' I slid out of the booth and paused to steady myself on the platform shoes. 'And for the record, if Nina doesn't take you back, she's a moron. I think you're probably the sweetest, most polite guy I've ever met in my life, and I've had a massive crush on you for years. I seriously *wish* you were the one for me.'

'Thanks,' Toby said. 'And if Wesley breaks your heart, I promise to . . . well, I would say I'd kick his ass, but we both know that's physically impossible.' He frowned down at his skinny arms. 'So I'll write him a strongly worded letter.'

'OK,' I snorted. I leaned across the table and kissed

Toby on the cheek. 'And thank you.'

He gave me one more perfect smile, one I would remember for the rest of my life, and said, 'You're stalling. Hurry up and go.'

'Right. OK. See you in class, Toby.'

'Goodbye, Bianca.'

I took a long, deep breath to calm my nerves as I locked eyes with Wesley again. Then, with a weak smile pulling at the corners of my mouth, I began to push my way through the crowded club, leaving behind the nicest guy in the world. The familiar techno music had stopped playing, and everyone on the floor stood around waiting for the band to go onstage. I had to zigzag between their stationary bodies, no one being considerate enough to step aside for even a millisecond.

I spotted Casey in the crowd – her blond head towering over everyone but the boy beside her, the basketball player she'd been eyeing for weeks – and I knew she wouldn't like my decision. In her head, it was Wesley's fault I'd neglected her. She'd be upset with me. She might even get pissed. She'd think I was leaving her behind again. I would just have to prove her wrong. Prove to her that Toby, whom she adored, wasn't right for me.

When I was about three yards from the bar, a sound filled the speakers, but it wasn't the Emo music I was expecting. Instead, a screech of feedback assaulted my ears – and totally scared the shit out of me. I was so startled that I jumped, which wouldn't have been a big deal in any other shoes.

My foot landed on the side of my platform, throwing me completely off balance. Before I could recover, my ankle gave way and sent me flying – face-first, naturally – into the wooden floor. Fanfreaking-tastic!

I couldn't help letting out a whimper as pain shot through my twisted ankle. 'Fuck!' I groaned. 'Ow, ow, ow! God, I hate these damn shoes.'

'Then why did you wear them?'

My skin tingled as two hands lifted me by the elbows and guided me into a standing position. Realizing I wasn't stable on my feet, Wesley wrapped his arm around my waist and walked me over to a bar stool.

'Are you all right?' he asked, helping me onto the seat. I could tell by his smile that he was fighting the urge to laugh.

'Yes,' I mumbled, letting myself smile a little. I didn't really feel that embarrassed. Not with Wesley. Had it been anyone else, I would have run – or hobbled – right out of the club, but with Wesley it felt OK. Like we could laugh about it together.

But the smile faded and his face became serious. He

336

stared at me for a long moment, and his silence was about to drive me up the wall when he finally opened his mouth. 'Bianca, I—'

'Bianca! Omigosh!' Jessica materialized at my side, her cheeks pink from excitement and exercise. Behind her, the band had started playing (or attempting to play) an Emo version of a Johnny Cash song. It was sickening, but Jessica managed to talk over the racket. 'Oh, Bianca, I finally found you! Did you see? Harrison and I were dancing together! I think he might ask me to prom. Wouldn't that be great?'

'Good for you, Jessica.'

'I have to go tell Angela!' Then she spotted Wesley. A knowing smile spread across her face as she said, 'See you two later.' And with a whip of her blond ponytail, she was gone.

Wesley watched her vanish into the crowd with an amused expression. 'She does know Harrison prefers men, right?'

'Let her have hope,' I said, smiling to myself.

He turned his attention back to me. 'Yes. Hope is good. Bianca, I—' He grinned wickedly. 'I knew you'd give in sooner or later.' He put his hand on my knee and ran it smoothly up my thigh. 'You're finally going to admit that you love me, aren't you?'

I swatted his hand away. 'First of all,' I began, 'I don't *love* you. I love my family and maybe even Casey and Jessica, but romantic love takes years upon years to develop. So I don't love you. But I will admit, I've thought a lot about you lately and I definitely have feelings for you . . . feelings other than hatred for the most part. And maybe it's possible – in the future – that I . . . could love you.' I hesitated, a little scared of the words that'd just left my mouth. 'But I still want to kill you most of the time.'

Wesley's grin turned into a genuine smile. 'God, I've missed you.' He leaned down to kiss me, but I held up my hand to stop him. 'What's the matter?' he asked.

'You're not getting into my pants tonight, asshole,' I said, remembering Vikki and the scare she'd gone through. I wasn't going to suddenly become a nun or anything, but after realizing how easily we might have swapped roles, I knew a few things would have to change. 'If we're going to do this, we're going to do it right. We're going to move at the speed of a normal high school relationship.'

He reached forward and touched the little white *B* that lay right between my collarbones, twisting the charm that Mom had given me between his thumb and forefinger, almost absentmindedly. 'But neither of us is normal.'

'That's true,' I acknowledged. 'But this part of us will

be normal. Look, I'm not saying we can't build back up to that point. We'll just . . . take it a little more slowly.'

Wesley thought about this for a moment before letting that crooked grin slide across his lips again. 'OK,' he said, leaning forward a little to look me in the eyes. 'That's fine. There are other things we can do.' His fingers released my necklace and moved across my collarbone, gliding down my arm and sending a shiver up my spine. 'I have a job to finish, I believe. We were interrupted last time – in your bedroom – but I could show you again. I look forward to showing you.'

I took a deep breath, trying to ignore this statement and the burst of excitement it gave me. 'You're going to take me on dates,' I continued, clearing my throat. 'Nice dates. And you're never ever going to call me Duffy again either.'

Wesley's smirk faded and he bit his lip. 'Bianca,' he said quietly. I could barely hear him over the music. 'I'm sorry. I didn't know how much it hurt you. I should never have called you the Duff in the first place. I didn't know you then. I didn't—'

I shook my head. 'Don't bother making excuses,' I said. 'Don't waste your time because, the fact is, I am the Duff. But so is everyone else in the world. We're all fucking Duffs.'

'I'm not the Duff,' Wesley said confidently.

'That's because you don't have friends.'

'Oh. Right.'

'And,' I continued, 'I'm probably going to be a bitch most of the time. I guarantee I'll find a reason to yell at you almost every day, and don't be surprised if a few drinks get dumped on you from time to time. That's just me, and you're going to have to deal with it. Because I'm not changing for you or anyone else. And I—'

Wesley slid off his bar stool and pressed his lips against mine before the words could get out. My heart pounded as every thought vacated my mind. One of his arms encircled my waist, pulling me as close to him as possible, and his free hand cupped my face, his thumb tracing my cheekbone. He kissed me so passionately I thought we would catch fire.

It wasn't until after he pulled away, both of us in need of some air, that I could think straight again.

'You jerk!' I yelled, pushing him away from me. 'Kissing me to make me shut up? God, you're so obnoxious. I could just *throw* something at you right now.'

Wesley hopped onto his bar stool with a big grin, and I suddenly remembered him telling me that I was sexy when I was mad at him. Go figure. 'Excuse me, Joe,' he called to the bartender. 'I think Bianca wants a Cherry Coke.'

Despite my best efforts, I smiled. He wasn't perfect, or even remotely close, for that matter, but, hey, neither was I. We were both pretty fucked up. Somehow, though, that made everything more exciting. Yeah, it was sick and twisted, but that's reality, right? Escape is impossible, so why not embrace it?

Wesley took my hand and laced his fingers with mine. 'You look beautiful tonight, Bianca.'

Acknowledgements

Thanks to the amazing people I was given the honour of working with. My editor, the incomparable Kate Sullivan, whose thoughtfulness and insight have helped me make this book a million times better than I ever thought it could be. The entire Poppy crew for their overwhelming enthusiasm. And my fabulous agent, Joanna Stampfel-Volpe – who is, without a doubt, this book's biggest fan – for always understanding *exactly* where I was coming from. Thank you all for making my dreams come true.

Special thanks to my cheerleaders: Hannah Wydey, Linda Ge, and Krista Ashe for reading this book in its earliest form and still managing to love it; Amy Lukavics, my 'online BFF' and all-around awesome woman, for cheering me on from chapter one – fate has truly made our paths cross!; and Kristin Briana Otts, Kirsten Hubbard, and Kristin Miller for being the best support group *ever*.

I hope we can have a K4 Book Tour one day. And a general gush of gratitude for the people at Teens Writing for Teens, YA Highway, and Absolute Write. I couldn't have done this without you.

Undying appreciation belongs to my supportive friends: Shana Hancock, Molly Troutman, Stacy Timberlake, Aja Wilhite, Kyle Walker, Cody Ogilby, and Allison Austen. Thanks for putting up with me while I wrote this book, even when I probably drove you *insane*!

And, most of all, thank you to my family, Mom, Dad, and Chelle: you knew I would be a writer, even when I thought it was impossible. I would be nowhere without your encouragement, patience, and love. Not everyone is blessed with a family who supports their artistic fancies. Thank you so much for believing in me. I love you.

Can't get enough of
BIANCA and **WESLEY?**

LOOK OUT FOR THEM IN

LYING **OUT** **LOUD**

A companion novel to **The DUFF**

Starring Amy Rush, AKA Wesley's sister, and
Sonny Ardmore, the most inventive liar in
Hamilton High. With major cameo appearances
from Bianca and Wesley that you're not going
to want to miss …